News from the Front

By

Lazette Gifford

©2018, Lazette Gifford

An ACOA Publication

www.aconspiracyofauthors.com

ISBN: 978-1-936507-81-8

News from the Front
A Conspiracy of Authors Publication
www.aconspiracyofauthors.com
©2018, Lazette Gifford

Cover Art ©2018, Lazette Gifford
ISBN: 978-1-936507-81-8

First Print Edition, September 2018

DEDICATION

News from the Front is dedicated to Holly Lisle, who helped to instruct me about how to write when she taught a Snail Mail class for Writers' Digest. With incredible patience, she edited, made notes, showed me what I was doing right and what I'd done wrong. Only rarely did she threaten to beat me over the head with my own manuscript if I didn't remember something she taught me.

Thank you, Holly. You will always be a great inspiration to me and to all the others whom you continue to help along this insane writing path

Any mistakes are still my own. I am a slow learner.

TABLE OF CONTENTS

CHAPTER ONE

O ne last time....

Alyn Naevon fed his ID into the table's menu slot and ordered dinner with three quick stabs of his finger: hot spicy chicken sandwich, orange cola, fried sweet chips. The servo chimed, and the countdown appeared on the screen. Barely four minutes later the food slid out, the welcome aroma winning a rumble of appreciation from his empty stomach. Even the cheap food on Mars came seasoned with real spices imported from Earth. Alyn had come to savor the exotic tastes from a world well beyond his meager and often ephemeral income as a freelance reporter. This short assignment on Mars was as close to Mother Earth as he was ever likely to get.

The menu kicked his ID back, and he took the card with a sigh of regret. The green line of food credit showed dull black now. The account was empty, and in another six hours, all benefits of the card would expire. Luckily, he had no reason to remain, and flights out from Mars were numerous and relatively cheap. The trial he'd covered had ended, and he'd soon have to pay for the honor of being here. The Inner Worlds Council

Complex maintained the price of lodgings at a level that discouraged vagrants and the unemployed.

Despite the impatient protests of his stomach, Alyn slowly nibbled at his sandwich, relishing his last free meal. Besides, this gave him time while he pretended to decide his future. There was only one option for an unemployed free-lance reporter on Mars. He had to book passage out of this costly settlement before he ran up expenses that he had no way to pay without another job. He needed a direction and a new story to cover. Unfortunately, his last few scans of the news lines hadn't produced anything promising.

Alyn took another small bite and stared distractedly across the nearly empty cafe. His eyes locked on the dark brown wall as though he expected the Hand of God to write him his traveling orders there. A few minutes with a comp might be more rewarding.

Sudden noise filled the dining hall as several families appeared from the lifts. Children, loud and anxious, rushed between tables while the adults shouted greetings across the room to one another. Alienation struck as he watched. The others found comradeship here, and the few faces glancing his way were neither friendly nor hostile. To these highly placed professionals, a free-lance reporter without permanent credentials was a non-entity.

Alyn wouldn't have come within their private lair, except as a temporarily verified member of the press he rated certain privileges. He wasn't too proud to forego Vidline and the Inner Worlds Council's generosity of a sleeping room and at least one free meal a day. After all, permanently assigned reporters had suites and took meals whenever they chose.

Alyn didn't want a permanent post, even one with free meals. He enjoyed the travel and the excitement of covering even minor stories. That was lucky, or else he might envy these reporters with their steady incomes, suites, families, and friends.

Someone stopped by his table and fingers touched his arm to draw his attention. Alyn looked up with a start, sandwich still in his hand. The woman who stood over him was small and dark, her bright gray eyes too large for her thin face. He recognized her. Marquesa was the most notorious of the local reporters and famous far beyond the IWC Complex. Her smile was unexpectedly friendly.

"You did a nice job on the trial, Alyn Naevon," she told him. Her pleasant voice rose loud enough to draw the attention of the others settling nearby. "You have a good eye for news. You're going to make it in the field."

"Thank you." He grinned and put aside the sandwich hoping he hadn't blushed too noticeably. Alyn took a chance and waved her into the seat across from him; he hadn't had company in days.

Marquesa accepted the invitation and nodded a distracted greeting to friends as she settled into the chair. Marquesa didn't work for Vidline News, any of its affiliates, or even the respectable home-based news services from one of the colony worlds. She was Private Line's reporter in residence. PL specialized in uncensored and often compromising vids of any person with a *Name*. She enjoyed targeting politicians who pretended to be above reproach. Rumors credited the downfall of at least three people to her vidcam. Though expelled twice, Marquesa had proven she was scrupulously honest. Now that Private Line was so successful there was little chance she'd be run out again.

The woman was famous and Alyn wasn't clear why she bothered to notice him -- and then felt a little trepidation at the thought that she might know something he'd worked hard to hide. He did have a *Name*, once, but it wasn't one he'd been known by for years.

If that was the reason for her interest, he might as well find out now.

She put her elbows on the table and settled her chin in the palm of one hand as she watched him. He could see that the silver-tint of her eyelashes matched the slinky singlesuit she wore. Her smile appeared genuine, but he knew well enough that she was beyond his reach. Marquesa had an equally scrupulous reputation regarding her rare personal relationships.

"Where are you going next?" she asked.

"I was considering one of the fringes. Few of those worlds have full-time reporters yet," he answered, wondering what this woman really wanted from him. "Something odd is always happening out there. And odd sells."

"True." She nodded thoughtfully. "Aquila Fringe?"

"No. They've had an infestation of reporters since the end of their war. I don't mind competition, but I do like to earn enough to eat. I was considering the newer areas, perhaps the Pavo Fringe."

"Are you looking for a permanent post out there?" she asked with sudden interest he didn't understand.

"Not yet. I still like moving around."

She nodded, a slightly wistful look slipping across her thin face. This was her second decade of reporting from the Inner Worlds Council Headquarters. The work might be rewarding, but he suspected she had grown bored of the dull Martian sunset years ago. He'd tired of them after two days. Even expensive vacations to far-famed Mother Earth must lose their magic after so many repetitions.

"Eat your food." She waved a slim, perfectly manicured hand toward the plate. "You're too thin."

He bowed his head in embarrassment and took up the sandwich before his stomach made another untimely protest. He noticed his own fingers were tan, scarred here and there from other work he'd done. He didn't like to make the comparison.

When he looked back, Marquesa was studying him still, and he felt distinctly uneasy beneath her critical stare. He'd been working for several years to remain, if not entirely anonymous, at least personally unremarkable. Her stare made him feel conspicuously out of place once more.

"What attracted you to this story?" she finally asked after half the sandwich disappeared. "The sensationalism?"

"The Port Rats," he corrected automatically. She nodded, even looked as though she approved, this woman who made her fame on sensationalism. "Can I get you something to eat or drink?"

"No, I ate earlier." She waved that politeness away with another slight movement of her long dark fingers. "Do you always look for an incident involving the exploitation of the poor?"

"I look for anything that will pay," he answered truthfully. "I'm just drawn to those where I can bring some wrong to the attention of others."

"You have a feel for real news, Alyn," she said again, a slight flicker of emotion crossing her face. Regret? "You honestly embarrassed the local reporters by your success with this one, a free-lancer who took the chance to come into their territory. They never considered that a trial about exploited Port Rats on a backwater world might be important. Hell, Caliente doesn't even rate an ambassador to Council, let alone a reporter! Besides, their Chief Magistrate was so blatantly guilty of misuse of power, we all knew the trial would hardly take longer than the filing of formal charges. It hadn't occurred to us that people elsewhere might not be as jaded about such things as we are. And you were smart enough to make certain you'd filed with Vidline, so the story remained yours when we did finally notice."

"I saw another free-lancer lose a good story by making that mistake," he explained. "She didn't register the story with the nearest Vidline office, and they sent in one of their own local reporters. She ended up selling her raw footage for about a tenth of what she could have made if she'd filed with Vidline right away. I'm not stupid. I can even learn from other people's mistakes. I always file, I don't care how minor the story looks at first."

"The locals have forgotten there's actual competition out there. Most gather their best news here in the cafe rather than out in the meeting halls. We're a tight-knit group, but we're too intent on local politics. You recognize news, and you know what to ask to learn answers. What you really need is newer equipment."

He nodded, though his hand protectively patted the worn brown bag beside him.

"The new vidcams are out of my league," he admitted with a slight shrug. "This one's held up well enough. It doesn't have the new wide-scan view, and the night lens is a bit fuzzy, but that adds to the nuance sometimes."

"Nuance is fine if you're selling to Private Line, but Vidline has more exacting standards, I've heard."

"I've sold enough -- to Vidline and others -- to keep in the business."

"I watched your reports. You have a good eye," she answered. She stared off at a wall for a long moment. Perhaps everyone picked up that habit here. "Eat your food. I'll be right back."

She slipped out of the chair and glided quickly across the room to the lifts, then glanced back, one thin eyebrow raised. Alyn grabbed his sandwich and began to eat as the lift door slid closed.

He wondered what had prompted the woman's attention in him. Maybe she'd only felt sorry for someone, sitting there alone. Marquesa had been a pleasant distraction, but he still had important decisions to make.

For a few more hours he could continue to use his temporary Vidline status to make a last quick sweep of the Complex, picking up short vid pieces. He lost himself in imagining artful shots, unique perspectives. Now that the trial was over he could linger in those areas he found fascinating: the enormous Martian red stone columns carved in intricate spirals, the excellent Earth-wood doors and inlaid marble floors, the eclectic art collection donated by the many colonies. Then he'd wander the main hall with the holo-covered walls where famous politicians whispered their greatest speeches in monotonous repetition, day after day after day.

A vid of the walk might net him a little extra at one of the travelogue services. Beyond that, he still couldn't formulate any tangible plans.

Marquesa returned before he finished his sandwich and chips and she carried a narrow black case in her hand. A couple reporters looked up as she passed and nodded in a way that made him think there was some conspiracy here. That made him nervous again.

She sat the case on the table and slid in across from him again.

"Open it."

He pushed the locks aside and lifted the lid. Inside he found a new vidcam still nestled in the sealed plastic. The cam had never been touched.

"What do you think?"

His fingers moved appreciatively over the thin plastic and linger on the expensive lens. Alyn nodded when he saw the quick change vidchit slot. The body of the vidcam was barely twenty by ten centimeters and only another ten centimeters thick. Key controls showed all the functions of his older bulky model, plus a few fancier editing features. Even the accessories looked impressive. The pliable surface around the eye patch apparently molded to the face more comfortably than the strap on the one he used. The padded shoulder brace didn't look as though it would cut off the circulation to a person's arm while shooting. A small handheld remote had both key code and voice activation.

"Damn nice piece of equipment," he admitted. The lens had the wide view feature that was almost the equal of holos. This was as good as equipment got for reporters since people had shown they didn't like most of their news in holographic splendor. They wanted to see it, not live it.

"Glad you like it. It's yours."

"Oh no," he protested. His hands instinctively drew back from the case. "I couldn't even begin to afford--"

"I didn't say you had to buy it," she replied and shoved the case closer toward him. "Alyn, Private Line buys me a new camera every year. I haven't unpacked the last three. I got tired of learning all the new little tricks and the new keys for the same old functions. Apparently, the execs at PL think my reports must burn out vidcams, and I throw them away. I've even given a few to the local clowns, for all they appreciate it."

She shot a playful glare at the woman sitting at a table halfway across the little area. The woman looked momentarily contrite and then grinned back. This wasn't a conspiracy; it was an old game, and they included him for reasons he couldn't begin to imagine.

His hand touched the edge of the long sleek cam, noting the quick edit innovation, the image magnification features, and the incredible telephoto range. He drew his hands back, uncertain.

"If you don't take it, I'm leaving it here on the table for someone else to grab. I get tired of dusting the cases, all stacked so nice and neat in my closet."

He still couldn't believe she was serious. The vidcam wasn't the most expensive one on the market, but it was more than he could have afforded on a freelancer's income. This wasn't something a tourist would pick up to cover a vacation out to Paradise. The vidcam was a professional piece of equipment with features for serious work.

"I don't know what to say," he confessed as he looked back up at her.

She smiled more brightly this time. "Then we've agreed? You'll take the damn beast?"

"I -- I guess so." He looked down at the vidcam and let his fingers brush across the surface again.

"Good. You better go check your email." That brought his head back up with a start followed by a whisper of excitement. Email? No one would send messages to him here unless he had an answer to one of his queries about a story. "I saw your name on the queue at the public station when I went past. It looks a message from Vidline. I think they might be offering you an assignment, Alyn."

"Assignment," he repeated the word automatically. Marquesa's eyes brightened as though his good fortune meant something to her. "An actual assignment?"

Vidline offering a freelance reporter a job was the first step to full-time employment under their auspicious shield. Vidline News credentials opened doors no freelancer would ever get through. And if a reporter did well on the first assigned jobs, Vidline usually put them on the payroll with a steady income, even paying reporters between assignments. Vidline represented success, prestige, and stability. He'd worked hard through the last four years for this opportunity.

Alyn stood, telling himself not to hope for too much as he crossed to the old battered comp by the lift where transients picked up their notes. The screen did show that he had a message from Vidline on file. They'd already posted him his pay for this job. There was no reason for them to send him another message.

Unless Marquesa was right. He keyed in his code and let the wall spit out a stiff thin sheet of paper. He didn't even look at it until he went back to the booth and sat down.

The vidcam was still there. Alyn had half expected it to disappear. He closed the lid and laid the paper on top. Marquesa leaned over the table and read the news upside down, still grinning.

An offer of employment: standard pay, single assignment, with an option for further work if he proved competent. Unknown time frame. Full expenses paid to and while on Tempest.

He must have gone white.

"Alyn?" Marquesa slipped her dark fingers over his hand where it held the paper far too tightly. "Are you all right?"

"Yeah," he answered. All the hopes of his career disappeared in that single sheet of paper. "Just -- Tempest --"

"Tempest!" she laughed. "Hell, that's a great assignment for a freelancer! That's an Inner World, only a couple days away, which means you are staying in civilization, even if they are having trouble there. Better work there than in the Pavo, friend. And the trouble the Port Rats are having on Tempest should be perfect for you!"

"Inner World," he repeated, trying to cover his discomfort. "Oh. I must have had it confused with somewhere else."

"Congratulations!" She took his hand firmly in hers, delighted at his success. "There are reporters here who couldn't *buy* that good of an assignment from Vidline. They must have really liked your work! It looks as though they've booked you on a ship that leaves in about three hours. You better go get packed and send your belongings off to the port for clearance, or you're going to miss the opportunity of a lifetime. Vidline doesn't give away these chances twice."

That was, unfortunately, the damned truth. His career was over.

"Go on!" She shoved the vidcam case at him again, and he automatically picked it up. "I've already filed ownership on that thing in your name. Get it packed and sent to the ship, then come down and we'll have a last drink before you go. I'll get your Vidline credentials made up here. That'll save you time and annoyance on Tempest. Go!"

Despite himself, Alyn grinned and stood. What choices did he have? If he didn't go to Tempest, he'd lose his only chance at a real career. He could change his name again. Start over. It would take at least another four or more years to get this far unless he decided to count these as wasted years and try an entirely new profession.

Alyn liked being a reporter. He'd worked hard to get this chance. So, he stood with one vidcam case in hand and picked up the older one. Nodding politely to Marquesa, he turned to the lifts that led up to the sleeping rooms above them. Hopefully, she would think his reaction as only a show of surprise.

When the lift door closed, and he was finally alone, Alyn growled with frustration and crumpled the stiff paper into dust, blowing the debris into the air vent beside him.

Tempest. Damn!

The last place he wanted to go was *home*.

CHAPTER TWO

As he stepped from the ship's sterile airlock, Alyn Naevon immediately tasted the peculiar acidic taint in the air of Tempest. Metallic: The locals called it the taste of money. The familiar tang left his skin tingling and his mind filled with a sense of dread he had kept at bay until this moment. Now he faced the undeniable truth. This was home, and he shouldn't be here.

The passengers disembarked through a narrow, transparent tube connecting the shuttle to the Port Tower. Though hard weather had pitted the outside of the conduit, Alyn could still look to the right and see the city. Searching the late afternoon skyline, he took in changes in the once familiar landscape. The most noticeable alteration was a needle-like structure near the Port Tower, a uniquely elegant form against the outline of otherwise square, ordinary buildings. Farther inland he saw the skeletal shapes of unfinished offices profiled by the sinking sun. Those new shapes replaced buildings destroyed in an explosion a few years ago. He would have thought they would be finished by now, which made him wonder -- reporter's instinct -- what caused the delay.

The glass and metal of Tanton Steel's twenty-floor corporate office still dominated the city skyline. There were no other changes that he could see from here and that depressed him. He'd wanted to see differences so that he wouldn't feel so uncomfortable coming back.

Scattered patches of gray and black dotted the open skies beyond the bleak contour of the city. The massing clouds promised one of those storms for which the world was well known and named. That was the final, perfect touch for this injudicious homecoming. Alyn hated getting drenched.

Midway through the tube Alyn stopped once more and looked opposite from the metal city and closer to the port. The Rat Maze hadn't changed much either. Packing crate walls and preform plastic roofs made a strangely colorful pattern against the otherwise empty gray and brown landscape. In an odd sort of way, and at a distance, the Maze was far prettier than the plain steel of the citizen's capital. He tried to pick out familiar landmarks within those less stable structures. There were a few permanent buildings at the heart of the Maze, but the expanding walls of makeshift huts obscured the view.

"Do you mind moving?" a voice growled behind him. "Some of us have better things to do than stare at the damn Rats."

Alyn slowly turned, keeping his unexpected surge of anger in check. The portly woman standing behind him mimicked all the latest dark fashion of the Inner World elite: black clothing, black hair and black lips. The style also included a show of boredom and bad manners, though really, that was nothing new. Alyn had the pleasure of watching those annoyed brown eyes go wide at sight of the Vidline ID pinned at his right shoulder.

"A -- pardon me." Her head bowed in a gesture that might almost have been an apology. "May I get by?"

Amazing how even the most respectable and law-abiding citizens got nervous around reporters and Port Guards. Alyn graciously moved out of the way and let the woman and others go past. He was in no hurry to reach the far end of the tube where Port Administration officials would pass him through customs.

Or not, if someone recognized him. Damn, damn, damn! Sanity struck unexpectedly. This was, without question, undeniably and unequivocally stupid! No job could be worth the risk he took coming here! It wasn't just recognition by the authorities that could prove dangerous. He'd made worse enemies among his fellow Rats when he fled the cause six years ago.

Alyn had made a few small changes in his physical appearance during those years away from home, but they weren't much of a disguise. With shaky fingers, he pushed long black hair from his eyes. His hair had been shorter, and several shades lighter, before he left. Alyn had also paid for the removal of a distinctive scar that once ran from his left eye to his chin. He'd had that work done to help in his career, and not for vanity, since Vidline reporters had to look respectable. Now Alyn found a new reason to be grateful for having made improvements although the changes weren't enough to fool anyone who knew him well. He hoped there was no reason for the port to have set up a DNA scan on people coming on-world. There had been a protest throughout the Inner Worlds over that one a few years ago, and now it was only done in times of crisis. The trouble here hadn't quite hit that point. His Vidline ID should get him through.

Alyn hesitated.

The sign at the end of the connection tube began to flash with large red lettered words, warning him that they wanted to disengage. He was the last person in the passage.

He could slip back aboard the ship and never set foot on Tempest. No, that wouldn't work. Someone would wonder why he came all this way only to turn around. They'd ask questions, make checks -- and he had little doubt the Captain would turn him over to local authorities if they asked. He was safer going on and taking his chances rather than inviting questions.

Alyn picked up his pace and forcibly settled his nerves. He finally reached the end of the tube, trying not to let his step falter as he scanned the admissions foyer. Alyn had only been inside this part of the Port Tower once before. On that day he'd made his nerve-wracking escape with forged papers and a horde of 500 credits that were not entirely his own.

Madness to come back here.

They'd remodeled since then. The walls that had once been a dull green now sparkled with silver traces in black stone. A metallic customs table lay flooded by the illumination from a large window that framed the gleaming spire Alyn had noted in the tube. An arch of lacy metal filigree divided customs from the nearly deserted reception area.

Like most habitable worlds, Tempest was metal-rich. Unlike many new colonies, the First Settlers had turned their initial resources to exploiting that metal rather than farming and other traditional survival crafts. Other new colonies in the sector soon found it less expensive to import sheet metal from Tempest rather than build extensive works of their own. Metal made Tempest rich.

They flaunted it.

"Here he finally comes," someone testily reported.

Local kids worked the port with Rat kids doing the heavy work outside and Citizen brats at the admissions area inside. Three of the brats impatiently awaited the last passenger. A Port Guard in the familiar tan uniform seen on all Inner Worlds stood at the custom's table. Happily, Alyn didn't recognize any of them.

He didn't rush forward. The glares of those poor bored Citizen children set off old reactionary triggers despite himself. Damned if he'd make life easier for them.

He took his time studying the new layout as he casually crossed to the patient Port Guard. His two vidcases and one other piece of luggage were already on the custom's table. Alyn passed through an inspection grid which did a quick scan; the outcome matched the ID he carried.

"Welcome to Tempest, Citizen Naevon," the stocky Port Guard greeted him with a bow of his head. The tag on his named him Captain Bauer.

"Not Citizen," Alyn corrected automatically and with too much intensity. The guard looked up, curious. "I'm just a visitor. I avoid association with either side in a political conflict."

"Ah." Bauer slid the travel case in front of them. "Then you do know about the local situation."

"That's why Vidline sent me."

Bauer flashed a quick, embarrassed grin as Alyn began keying open his cases for inspection. The soldier's fingers expertly flicked through the first case with a scanner-gloved hand as he quickly rifled through the clothing.

"There is a local Vidline reporter stationed here, you know," the guard said as he closed the case and reached for the older brown vidcase. "And we have several local on-world reporters as well. Why did they send in another one?"

"The Vidline reporter is a native woman," Alyn replied. He was less nervous since no one had rushed out to arrest him yet. "They sent me for the same reason they bring you Port Guards in from off-world. They want an outsider with no local involvement."

"I ran your ID while we were waiting for you," Captain

Bauer reported. Alyn quelled the instinct to step back and prepare for trouble. "It said you were born on Tempest, that your parents were itinerant engineers. We found some reference to the Naevons, but not to you."

The trickiest part of his new identity had always been the question of a homeworld. People often asked about his background, and he needed a solid core to of memories to draw upon. Tempest was the only world he knew well enough to use, but it was also the most dangerous.

The Port Guard still watched him, hazel eyes slightly narrowed.

"I left a long time ago." He finally shrugged and tried to look calm. "Vidline thought I'm a good choice for this assignment since I know the world but have no ties here. I never applied for citizenship."

"Why not?"

"My parents often moved from world-to-world. I only spent a few years here, mostly in the backcountry where my parents helped set up power stations for new villages. I always thought I'd take my citizenship wherever they settled down."

"And?"

"They never settled down. Now I'm just about as bad. Forgive me, but Tempest was just another stop along the way, even if I was born here."

"Don't apologize to me." Bauer suddenly smiled and looked relaxed. "I'm an off-worlder Port Guard, as you pointed out."

Alyn felt the tension start to ease in his shoulders as the man pulled the last black case over to have a look. Alyn realized he would make it past customs, at least.

"Looks good Cit--" Bauer looked up and stopped himself.

"Alyn."

"Alyn," he agreed and closed the last case. "If you don't

mind, Commander Kalison would like a few minutes of your time before you go to the hotel."

"A problem?" Alyn ventured as he picked up the brown case, slipping the long strap over his shoulder. With his other worries, it hadn't occurred to him that the local establishment might find the appearance of a new reporter troubling.

"I think he wants to make certain you're aware of local problems. He doesn't want a martyred Vidline Reporter to add to the files."

That sounded like a probable enough reason for the meeting. If the Port Commander suspected anything else, he'd have had Alyn picked up by now.

"I'd be more than glad to meet Commander Kalison." A face-to-face encounter with this man wasn't a danger. Commander Kalison had arrived with the off-world Port Guard more than two years after Alyn's escape from Tempest. They'd never met. "Do you think he'll give me an interview?"

"Maybe." The guard took the travel case, leaving the precious black one for Alyn. Then Captain Bauer looked to where the three Citizen children still waited impatiently behind the customs table. "Oh -- you can go on home now. I'll see to Alyn myself."

The casual dismissal, after making them wait this long, won three scorching glares. Alyn kept his own face steady until they were past the group and heading for the tower lift. When he grinned, Captain Bauer did the same although he remained silent until the door had closed behind them and the cubicle began to move upward into the tower.

"Are they a bit too much for you, Captain?" he dared ask.

"Off the record?" the Captain raised an eyebrow.

"Let's just say at best I'll list it as an anonymous source if I find a reason to use it at all."

"Good enough. I think they're pretentious spoiled brats

who couldn't manage a real day's work to save their lives. The ones who work in the Port Tower are the worst. They're the Elite Citizen's offspring. The older boy in the middle was Governor Bramis Tanton's grandson."

"I wish I'd been paying more attention," he admitted calming the flutter in his stomach at that name. Bramis Tanton was the epitome of power on Tempest and a name that still brought a surge of emotion to him. Alyn took a couple deep breaths in the lift. He needed calm to face the Port Commander.

"Here we are," Bauer signaled him out as the door slid back.

Alyn had never been up into Guard HQ, although he had spent time in the lower holding cells. The ostentatious display of metal from the lower level was missing here. The dull beige walls made the numerous tan uniformed guards less conspicuous. Alyn wasn't sure how many he saw as they stepped out of the lift and into a square lobby.

The wall was decorated with the star-and-ship symbol of the Port Guard. Five cluttered desks stood sentinel in an imposing half circle a dozen steps from the lift. Behind the central desk sat an older woman in perfect uniform who looked up and gave a regal nod at Captain Bauer's salute.

"He'll see you right away," the woman stated. "Go on in, Bauer."

"Thanks." Bauer sounded relieved, and he gave Alyn a slight nudge. "The door straight ahead."

The indicated door stood open, an unsettling invitation to someone with already rattled nerves. Alyn steeled himself as he and Bauer crossed the short distance and walked into the equally cluttered office. People were very busy, and Alyn didn't think this was an act put on for a low-level Vidline reporter. He had studied the current unrest on his way in, having avoided looking at news from Tempest for years. Now he suspected the occasional Port Rat unrest reported outside of Tempest wasn't the entire truth.

And was that why he was here?

The man behind this desk was thin with blond curly hair liberally sprinkled with silver. Alyn suspected the gray came with this assignment on Tempest since Commander Kalison didn't look old. The man belatedly looked up from his comp and offered a ghost of a smile in greeting. He waved Alyn to a chair while Bauer waited patiently by the door.

"I'll be frank with you, friend," the Commander stated as Alyn settled into place. Kalison had a tired, gravelly voice and his gray eyes flickered back to the comp, as though he had far too much else to do. "Naevon, I don't want a reporter wandering around these streets honestly *looking* for trouble."

"I intend to interview as many prominent people as I can and shoot some filler, and then head on to new assignments," Alyn answered truthfully. "I don't want to get caught up in the local war, Commander Kalison. I just want others to understand it."

Kalison's eyes stopped shifting from him to the screen and stared at Alyn for a long silent moment. Bauer moved slightly at the door while Alyn awaited judgment.

"You do realize I have the authority to have you removed from Tempest the moment I think you're causing a disturbance. And I will, Vidline credentials or not. This is a sensitive situation. We don't need any outside factor adding to the tension."

"That's fair enough." Alyn leaned forward, letting reporter's instincts overcome worry. "But maybe I better ask a question right now, so I'll know whether to get back on a ship and not bother to even leave the Port. Do you consider showing that the Port Rats have some legitimate grievances as a cause for my removal?"

"No, I don't."

Alyn grinned with relief and saw a faint whisper a smile in the Commander as well. So, the man remained un-swayed by the more radical Tempest Citizens. That explained why there hadn't been a pogrom against the Rats when trouble escalated into random acts of terrorism. The Citizens, despite holding far more power, couldn't get past the Port Guard.

"Commander, I realize you're busy, but would you have time for a short interview? I'd like to get my bearings here, and I think you can give me an excellent overview of the situation."

"As long as it's quick," he said with another glance at his comp. "I have meetings in ten minutes."

"No problem," Alyn replied and was already flipping open the black case.

He no longer felt shaky, but rather anxious to get to the work. He slipped the eye patch into place, and keyed on the cam, giving his brain a moment to compensate for the distortion of double vision. Using the comp board on the remote, he jotted down the time -- local and standard -- the location of the interview, and Kalison's name and rank. That data automatically encoded on the vid chit for Vidline's records. When he looked up, Kalison nodded, ready.

Get straight to the point, he decided. Kalison didn't have time to waste.

"Commander, how long have you been on Tempest, and what is your opinion of the situation?"

"I arrived here from Terra Nova three and a half years ago standard," he replied evenly. The man knew how to give statements to the press. "I believe the local situation should never have deteriorated so far before the IWC sent in a new force without any long-term ties to the world."

"What was the situation and how has it changed?"

"The first week I arrived, we faced three acts of serious sabotage within the city. The next month a bombing in one of the major banking facilities also claimed the life of Federico De Velera, the man whom everyone thought responsible for the acts of Port Rat terrorism. However, after his death, the situation drastically deteriorated. Apparently, Federico De Velera was a more moderate influence among the Rats than the Citizens believed. Following his death, we had several assassinations of both Citizens and Rats. We've had more bombings, and it's become obvious that the Rats have acquired outside help. Someone is supplying them with weapons and explosives, despite our best efforts to intercept any such shipment."

"Do you have suspects in these incidents?"

"I have a suspect for the leader of the militant Rats: Federico De Velera's daughter, Miranda. She had her hand in her father's work, and from what we know about her, she's far more radical."

"You've made no attempt to capture her?" Alyn asked.

"Miranda wisely doesn't come out of the Rat Maze, and we're limited in our available options to go after her. We're Port Guards, not the regular troops; if we went in the Rats would shoot back now that they have the weapons. Yes, someone is supplying them with laser pistols and probably more. Given the chaotic nature of the Maze, there's also no guarantee we'd ever actually find her. I don't believe the possible loss of life to my men and the Rat non-combatants would be worth the cost. Also, though Miranda's their leader now, she could as easily serve as their martyr. They'd have another leader before I got my troops back to the Port."

"What is your relationship with the Citizens?"

"Those who believe I'm only here to chastise the Rats and will ignore the indiscretions of Citizens had better take a closer look at my record."

"What are the issues?"

"There is only one true issue: Do the Port Rats have the right to demand equality with the Citizens? Don't ask me my opinion, Alyn Naevon. I'm here to make certain they don't destroy each other before they work out that question among themselves."

"Do you see any end in the hostilities?"

"Until both sides confront each other across a table rather than across a weapon -- no."

CHAPTER THREE

Kalison reluctantly allowed Naevon to walk out of his office. He wanted to trust the reporter, but he still felt all the misgivings of someone watching a preventable disaster about to happen. Naevon, by his very work, would go out on the streets to look for trouble. On Tempest, the reporter might find more than he expected.

Kalison crossed to the door in time to see the lift seal closed over Naevon and Bauer -- too late for any last-minute warnings or threats.

Kalison's second-in-command still sat at the entry desk where she liked to work, rather than in an office. Outsiders sometimes mistook her for a clerk if they didn't pay attention to her uniform. Today she apparently dealt with a disagreement about funds between two department heads who stood over her desk. Shanley was excellent at handling all those little problems, leaving him free for more serious trouble. However, he needed her help in the more critical cause right now.

"Shanley? I'd like a couple minutes before my next meeting."

Shanley stood, brushing a hand down her always immaculate uniform. With one regal nod, she dismissed the others and turned to him. All the Junior Officers thoroughly disliked Shanley. She could often be an implacable tyrant who demanded that even the least job be done to her satisfaction. Kalison wouldn't trade her for anyone else in the ranks.

Both risked their careers here. If they didn't get this problem settled soon, the situation would be a blot on their records they'd never live down. At least once every three months Kalison offered Shanley a chance at transfer. She consistently turned the opportunity down. If he'd been wise, he'd have applied for reassignment the first year. Now, like her, he felt some morbid need to see this disaster finished. And like Shanley, he wanted the job done properly and wouldn't settle for less.

They were fools to care more about what happened on Tempest than about their own futures. Neither Citizens nor Rats were without blame in this trouble, and neither side would back down. All Kalison could do was to stand in the middle and take the fire from both sides.

"Commander," Shanley said as she came through the door. At least he'd convinced her to stop saluting at every turn. Kalison reached over and keyed the door closed, watching it slide into place with a quiet click before he settled on the edge of his disorganized desk. Shanley took the chair across from him.

"Shanley, I'll be meeting with Jeffries in a few minutes. Is there's anything you think I should know before I go?"

"Jeffries." She grimaced at the name. None of the Port Guard liked the fanatical head of the local militia. "There's nothing current that will help you deal with him. Was that the new reporter with Captain Bauer?"

"Yes." He frowned, then shrugged. "He looks competent

enough, and he definitely doesn't intend to follow in our Janith's footsteps. The Rats are going to have their say."

"Do you think that might instigate trouble?" Shanley asked, her eyes narrowing slightly. Anything that might start fresh trouble interested them.

"I think his views might make him unpopular among the Citizens. Hopefully, he'll do his work and be on his way before matters escalate again. He indicated he doesn't intend to stick around for long. I hope he works fast. I can feel it in the air; trouble is coming."

"What did you tell him?"

"Nothing that Janith doesn't know. I'll decide if I'm going to tell him more after I see how he handles himself during the next couple days."

"We only have five weeks before the IWC sends in the regular troops," Shanley reminded him. Her voice remained remarkably calm at that reminder and the problems it meant for everyone. "We'll have to tell the population sooner or later that they're coming."

Once those troops arrived, the Port Guard lost control, and the army took over. Then Kalison would find himself in Jeffries position, under the command of another off-worlder. A new layer of bureaucracy would settle at the top, and with orders far more stringent than Kalison's injunction to work things out between the two groups. The IWC troops only came in to settle problems, and they were rarely big on talk.

"The army only ships in if we don't get this mess in order by then. We still have time to work things out," Kalison reminded her. They both knew that was an unlikely occurrence given how long they'd already been struggling with the situation. "If I let the Citizens know they have IWC Whites on the way and might find themselves under martial law before long, they're going to panic."

"And hysteria in the Citizens inevitably turns to anger against the Rats," Shanley added, leaning back in the chair. This was an old discussion of an old problem. The statements seldom changed. "I don't want to pit the troops against the population of either side."

"I want to get Miranda De Velera and her accomplices -- especially the ones I suspect live in the City, not the Maze."

"She's not coming out, Commander. If you want her, it's either gas, or we take Jeffries suggestion and begin systematically destroying the Maze."

"Anything from Ino Mythrin?" he dared to ask.

"That slimy little bastard?" Shanley snarled. Apparently, she disliked their rat informer more than she hated Jeffries. "He'll come to us when he has something worth his while to sell. Or, more likely, something Miranda wants us to know. You know he's not doing anything without her consent."

Kalison nodded weary agreement, then looked with startled worry when his comp beeped for attention. The screen momentarily flashed red before a new report popped up over his own work. Shanley made a slight noise of frustration as she stood so she could watch the words scroll across the screen.

A regular patrol had found three more murdered Rats near the Tanton Mines just outside the city. There were no witnesses, of course. Laser shots through the head, close range. No way to find the killer until they obtained the weapon and could match the burn patterns. Commander Kalison made an inarticulate sound of rage as he cleared the report with one furious jab of his finger.

"I'm going out to look over the scene. Can you cancel my meeting with Jeffries?"

"I'd love to," she replied, and apparently meant those words. Jeffries would rant and rave, but if anyone could handle him, it was Shanley. "This news is going to spread fast through the colony on both sides of the port. You'll have to give some statement to the press."

"And now we have *two* damn Vidline reporters." He keyed open his door from the desk comp and paused only long enough to grab his heavy jacket from the hook. The weather department had predicted rain today, and he could see the build-up of ominous gray clouds through the window across from his office. Kalison hated getting drenched.

"I don't know about this Naevon but at least Janith knows enough to stay out from underfoot in this type of situation," Shanley offered as she followed him out of the office.

"Right. She stays out from underfoot because she couldn't give a damn about the murder of Rats. She's so blatantly one-sided I stopped giving her interviews. This Naevon kid looks like he'll do a better job, and that might make him very unpopular in certain circles. If he starts stirring up any kind of trouble, we better keep an eye on him."

"I'll arrange a watch at the first sign of trouble," Shanley declared as they crossed to her desk. The two department heads still waited with their credit vouchers in hand. "Captain Bauer apparently got along well with the man. I'll detail him to set up friendly surveillance."

"Surveillance but not interference, Shanley. Tell Bauer that if the reporter walks into something he can't handle to pull him out. Don't stop him before he gets there. We don't want Vidline believing we're interfering with their work. If they think we're hiding something, we'll have a couple dozen more reporters on hand. That could be more than even you and I could handle."

"I understand, sir," she said, almost daring a smile. Then she saluted as he started away.

He sighed and saluted in return. They did have a show to keep up for the troops and the Citizens. The Rats didn't seem to give a damn about useless formalities.

Sometimes it was hard for Kalison to remain neutral.

CHAPTER FOUR

Alyn gladly accepted Bauer's offer of a tour around the Port Tower. They'd moved leisurely through halls, past the barracks, armory, cafeteria, and more offices. Bauer told him what information he could like the number of Port Guards stationed on Tempest, how long most of them had been posted here and even some of the moods of the men. There was, Alyn learned, more sympathy toward the Rats in general though that became eroded with every new act of terrorism.

When Bauer finally led him down to the ground level terminal, Alyn almost betrayed his secret in a moment of panic and surprise. He'd never ridden on the famous Silver City transit system in his other life. No Rat was allowed the luxury.

Bauer slipped into the rounded pod ahead of him, patiently holding the door while Alyn fumbled at his case. Finally recovering from his surprise, he uneasily stepped forward and peered inside.

"They're safe enough sir," Bauer assured him, patting the single narrow black couch. "If there's a power failure, each pod has a built-in emergency drive. We can't get trapped in here.

These are new since you lived here, huh?"

"I believe the system was built the year I was born," Alyn answered with a partial truth. "We never spent much time in the city."

"It's funny how many people trust themselves to a spaceship jumping between realities but get skittish when they look at one of these." Bauer grinned with good-natured humor and took one of the cases as Alyn slipped inside.

Alyn took the gentle chiding with an embarrassed smile. He wasn't the militant Rat who'd left Tempest six years ago. Alyn could ride with the Citizens now since he was a real person in their eyes. He purposely turned away to needlessly adjust his baggage and hoped Bauer couldn't see the sudden flash of anger in his eyes. Alyn knew he had to get better control of his emotions if he was going to pull this off. He had to believe he was as good as any of them.

Strangely, as a Rat living in the Maze, he'd never felt he inferior and had fought hard to prove it. Now, sitting in this pod, he only felt as though he was living a lie.

A belt restraint slid into place, and the dome snapped shut over their heads. Bauer quickly keyed in their destination, the Tempest Pride, where Vidline had registered him and was paying the bills. The pod abruptly slid forward and out of the enormous Port Tower. They glided effortlessly onto the main transline falling in among other travelers in the computer-synced pods. The craft's transparent dome showed only the drenching rain. Even the nearest buildings remained invisible behind the pounding sheets of water though they were occasionally outlined by a flash of lightning. Alyn grinned with a touch of ironic humor. He wasn't going to get wet after all.

"Ah, another wonderful day in paradise," Bauer said with a sigh and leaned back on the couch. "I'm just glad I'm not walking the streets tonight. Getting wet is bad enough but stormy nights are the worst for the other trouble too. Should I be telling you that?"

"Someone has to." He grinned back at the affable Port Guard.

"True. Well, consider it a warning then," Bauer replied. The humor unexpectedly left his face. "This really isn't a safe place, Alyn. And if these people don't respect authority in uniform, I doubt they will honor a cam and Vidline credentials, either."

"I'll be careful."

"Good," Bauer said. He stretched as the pod began to slow and slip onto another fork from the main transline. "Here we are."

Startled, Alyn looked out the dome again. They began descending from the main line to the entrance of that needle-like building he'd seen as the left the ship.

"This is a hotel?" he asked, surprised and unexpectedly pleased.

"Best in Silver City. Hell, the Inner World Tourist Board ranked Tempest Pride as one of the best in the entire Ursa Minor sector. Vidline must really think you rate. Staying here doesn't come cheap."

The pod slid into the building and settled at the edge of the hotel's bright and busy lobby. When the dome popped open, two people dressed in the blue uniform of the hotel waited to help with the luggage. A third woman in a modern street dress came closer with a scowl on her face. He hadn't expected another welcoming committee.

"This is Alyn Naevon," Bauer addressed the first person in the line. Her smile of greeting looked friendly rather than just professional. "You have his reservation. Take care of him. Kalison likes him."

"Does he?" asked as she retrieved one of the two cases Bauer handed out. "What a rarity. Thank you for delivering him to our doorstep, Captain Bauer."

"My pleasure, Fiona." Captain Bauer gave a quick gallant little bow, and the woman laughed and patted him on the arm. Apparently, they were more than passing acquaintances. "Good luck, Alyn. I'll probably be seeing you around."

"Thanks," Alyn said, belatedly realizing the Captain was about to abandon him here.

He wasn't a child. He could manage to get to his hotel room without a guard. He nodded good-bye to the Captain and watched until the pod slipped back out into the rainy night.

"Take our guest's luggage to 1503," the woman nodded to one of the people in uniform, who took the cases expertly in hand. "If you follow me, Citizen, we'll get you properly registered, and palm scanned."

"Call me Alyn," he corrected automatically. "I'm not a local."

"Too good to be one of us, right?" a woman behind them finally spoke. It was not a friendly statement.

Alyn recognized the voice though he hadn't the face. He'd listened to her summarizing background on the few recent reports Vidline had passed on to him with this assignment. This was Janith, the local Vidline reporter.

Janith glared at him and waited for an answer to her childish accusation. The man who took his luggage promptly disappeared, and the woman who remained to register him looked dismayed. Other people in the moving crowd glanced their way, but none did more than slow to watch the exchange. There were not, Alyn noted with his usual reporter's instincts, all that many friendly looks directed at Janith even in this group of Citizens.

"I'm just not local, Janith," he finally answered when realized she wouldn't move out of the way without some exchange of words. This was another problem he hadn't foreseen. "And I doubt I'll be here long enough for it to matter."

"Better places to go? Hell, you're just an up-start free-lancer."

The hotel woman winced and gave Janith an unfriendly look, although she refrained from stepping into the battle. Janith glowered with her hazel eyes narrowed to slits, her pale face showing red in spots. Alyn didn't want to stand here in front of strangers and trade caustic conversation with a supposed colleague. He considered inviting her to his room to finish this discussion but decided he didn't want her there either.

"Janith, if you have a problem with my presence, send a message back to Vidline central. I think it would be a waste of time and credits, though. They sent me. If they thought you were doing your job, I wouldn't be here."

Her face went from splotchy red to dead white. Maybe he should have considered a more amiable and conciliatory tact. After all, she wasn't just another reporter: Janith was a Citizen with local fame and personal power. However, she'd already made it clear she wasn't going to work with him, and he didn't see any reason to prolong this useless conversation. The ploy worked in that respect, at least. Janith spun and stalked off across the foyer toward the cafe at the far end. She held her head high and never looked back.

"You did that very well, Alyn Naevon," Fiona mused softly.

"Well, but perhaps not wisely," he admitted, watching uneasily as Janith disappeared into the crowd. "She must have friends here. They might be people I want to talk to."

"They'll talk to you anyway. And you might get more truth out of some locals if they aren't pretending to be pleasant," she answered. When he looked at her, she grinned. "I'm Fiona Salend, the hotel manager. And I'm not a Citizen either, though

I have to pretend to be quite often."

"Then you're from off-world?" he asked, keeping pace with her as they headed towards the admission's desk. He couldn't place her slight accent.

"When they finished this hotel four years ago, the Tempest Government hired me because I ran a popular hotel on Rose. I didn't know about the local trouble with the Rats until I got here."

"I would think that would have been reason enough to have your contract legally voided," Alyn offered.

"It was, and they would have had to pay me until I found another, equally good position," she replied. They reached the desk where two others in hotel uniform were intent on comps. She slipped behind the counter and keyed on the third computer, pushing a palm scanner around so Alyn could use it. "I still hold the possibility over their heads, which keeps the local government from trying to run my business. If the Rat problems get much more out of hand, I may go, though. Business is still good. There's just the whisper enough of real trouble to draw tourists looking for a thrill. If it does turn worse, those tourists will stop coming, and I'll leave. For now, I enjoy the work. This is a nice hotel."

Alyn nodded, letting her take his hand and press it against the cool surface of the scanner. He didn't worry what this one would call up. The scan was only so he could use the palm lock on his door.

"This really is a mess," Fiona said as he pulled his hand away. "I don't want things to get worse. Maybe you can help. Janith and her friends aren't."

"I'm not here to make things right, only to report on the situation," he reminded her.

"We both know nothing changes if the truth isn't fully known." She stopped and looked nervously around the hotel lobby. Whom did she fear would be listening? Government officials? Or just Citizens whom, she admitted, she had to placate by pretending to be one of them. "I'm not saying the Rats are right. I'm just saying there's more truth here than what Janith reports. She forces the other local-based reporters to stick to lesser issues making certain she's the only one reporting on the Rat trouble."

"How strange. All the off-worlders I've met here today apparently think I'll find more than Janith has." Alyn laughed. "I wonder what the natives are going to tell me."

"Lies," Fiona answered automatically, then shrugged. Her eyes flickered nervously around the lobby again. "Lies all the way around."

"We'll see what I find out -- tomorrow. I'm unfit to make any reports tonight, and Captain Bauer warned me not to go wandering about in the rain."

"Ah, true. If you like just ring down to the restaurant and you can have dinner delivered to your suite. That might be a good idea. Janith usually spends a few hours in the hotel bar, and I doubt another confrontation with her would make a meal pleasant."

"Thank you for the advice, Fiona," he replied, grateful for that warning. "I don't need to look for a war with her. There's bound to be plenty to occupy me as soon as I hit the streets."

She nodded grim agreement.

CHAPTER FIVE

Fiona Salend's life had been full of surprises and most of them less than pleasant. She had come to Tempest hoping for a new start. She liked this world and had made a good life here.

So, why had she gotten involved in aspects of the world's current problems that could lead to ... well, those unpleasant surprises again.

Every time she let one of the secret group into the private room, Fiona's heart beat double time. With the new reporter in residence, Fiona found an entirely different reason for worry. Alyn Naevon might look young and nervous, but he'd shown considerable perception in his first meeting with Janith. Naevon wasn't stupid, and if the reporter saw anything out of place, Alyn would investigate. She only hoped he remained exhausted tonight after his long journey. She wished him to sleep well and not go wandering around the hotel.

"I'm the last," Caden needlessly told her as he paused by the open door.

Caden looked down the empty, blue-walled hall and started

at a slight whisper of sound. It was only the air conditioning kicking in, and that won a nervous grin of embarrassment. He was a Rat and had every reason to worry about his presence in the city. Caden slipped into the relative safety of the room, nodding to the others as he settled into his usual chair. No one looked happy about being here tonight.

"Let's get the meeting going," he suggested.

Fiona sealed and locked the steel door behind her. No one else could follow them in since the hotel records listed this storage room as having a restricted entry. They kept all hotel comp records here, safe from the eyes of competitors and their spies. Fiona and her chief comp tech were the only members of management with access to the room, and he was safe at home tonight. They always planned their meetings on his nights off. Getting into and leaving the place was, of course, the riskiest part of this encounter. Even if what they did here was not illegal, there were people who would frown on it and not only make their lives miserable, but also put them in danger.

Two auxiliary computers sat against the far wall, nestled between tall storage compartments. Lights on the boards occasionally blinked as new info shuttled down from the main comp in the lobby: the request for coffee, a complaint that the blanket was too hot. During the day, the lights remained nearly steady with the stream of information. This late at night, though, they blinked in a slow random fashion, relating that nothing was seriously wrong. Fiona never felt that she ignored her duty when she sat here with the others. She always kept an eye on the comp info.

Fiona had added the long narrow table and stacked chair in the corner when she became involved with these people. Laten, her chief comp tech, never asked why. Maybe he thought she came here to get away from the hectic rush of her upstairs office. She did exactly that, sometimes, when she needed to get work done. She'd even held a couple hotel-related meetings here, but mostly it went unused. The quiet little room still smelled faintly of fresh paint and new carpets.

Tonight, four others joined her in this private hideaway. Caden was the only Rat in the company, and Fiona the only off-worlder. She again wondered how the hell she'd ever gotten drawn so far into this mess. Granted, in the beginning, they were only a group of concerned people hoping to maintain working relationships on both sides of the port. She needed that cooperation to manage her business. Now that very concern made them targets of mistrust. Citizens didn't trust anyone who worked with Rats. Rats distrusted all Citizens. People from off-world -- well, what business was it of theirs? Fiona wondered if anyone of her companions still hoped to do something positive in this environment.

Ember leaned forward, her hand brushing the unruly brown hair from her face. She, too, appeared anxious to set the meeting in motion. She likely had more important work to get to yet tonight. Ember Tanton was a cousin to the Governor and one of Tanton Steel's top executives -- by far the most illustrious member of this secretive gathering.

The last two Citizens in the group were male, middle-aged, and government clerks: Sonio from Transportation, Wintas from Education. There was supposition among the others that Wintas represented someone notably higher in his department. He never admitted to it, and the others refrained from asking what he didn't offer to tell them.

They were a taciturn group when it came to anything personal.

Fiona took her usual seat beside Caden and again wondered about her involvement in this madness.

"Do you have any news from the Maze?" Ember asked.

"Miranda doubled her personal security," Caden replied.

His dark and callused hands ran over the top of the table in a familiar nervous gesture. "No one's hinting at new trouble but everyone's nervous. I'm beginning to doubt she tells even her closest friends about her real plans."

"What about Sebastian? Anything you can get from him?"

"It's hard to talk to Sebastian these days." He shrugged and gave them a nervous little grin. "Miranda put a guard on her precious little brother. Nothing obvious -- but one of Miranda's younger followers has romantically attached herself to him. Lauren is seldom more than a couple meters away from her charge."

"You're certain she's working for Miranda?" Fiona asked. "Miranda's never been this subtle before."

"Lauren's older brother is Niel Taress, Miranda's current top aide," Caden replied.

"Another new top aide?" Fiona mused. "She changes them faster than I do lobby clerks."

"I don't see why she's so careful with Sebastian," Ember said. She looked thoughtful. "Surely he isn't much of a threat to her."

"She's moving carefully because Sebastian is popular in the Maze," Caden explained. "Even Miranda has to move carefully when dealing with him. The Rats like him -- but he's no threat to her power. She just wants to make sure she has him under her control."

"If he's so well liked maybe this girl is infatuated with him," Wintas offered. "Not everything is a conspiracy, Caden."

"Miranda sends someone to pick up a daily report on her brother's activities. Lauren hands it over in writing. My people watch the transactions. We even managed to read one of the reports before Miranda destroyed it. Lauren doesn't think much of Sebastian at all."

Ember made one slight snickering sound and leaned back.

"A shame we've lost him. I was beginning to believe he wasn't really so naive and maybe we could trust him as one of the group."

"Safer to ask occasional questions rather than take him into our confidence," Caden replied. His hands stilled, and his gray eyes swept around the table. "Safer for him and us. The boy's total dedication to his art leaves him, in some ways, vulnerable to being used by one side or the other. I don't want to put him in a position that makes him look unsafe for Miranda. I don't trust what she'd do."

"True," Sonio said and nodded with a frown of worry. "Bad luck that we won't have even that little link to his sister."

"Wait them out," Caden replied. "Lauren will get lax in time. She doesn't really care about the boy."

"Good," Ember said again. "Anything else? Any chance of contacting someone else in Miranda's group?"

"Not yet. There's no sign of a weakening in Miranda's power structure despite the constant changes in top personnel. And there's no Rat we can put up as a rival to her, at least not one who would survive for more than a few hours, anyway."

There was nothing new in that assessment.

"Three more Rats were killed on the way home from the mine this afternoon," Ember suddenly reported. She lost some of her usual poise as she related the unwelcome information. "Bramis took the news badly. I think we're going to face some new action there."

"She wouldn't close the mine, would she?" Fiona asked, worried again.

"She's Governor of Tempest and the nominal head of Tanton Steel, though most of the work falls to the board of directors. She does have final say in any major decisions. I don't know which position is going to win out," Ember admitted. Her hands remained still on the table, the way they did whenever she considered something bothersome. Fiona had gotten very good at reading some of the reactions from her companions. "Tempest World Stock took a loss on the market in the last quarter. Tanton Steel also lost credits for the third time in two years standard. She has to do something drastic."

No one was happy with that revelation. Tempest didn't need any more pressure, and Tanton Steel's stock -- on world and off -- kept the world solvent.

"Bauer let anything drop lately?" Sonio dared ask.

"Nothing." Fiona frowned at the man, and he turned quickly away. He'd been a fool to ask, and the others didn't pursue his opening. Her relationship with Bauer was outside this group's jurisdiction, as they had quickly learned in their first meeting here. However, he did occasionally tell her about the attitude shifts in the Port Guard. He was too good an officer to casually discuss anything could prove dangerous, but sometimes his insights did help them understand more significant issues, though it was nothing any of the others couldn't learn by hanging around a local bar.

"We have a new Vidline reporter on world," Fiona announced, drawing surprised looks from everyone. "Alyn Naevon. He's staying here at the hotel."

Ember made a shift in her chair, a clear sign of worry, which didn't calm Fiona's nerves anymore. None of the others looked very happy either.

"Don't worry," she assured them. "Unfortunately, I doubt Naevon will be on Tempest for very long."

"Unfortunately?" Wintas echoed, confused.

"He ran into our Janith in the lobby and put her in her place. I admit I did enjoy watching the show as long as I wasn't involved."

Caden grinned, but then he had the most reason to dislike the obviously bigoted native reporter. Fiona wanted Naevon to stick around at least long enough to set a few of Janith's mangled facts straight.

"He might make our work more difficult," Sonio suggested. Then he too shrugged. "Though it hardly matters at this point. We're at a standstill until we either learn what Miranda plans next or we find someone strong enough to oppose her. I hate to admit that everything is really in her hands -- and that's not because she's a Port Rat."

Fiona tried not to look relieved as the other three agreed. The thought of any blatant action on their part scared the hell out of her. She still believed in their original mission to try and help find common ground between Rat and Citizen, but the current trouble made anything more than talk impossible.

They parted company a few minutes later, intending to meet again the next night since Ember thought she might have more information on what Governor Tanton would do. Caden hurried away first, heading towards the service entrance. The four knew the keycode to get in and out there, the least noticeable access to the building. Surprisingly, Ember and Sonio left together, speaking softly as they headed down the hall. Usually, each member was very careful to slip out of the building alone. Even Wintas eyed the two with nervous worry and then hurried after them. Fiona watched tensely until they were all around the first turn in the hall. She glanced back into the storage room, making certain nothing incriminating remained behind, and that the chairs were all stacked back in the corner. Then she sealed the door and headed in the opposite direction.

Knowing she wouldn't fall asleep soon, Fiona went to the bright lobby. The place was empty except for hotel personnel, which was always a good sign. She paused by the counter and pretended interest in the comp board with its lists of breakfast meals and morning activities. She didn't like clandestine meetings or the case of nerves she always had afterward.

Nevertheless, Fiona remained actively involved with the little group. She knew the hostilities would never end without cooperation on some level. She liked Tempest, both the world itself and most of the people. She didn't want to see it irrevocably changed by this growing hostility. Even the remote chance that her group might help was better than hopeless despair.

Something had to change.

CHAPTER SIX

As he awoke, Alyn felt unexpectedly contented. The gravity felt right. He hadn't slept this well in years.

Not since he'd left home.

A faint hint of yellowish light drifted through the partially opaqued window, softly illuminating the casual opulence of the room. Alyn had never stayed in any place so nice, but despite the comfort, Alyn knew he wasn't going back to sleep. He had work to do. The sooner he started the interviews, the quicker he could leave Tempest.

The full night's sleep had cleared his head. Alyn realized he didn't dare approach this job haphazardly. He'd come to Tempest to save his career, and it would be stupid to throw it away now on sloppy work.

If he could pretend this was only another assignment, he might make it through the next few days without any revealing mistakes. Yesterday he'd reacted as though he was just a Rat pretending to be a reporter, and that was untrue. He was a damned good reporter, and even Vidline thought so.

With that daring thought in mind, Alyn finally threw

himself out of bed and wandered into the bathroom. The clock on the wall stated local and standard time, and both were far too early to go asking for interviews. He took his time in the shower and then settled down in the enormous outer room of his suite and ordered breakfast through the comp. The quiet opulence of the rooms unsettled him as he took a chair by the window with an incredible view of the port and part of the city. Vidline was apparently aware of local attitudes and knew riches were a sign of power; staying at the Tempest Pride made him more legit in the eyes of the Citizens.

After breakfast arrived, Alyn keyed up the Tempest Newsline to get a feel for the current situation. Janith's sketchy report on the deaths of three more Rats fell far into the broadcast. The high point of the news had been the time given to cover the decline in Tempest world stock at Earth-based markets.

Money over murder. He was neither surprised nor annoyed and would have expected the same reaction if they had found a Citizen murdered. Here in Silver City the lives of people often meant less than income. The entire world rested on how the markets did.

This also made the local tensions harder to work around, especially when not everything could be corrected with money. More income in the Rat Maze would help ease the problems, but it wouldn't fix them.

He wasted as much time as he could accessing old newscasts and government reports for more information. Finally, with his hand hardly shaking at all, Alyn keyed up a directory to the local government offices and quickly typed in requests for interviews with the heads of every department listed.

He received three acceptances almost immediately and arranged times with the Transportation Department, Education

Department, and the Tempest Militia. The last was still nominally the local police force though primarily superseded by the Port Guard. Their notoriously anti-rat leader would probably have plenty to say.

Alyn managed to remain calm and professional right until he stepped into the office of the Head of Transportation. He hadn't recognized the name -- Lisbonne -- but he knew the face. Six years ago, Lisbonne had worn the uniform of the local militia.

They had met.

The woman looked up, nodded a greeting, and waved to the chair in front of her desk.

"Alyn Naevon," he introduced himself. His voice remained remarkably steady though his heart pounded so hard he could feel his blood pulsing.

"Citizen Lisbonne," she said in return, looking up from her desk again. Her gray eyes narrowed, and Alyn's hands tightened on the vidcam, ready to run, for all the good that would do him. He'd never get past security in this building. "Janith says she's checking on your credentials. She doesn't believe you are legit."

"Port Authority checked me out." He shrugged and refrained from showing any worry. Janith would hear of his reaction, and that would only further fuel her vendetta. "As soon as I finish this work, I'll leave. I'm not here for Citizen Janith's job. I'm here because Vidline sent me."

"Right," Lisbonne said. She appeared satisfied with his answer. "Then the sooner you get your interviews over, the better, right?"

"Absolutely."

"Janith thinks you're a Rat-lover here to cause the Citizens new grief."

"I'm here to ask questions," he answered, still maintaining his calm. "You answer them as you see fit."

Lisbonne scowled. He hoped the woman didn't look at him for too long. "Ask your questions," the woman ordered. A whisper of open hostility came and went. "I have real work to do."

Alyn refrained from reminding Lisbonne that she'd invited him to the office. There was no reason to antagonize her. Instead, Alyn keyed on his vidcam and prepared for the interview. He even put the eye patch in place though it wasn't needed with the subject this close. He felt safer behind the little disguise.

"How long have you been the head of the local transportation system, Citizen Lisbonne?"

"Three years standard. The last person in charge of the department retired when the Rats made the position dangerous."

"How does the trouble with the Rats affect your department?"

"They've twice stopped the pod system in-city. On three other occasions, they hijacked transports heading for the smaller villages. In those instances, they delayed valuable supplies in shipment. That could be extremely dangerous, especially for the outer communities."

"I believe the Port Guard has now taken over those shipments, have they not?"

"Yes," the woman's eyes glared for a moment. "However, this imported Port Guard is causing considerable problems of their own."

"They're not getting the supplies through?" he asked, his cam focusing in closer on Lisbonne's face.

"Oh, yeah, they manage to do that work." Her fingers carelessly waved away what had been so life-threatening a moment before. "They're here to stop the Rats from causing trouble. They've done nothing."

"I studied the reports on the last decade. Since their arrival, you've suffered from less trouble. What more do you expect them to do?"

"Go in and clear the Maze out," she answered, then frowned, as though tricked into the answer. "At least go in and drag out that bitch leader of theirs, Miranda De Velera."

"Commander Kalison states that such an attack might be hazardous."

"Well, what the hell are they here for, if not to do what's dangerous?" Lisbonne growled with another wave of her hand. She was growing very visibly angry. "The Rats kill Citizen's on the streets, and they just stand around watching."

"I understand that the number of Rats murdered in the last year standard has topped one hundred."

"Yeah, well -- someone has to do it, don't they?"

Apparently, they both realized that Lisbonne had said enough. Alyn lowered his vidcam and peeled away the eye patch. He gave Lisbonne a civil enough nod. Lucky for the woman Alyn still had that career to consider.

"I'll let you know if there are any more questions," Alyn told her as he stood.

"I'll let you know if I have the time," the woman answered with a slightly surly growl.

"Of course. Good day, Citizen Lisbonne."

He walked back toward the door. Lisbonne childishly forced him to wait a moment before keying it open. Thankfully, the hall remained empty. He took a moment to lean against the wall and take deep breaths to get control again.

Whether the woman recognized him or not no longer mattered. He felt righteously infuriated at the attitude of Tempest Citizens who thought Rats were an infestation and the Port Guard just a fancy extermination squad. It wasn't a new attitude, and it wasn't even limited to Tempest, but having lived on both sides of this particular line made Alyn feel the sting all the worse.

In the end, it always just came down to riches. Alyn had bought his way out. They never even considered he could be a Rat.

His next interview was in an office halfway around the building and five flights up. He avoided the lift. The walk gave him enough time to calm before he faced another Citizen. He wondered if he'd ever met the head of the Education Department. Probably not. It was unlikely he knew more than one high-ranking Citizen.

Guards stopped him twice and checked his ID. People working for the government were nervous about strangers walking in such a high-risk location. After the morning's interviews, maybe he'd try to question the person in charge of the building's security. That might add more insight into how people worked with this problem rather than how they created it.

He arrived at the Education Offices just barely in time for his appointment. The clerk quickly ushered him into Nedra's suite. Alyn prepared himself for another unpleasant interview. The woman greeted him far more civilly than Lisbonne which at least meant it wouldn't be as uncomfortable a meeting. He didn't recognize her either, easing another worry.

"Citizen Nedra, will you tell us how long you've been the head of the Education Department, and any views you have on the current situation?"

"I've held this position for ten years standard," she told the cam. She looked weary, as though she'd been working for days rather than a couple hours. "And if even five years ago, I was given half the new equipment I asked for, we wouldn't have this problem now."

"Pardon?" he asked, honestly surprised.

"I wanted to build a real school out by the Maze. Something more than that bunker where they waylay Rat Children and tell them they're second-class humans."

Alyn chilled slightly with the memory of his own days in that school. He hadn't gone there often and not at all after his father became famous. He couldn't remember learning anything from the hawk-faced teachers who were volunteers from Silver City, and now he wondered if they had even possessed teaching credentials. Young Rats usually received their serious education from community adults who still believed their children had a future.

"I wanted to stock a real school with comps, teachers, and techs who could teach the Rat kids some profession," the woman continued softly. "I've submitted that proposal every three months for nine years, Alyn Naevon. They won't even let it get as far as a public meeting. They vote it out in private committee."

"They?" he asked, surprised to learn the head of the Education Department sided with him.

Sided with the *Rats*. Alyn had to remind himself yet again not to take this all so personally.

"The other Department Heads. They say giving Rats an education would only make them less happy with their position. Damn right it would!" Nedra nodded vigorously, blond hair falling into her eyes.

She brushed the strand back away with an angry swipe of her fingers. Silent for a moment, she stared past the cam and him. The intensity of her convictions remained visible in her open face. This was another fanatic, of an opposite breed than Lisbonne, though just as dedicated.

"Do you know the only difference between you and me and the Rats, Alyn Naevon?" She asked, focusing on him again. She didn't wait for an answer. He wasn't certain what to say, anyway. "We have a profession. We have jobs that will pay us a decent income and offer a chance of advancement. They have nowhere to go. They can work the mines if they have the strength, though chances are the work will kill them eventually. Or they can work as street cleaners, window washers, gutter walkers -- and, of course hauling things at the port. Port Rats -- that's the term heard on every world. That's work no *Citizen* would ever do. The Citizens know they would suffer if the Rats stopped doing the dirty work so that they aren't going to let them have a chance at something else. There's no future for Rats on Tempest, Alyn Naevon."

"Are you from Tempest, Citizen Nedra?" he dared ask.

"I was born in Farrow, a farming community about a thousand kilometers south of here. We didn't have real Rats there. We did have poor people who were willing to work and out in the farms, we needed the extra hands. We wanted to give them more, but old government regulations kept us from selling them any land. If someone moves to Tempest and doesn't have a permanent job within six months, the government designates them as undesirable immigrants, unless a Citizen signs for them. None of the jobs open to Rats are permanent, by the way. Even the mine work is only a weekly sign up, though Tanton Industries might yet change. The designation passes on to children, and some of these Rats are the fourth generation born on Tempest! It's a wonder this trouble took so long in coming."

"I assume the local Citizens are uneasy about offering an education to Rats because they don't want to deal with them as equals?"

"They can't *imagine* them as equals," Nedra replied, calmer again. She patted papers on her desk, looking away from the cam. "They say the Rats will take jobs that belong to Citizens. They fear they'll no longer find workers to do the dangerous work out at the mines. They could, of course. They'd just have to start paying them wages commensurate with the danger. If it cost them, they might even make the needed improvements in the working conditions."

"You think this is all a matter of money," Alyn supplied.

"Money," she nodded. The angry animation left her face. "Other members of the government constantly remind me that my job is to run the School Board, not change it. Other department heads tell me it's no use teaching Rats to even read or write since it only makes them less tractable. I've put up with this for ten years. I gave up a few months ago. They have my resignation on file. I'm just waiting for a replacement."

"That's a shame," Alyn said with a sigh. She looked surprised, and he realized how partisan he'd sounded. "You're a person who could offer considerable enthusiasm to the education of any child. They all need to learn, Citizen and Rat."

She nodded and looked away for a moment.

"I am emigrating to the Pavo Fringe," she said and smiled this time. "They want teachers out there. I quit fighting the people in charge. I want to teach again."

"Good luck," Alyn offered.

"Thank you."

Alyn left the office, remembering how he'd felt when he escaped Tempest. He understood why she also planned her escape, but he was no longer confident going elsewhere was an answer.

CHAPTER SEVEN

Sebastian frowned and looked over his shoulder at the haloed form blocking the bright light from the doorway. He patiently held the softly vibrating paint brush a centimeter above the porous plaster surface and schooled himself to patience before he spoke.

"Lauren, love, you're in the light again," he said with as much politeness as he could manage.

Lauren looked back at him, her glare of hostility quickly replaced by a brighter -- but far less honest -- smile. Lauren bowed her head and moved out of the doorway. Unfortunately, she came inside, and he suspected she would soon distract him once more.

Morning light once more flooded the small room, illuminating the bright greens and blues sketched on the wall. He steadied his hand and banished the discordant thoughts Lauren's presence brought. Sebastian let his mind drift as he savored the scent of fresh sweet bread cooked in the outside oven and the sound of men gambling in the room across the alley, laughing and cursing as the dice rolled on a plastic table.

From here he could even hear the continual hum of work out at the Port. The sounds and smells of life brought him calm and inspiration again.

Sebastian adjusted the brush and made two fine lines across the rough plaster surface, adding a hint of shadow to a scene of sunlight and alien flowers. After a few more strokes, the outline of a tree rose like a sentinel in the middle of rolling green hills --

"Doesn't look like anywhere I've ever seen," Lauren complained.

He hadn't heard her move up to his shoulder and her sudden comment startled him. Sebastian quickly drew his hand away from the wall and steadied himself. He wanted to order Lauren away and have a few, uninterrupted minutes to devote mind and soul, to his work. If he tried that tact, she'd only get angry, and he'd get no more painting done at all.

Forcing himself to remain calm, Sebastian looked back at her. His smile wasn't any more real than hers.

"This is from a painting done from a picture I saw of a place on Earth," he explained softly. *Again.* He looked at the wall and dabbed a bit of darker color at the base of the tree, nodding approval of the result. "I saw the holo in a book once, and I always wanted to paint it."

"Why don't you paint real things?" she demanded.

Sebastian carefully turned off the brush and put it aside, telling himself he needed to change the color tubes anyway. He didn't want Lauren to annoy him into a mistake.

"This is real, Lauren, but it is a reality Rats aren't allowed to touch which is why I paint it. We should know what we want, what we fight for."

"I know what I want." Lauren smiled. She leaned close to his ear, her breath warm against his neck. "Come on home with me, Sebastian."

"I have work to do," he said and tried to push her hand out

of his hair.

"Come on," she insisted again and ran fingers down the back of his neck. "This isn't real work. You can do it anytime."

His teeth clamped tightly closed. He wanted to ask what Lauren thought *real work* was but refrained. He didn't want to annoy her and Miranda. It wasn't like there was anyone in the Maze who didn't know why Lauren had become his shadow.

"Hey!" a voice called from the doorway. "How's it going, Sebastian?"

Despite his better judgment, Sebastian turned a bright, welcoming smile to Caden and didn't hide his sigh of relief. He disliked being alone with Lauren -- at least while he was working. Sebastian accepted the nights together as payment for the hell she put him through during the day. However, if Lauren wandered off and found some other poor soul to torment, he wouldn't complain.

He wished Miranda would find someone else who needed watching more than him. She had real enemies in the Maze; Lauren could drive one of them to despair instead of him. Send her after Ino Mythrin and one of the other disreputable Rats that Miranda had recently started drawing closer to her inner circle.

Not something Sebastian dared mention, though. Everyone expected him to be the artist with no connection of the real world.

"I haven't much left to do," Sebastian said and waved Caden over to see the painting. This was, after all, Caden's wall.

"We were just getting ready to leave," Lauren added testily.

"I'm going to finish the tree, love," Sebastian smiled in return. Her face reddened, hazel eyes narrowing with anger. "Why don't you go on ahead of me? I'll be there in an hour or so."

Lauren stomped across the small room and threw herself

into a battered chair by the door. Hardly subtle. At least Caden had the grace to pretend interest in Sebastian's art, which was more than Lauren could manage. Caden let him choose his own subject. The few credits the man paid wasn't worth as much as the artistic freedom.

Caden remained content to sit on the floor and watch him work which proved an excellent deterrent to Lauren's games. Sebastian worked slowly, savoring the peace. His hand moved to a rhythm no one else in this room heard. Children laughed outside, and the breeze whistled along the edges of Caden's roof. The air held the scent of distant rain. On inspiration, Sebastian painted a few feathery clouds into the blue of the alien sky. Slowly, the scene magically transferred from his mind to the wall. He wished he could find peace like this more often.

Sebastian wondered if anyone else understood his work, despite how many times he tried to explain. They only saw him as Federico's son and Miranda's brother. They expected him to want power, but he had chosen a different path. He dreamed of better places and tried to make others see them.

That was his real work.

CHAPTER EIGHT

After his pleasant interview with Nedra, Alyn slowly made his way to the suite of offices on the ground floor which was now occupied by the Tempest Militia. He'd traversed the building twice in the last few hours. At least the security people no longer stopped him at every corner.

The Militia possessed a building of their own, but just after Federico De Velera's death, they had moved in with the rest of the government agencies. Officially, they transferred to this building for security reasons, though Alyn doubted that answer on several levels. First, the Militia didn't run security in the building. Also, the reports he'd read off the comp skimmed over the involvement of the Militia's role during the worst of the local troubles. Janith had written most of the reports herself and Alyn suspected she wasn't mentioning their less-than-legal treatment of captured Rats. Kalison's Port Guard troops assumed even local police duties that should have been the Militia's work, and it was certain they weren't doing it because they couldn't find enough else to keep them occupied. Apparently, no one trusted them, even for security in this single building.

Alyn had never cared much for the Militia, but he swallowed his old dislike and headed down the hall with every intention of being if not polite, at least professional.

A guard in a gray Militia uniform waited at his commander's door. Despite the laser rifle neatly resting on his shoulder, the guard appeared more pretentious than protective. He hadn't seen armed guards on any other offices in the building, and that clued Alyn on what to expect. He didn't protest as the guard checked his equipment for weapons or bombs -- or hidden Rats with guns. Still glaring with unspoken distrust, the guard finally ushered him into a darkened room crowded with chairs, three desks, and chart-covered walls.

Jeffries certainly *looked* busier than Commander Kalison.

The guard silently slipped back out of the room, and the door sealed closed behind him. Alyn felt a slight tingle of mistrust and worry all his own. The Militia might have recognized him ... no. They wouldn't have let him go wandering around the building interviewing important people.

A ghost of gray movement to the right startled Alyn. An indistinct figure in militia uniform slipped from a dark corner and almost into the pool of light near one desk. Alyn barely recovered before stepping backward in reaction. This encounter already felt tainted with too much illusion. He remained unimpressed by the show.

"You are the reporter from Vidline?" a whispery voice demanded.

"I doubt they'd have let me in if I wasn't."

"This is no place or time for jokes."

Alyn bit at his lower lip and unobtrusively keyed on his cam, making sure the lights stayed off -- a nice feature for times like this where a reporter needed to get a record of events unobtrusively. He wanted this on record though he couldn't legally use it in a report since he hadn't officially started the interview. Vidline News held scrupulously to the law on invasion of privacy.

However, if Jeffries admitted to any wrong-doing, or made an overt action against him, this became news. Sometimes reporters got lucky. Sometimes they even survived it, if they remained cautious.

"I am Alyn Naevon, assigned on temporary duty to Tempest," he finally offered. "I've come for the interview that I requested, and you confirmed."

"Very good," the man slipped forward fully into the light.

Jeffries was a short, corpulent man. The top of his shaved head was barely level with Alyn's eyes. He had been the second-in-command of the militia before Alyn left Tempest and he remembered that fat face and the perpetual glare. Jeffries always had to look up at others, and it clearly annoyed him. The Rats had always despised the strutting, bully and the man never spoke a kind word about Rats. Now he might have the power to act on his bigotry.

"I don't approve of reporters."

"You didn't have to agree to an interview."

"Janith is the only reporter I trust," he continued as though he hadn't listened. He probably only heard what he wanted to. "Janith knows the truth about what's happening on Tempest. She knows better than to tell Rat lies. What kinds of lies do you tell, boy?"

"I don't tell anything at all. You tell me."

"Huh."

The commander of the Militia slowly walked around him. The hair on the back of Alyn's neck began to rise, and his shoulders tensed. Alyn wanted to turn and watch him, distrusting this person at his back. However, he stayed very still, hoping Jeffries didn't look closely at the vidcam and find it running.

Jeffries finally appeared around the other side again. Little eyes of an almost colorless blue narrowed as he stared up at Alyn's face. Alyn's heart pounded hard again with a renewed fear of recognition. Jeffries might well never forget an enemy of the state.

Unexpectedly, Jeffries turned and slipped behind the desk. He settled in his high-backed chair, looking back at Alyn with silent animosity.

"If you don't want me here, I can leave."

"You leave when I tell you. I want to know what Lisbonne and Nedra told you."

"Watch the reports."

"I could confiscate your equipment," he warned. His watery eyes brightened at the possibility. "I know you haven't left the building. You still have the reports on you."

"You could find yourself facing Vidline in a civil suit too, but I doubt you want that kind of publicity," Alyn replied evenly.

The face flushed, and the eyes blinked, then narrowed with new anger.

"I don't trust you."

"You don't have to. Commander Kalison passed me. Do you want to give an interview or not? Don't you have more important work than to stand here baiting me?"

"From now on you will check with me before making any new appointments."

"No, I won't."

"I am the head of the Tempest Militia."

"I have the Port Guard Commander's permission to do my job, and if you keep up this harassment, I can guarantee you'll have a visit from him. You had better check the laws on censorship of the news, Citizen Jeffries."

"You're pushing me, boy. Don't push."

"I'll make you a deal. You don't harass me, and I won't see you again."

The man snarled, and Alyn felt the sweat starting to make his hands slick. He wasn't clear about the extent of Jeffries's powers. Alyn hoped Commander Kalison's approval meant the man didn't dare anything more than verbal harassment.

He desperately wanted out of this stifling, dark room and back into the lighted hall where there were people. He wanted witnesses. He wasn't certain his recording chit would make it out of here, even if he did.

"I'll give you an interview."

The startling statement wasn't anything Alyn desired to hear after this exchange. He considered saying no and changed his mind. He didn't want to annoy the man even more. So Alyn made a show of lifting the cam and pretending to turn it on. Thank God this was a quiet machine, with no lights and bells to show it was running. They made this type of equipment for clandestine work and dangerous situations. Usually, those were combat or riot situations, though, where a reporter didn't want to draw extra attention. Alyn had never thought to use those settings, and he hoped never to find himself in a similar position again.

Alyn settled the cam on his shoulder, and for a panicked moment, all questions eluded him. He knew he needed caution: ask simple questions, nothing controversial. He didn't want to make this any worse.

"Citizen Jeffries, how long have you been in command of the Tempest Militia?"

"I've been Commander for seventeen months standard. Before that, I was second-in-command, with nearly equal powers," the man answered. He sat up straighter in the chair. His fleshy face almost showed a hint of pleasure. The man liked his job. "I have a special nickname around here. They call me Rat Catcher."

Alyn realized nothing he asked mattered because the man would say what he wanted. Fine. Alyn steadied his cam and went straight to the heart of the trouble.

"Please give your impression of the situation and your opinion on how to end the trouble."

"The Rats are rebelling. If we gave them a true show of force, they'd slither back into their Maze. Then we blow the Maze to hell, and we don't have this problem again."

The man said those words with perfectly straight-faced seriousness.

"Don't you feel that might be a drastic reaction, to kill even unarmed children?" Alyn asked, somehow managing to keep his voice calm.

"Rats start young," the man replied. His eyes narrowed again. "Unless the Port Guard starts doing their job, they're going to find more enemies than they could possibly deal with."

"Is that something you would like to tell the Port Guard Commander officially?" Alyn grinned.

"Don't push boy," he glared suddenly. "I am finished with the interview."

"Good," Alyn lowered his cam. "Time for lunch."

Jeffries reached forward to his desk, keying open the door behind them. Bright light from the hall flooded the cluttered room. Jeffries's eyes watered.

"Sir!" the guard slipped in.

"Show the reporter out."

"I think I can find the door."

He didn't bother to turn the cam off. That also went unnoticed by Jeffries. In fact, the man noticed little that didn't directly affect him. Once safely beyond the door Alyn stopped and shook his head in disbelief, which won an antagonistic scowl from the guard; they had fanatics guarding fanatics.

However, Alyn did want to go to lunch and try to unwind following that last encounter. After a quick meal, he would take to the street and start collecting impressions from the local Citizens. Once he edited the pieces together, he'd send his first preliminary report to Vidline central. Unless Kalison pulled it, the same report would run on local Newsline by noon tomorrow.

If the report ran, he'd soon find out how the locals liked having a *real* reporter on-world.

Alyn passed a work crew making repairs on the walkway outside the main entrance to the building. Alyn wasn't sure if he felt more fear or shame as he rushed past the sweating Rats and slipped into the nearest waiting pod. He didn't dare look back as he headed for the hotel.

CHAPTER NINE

Kalison squinted against the assault of the bright morning sunlight as he slipped from the aircar and narrowly avoided trampling the row of tiny blue flowers bordering the landing pad. They hadn't been there last month.

"I won't be long," he told the uniformed driver. "I never am."

The man behind the controls nodded, and the aircar door sealed shut. Kalison inched his way around the vehicle and headed for the front door of the palatial, red stone home. Nothing moved around the landing pad and even the usual morning breeze seemed languid. Nothing could get up much energy at this time of the morning.

Visiting Governor Bramis Tanton was rarely pleasant for either of them. She still considered Commander Kalison's appointment by the IWC as a personal affront to her ability to control Tempest. He felt that with a little cooperation and common sense, he could have left years ago. The first few months of outright antagonism had gradually given way to acceptance and occasional cooperation. Perhaps that was only because, individually, neither made any headway.

Nevertheless, the woman seldom called him to private morning meetings at her country estate. They would both attend the regular Council Meeting in a few hours. He wondered -- and worried over -- what was so important it couldn't wait that long.

A row of four Tanton Steel vehicles stood at the end of the pad. The spotless blue craft sat in a perfect line, as though the gardener arranged them with the rest of the immaculate grounds. Kalison's battered and dirty aircar appeared distinctly out of place. It clashed.

He grinned as he slipped up to the door then frowned when it opened before he could even touch the communit. He hated feeling as though these people remained one step ahead of him. That was a game the Citizens played with the Rats.

"Good day, Commander Kalison," the doorman bowed in greeting, all very proper. "Governor Tanton is expecting you. This way."

The show was an act of Old World manners to go with the antiquated morals they'd transplanted out here. The Citizen Elite insisted on their spectacle of superiority. Kalison never understood why people recreated the same archaic Earth problems on new worlds. He didn't like to believe it was because humans couldn't do any better.

He followed the nameless man. As usual, he saw no one else as they passed through the long hall lined with artwork from a dozen worlds, including Earth. Despite his uniform and rank, Kalison always felt like a shabby intruder in these corridors.

The doorman pushed open an ornate non-electronic door and carefully stepped aside with a nod to Kalison. The ritual remained the same with every visit, and Kalison still felt the urge to bow as he came into the regal woman's presence.

Windows at the far side of the room cast bright morning light into the cluttered interior. Small tables lined the walls, littered with glittering glass and carved stone objects. Four empty chairs crowded around the Governor's equally untidy desk. Bramis Tanton's austere office in the government building was the antithesis of this chaos. He often wondered which represented the woman.

"Good morning Commander," Governor Tanton greeted him as she looked up from her comp. As always, the lithe, white-haired woman was immaculate. Kalison instinctively straightened his jacket. "I apologize for the sudden call. Thank you for coming here so quickly."

"No problem, Governor," he replied, marveling that he'd gotten an apology from the Steel Woman. Then he felt a touch nervous, wondering what she wanted. "How can I help you?"

"Sit down. This meeting won't take long."

She turned off the comp as he settled into the chair before her. He'd never seen the computer screen go dark in all the years he'd dealt with her. Even at the Council meetings, she kept a handheld comp with the power turned on. All the unexpected innovations in this meeting put him on edge. He suddenly expected disaster -- ah, but what Bramis Tanton thought of as a disaster might not be one to him.

"I did not sleep much last night, Commander. I've had a great deal to think about lately and decisions to make that will affect both Tanton Steel and the Tempest Colony," she said. Her light gray eyes steadied on him, and her long-fingered hands stilled on the desk before her. "These last three deaths have convinced me that I must take some action. I can't keep losing workers like this."

For one fleeting moment, he almost believed she felt concern for the welfare of those murdered and not her potential loss in income. He held the anger that rose in the wake of her statement and gave her a stiff nod to continue.

"I only have two options, Kalison," she said and leaned closer. Something unexpectedly softened in her face. "I won't see any more of these people killed just because they still have the guts to work for me, despite Miranda De Velera's decrees. I will not be the cause of such suffering because of that madwoman's obsessions!"

Well. Not what he had expected after all.

"We can't go in and get her, Bramis. Not without death on all sides --"

"I know, I know." She waved that suggestion away. "I'm not Jeffries. I'm not looking to create a bloodbath so that I can get my name in some damned history book. These are my options: either I shut down the mines, or you provide the Rats with guards."

"Provide your workers with guards?" he echoed, surprised. "You dislike the Port Guard!"

"Try to be a little more politic about this, Commander." She grinned with good-natured amusement as he sputtered over his own words. "I didn't like the intrusion of your Port Guard, that's true. I thought their presence would add impetus to the trouble. However, I need guards. Do you think the Rats would be safe under Citizen guards? Should I go to Jeffries and put their lives in his hands? Or do you think I should provide Rats with weapons to protect themselves? Personally, I think they have far enough weapons already, don't you?"

She had him on all points. Closing even one mine wasn't an advantageous answer for anyone, except for those who wanted to see the world destroyed. Tempest already suffered from an economic depression. If the mine closed, Citizens would blame the Rats as though it was their fault someone stalked and murdered them. Troubles would quickly escalate again and might not die down before civil war broke out in earnest. They walked a very fine line.

"I'm surprised you didn't just ask for Guards to work the mines," Kalison mused.

"Why? Do they work cheap?"

Chagrinned, he bowed his head in deference to her better wit. "Why didn't you approach me over the commline or at Council with this?"

"I wasn't certain of your reaction. I wanted this private in case you rightly pointed out that I haven't had any use for the Port Guard before I saw profits sinking. I didn't want our private disagreements to become public rallying cries."

"Well, there's no doubt now. You are the better politician than I am," he acknowledged.

"And I admit you've managed to keep the peace longer than I considered possible. Three years ago, I thought the new Port Guard would fluctuate between annoying Rats and outraging Citizens. I mistrusted off-worlders who come in to set matters right. They don't know the world."

That was an old argument between them. Kalison pursed his lips and didn't bother with a comeback. She'd heard them all.

"Janith was out here last night," she said with an unexpected change of subject. "She wanted me to order this new reporter off Tempest. Janith was irate. She was also drunk. I want a more sober opinion."

"Vidline News sent Alyn Naevon. Apparently, they don't believe Janith is fully covering the news to their satisfaction. From what he told me, he'll do a few interviews, wander the streets for a couple of days, and then head to a newer field. He filed his first report late last night. I watched it this morning and passed it on to the Newsline. He presents Lisbonne, Nedra, and Jeffries side-by-side with people on the street. He doesn't manipulate anything they told him. With Jeffries, he doesn't need to. The report will run on Newsline in the next hour. Watch and see what you think."

She nodded, frowning.

"Do you want my opinion?" he dared. The governor looked intrigued. "Don't listen to Janith. Cooperate with Naevon, and don't, under any circumstances, harass him. The sooner he gets his interviews, the sooner he'll leave. Don't push him away for Janith's sake. He can only do us harm if we give him something harmful to report. Neither Tempest World stock nor Tanton Steel stock needs any more bad publicity."

She sat back with a startled expression.

"It isn't necessary to be born on Tempest to care what happens here, Governor Tanton," he told her. "Hell, you don't even have to be a Citizen."

She almost frowned again but then nodded. They seldom agreed on so many matters in any meeting. Kalison wished there were witnesses.

Her eyes darted toward the darkened comp screen, and her fingers brushed against the keys. He knew the signs of an ended interview.

"I'll go back to my office and see what arrangements I can make on the Guards," he offered as he stood. "I'll need a timetable for work shifts."

"I'll key them over to your office immediately. Let us hope these murders don't spread to the outer mines as well. I don't want more troops coming in. I especially don't want to see those IWC Whites in our midst though it looks increasingly unlikely that we'll settle this in the next few weeks. I find it difficult enough to work with you. I don't know that I could stand dealing with a *real* soldier."

He laughed at her obvious joke, and she grinned despite the grim reality of the situation. He was even amused when the doorman led him back out, as though he might lose his way or pilfer a trinket or two on the way to the door. He knew he'd never understand that woman. He'd settle for being able to work with her.

CHAPTER TEN

A lyn spent the early morning interviewing people at the
Trade Exchange. He learned that none of the minor
industries of Tempest were faring any better than mining. Only
agriculture was precariously holding its own in a plunging
economy. The candid opinions of these people, like those he'd
interviewed on the streets, remained less rehearsed and less
vehement than those of the government officials. The Citizens
of Tempest wanted the trouble ended. Many hoped for a return
to the old days when Rats worked hard and stayed to their
Maze, but many admitted they would accept peace on any
reasonable terms.

At midmorning, he arrived at the Government Building to
cover the weekly Council Meeting. People were already filing
into the crowded room near the front of the building. Alyn saw
Janith and Jeffries standing at the hall leading to the Militia
leader's office. Their stares when they turned his way could have
sent a chill down anyone's back.

"Sir? Are you Alyn Naevon?" He turned to find one of the

building's security guards at his right. A friendly looking man, at least. Alyn nodded, afraid to speak since his voice might not have been very steady. "Governor Bramis Tanton thought, if it was convenient, that she might give you an interview."

"Me? Interview?" he said.

"Yes, sir. Can you come now before the Council Meeting?"

"Certainly."

He dared a look at Jeffries and Janith. They didn't look any happier, and he couldn't tell if they had heard what was said or not.

The guard escorted him to the lift and directly to her upper floor offices while he followed in stunned surprise. Before he could recover, a clerk announced him and let him into the blue-walled inner sanctum of Tempest's most influential person.

He suddenly wondered what prompted the invitation. He hadn't dared ask for an interview with Governor Tanton. He had intended to spend a few days on local reports and hoped to prove himself competent before he dared approach her, and even then, he had doubted he would get more than a pre-written press release.

The immaculate woman sitting behind the earth-wood desk barely looked up as he entered, and she signaled him over to a chair with a negligent flick of her hand. That gave Alyn a moment to study the famous Bramis Tanton, the matriarch of Tanton Steel, and five-times-elected Governor of Tempest. The light in her Government Building office was dim, and her comp screen reflected an unnatural rainbow of color against her pale, thin face. He could see she hadn't changed in the years since his departure. He carefully placed his bag on the floor to his right, ready to grab and go. She intimidated him, even just sitting there. It wasn't only the Rat in him, faced with a powerful Citizen. Bramis Tanton was powerful to *everyone*.

Her fingers danced rhythmically across a comp board. Alyn

wondered what she wrote and how it shaped this world. Her power was both civil and political, and nothing this woman did was without some effect.

He sat very quietly and waited.

"Well," she stated and suddenly looked up at him. "I appreciate that you came so promptly. I only have a few free minutes before the Council Meeting."

"Yes, I know. I'm here to attend it," Alyn said.

"I imagine so. Janith told me you're usurping her work, boy."

Boy. Alyn managed not to squirm, though he probably blushed. At least the dim light worked for him there.

"I only go where they send me, Governor Tanton," he answered her with forced evenness.

"Kalison said I should talk to you." She pushed aside the comp board and faced him, pale eyes narrowed with distrust or distaste. "I suspect you could make us look very bad if we didn't cooperate."

"I can't imagine why you'd be uncooperative, Governor," Alyn answered. He sat back in the chair; not relaxed, only attempting to get as far away from those steel gray eyes as possible. "You've controlled Tanton Steel for more than seventy years standard and held the Governorship of Tempest for nearly fifty years, and you've never made a secret of your views. I only want an up-to-date interview with the most influential person on this world."

The thin lips parted, showing a slender line of teeth.

"Well then, unpack your equipment, Alyn."

From boy to first name in exchange for one flattering little statement? Not damned likely, not from a woman with this much intelligence. Though he mistrusted the change, Alyn swung his bag up into his lap and unlatched the top. He slid out the cam and keyed it on while the woman patiently waited. Alyn never once worried that the Governor might recognize him. He and Bramis Tanton had never truly lived in the same world.

"Will you begin by telling me your views on the underlying problem with the Tempest colony?" he carefully asked. He didn't want to overstep himself now.

She nodded and sat back, looking relaxed as she spoke.

"The first settlers came and made this into a viable, even profitable, settlement. They invested their time, their lives and the futures of their families. Then, when the world began gaining monetary momentum, they needed some unskilled labor for the less popular jobs.

"Unfortunately, with the workers came another element that believed they could live on the bounty of the hard work done by others. Originally transients -- the gypsies of the early star faring days -- they traveled from world-to-world. As economic conditions in the Colonies changed, they lost their mobility. By their own bad judgment, they became trapped in a place that never wanted them. These Rats now want -- demand -- equality with Citizens without taking any of the risks."

"Most Rats were born on this world. So were their parents, and for many, even their grandparents. Are the Citizens of Tempest punishing a generation for mistakes made by others?"

"Attitudes are beginning to change, Alyn. They won't transform overnight. We are willing to give the Rats autonomy within their community. We might even be willing to work on limited rights for those who prove they can contribute to the betterment of Tempest." She stopped and leaned closer, eyes narrowed slightly. "Maybe that would eventually expand into full equality. However, they must prove themselves first."

"You are asking for proof but is there any opportunity for the Rats to provide it? Even those who find work are under threat from both Citizens and more militant Rats. Do you have any suggestions?"

Her eyes narrowed even more. Alyn stopped, cautioning himself to proceed more carefully and with less personal animosity.

"We need calm again before anything positive can happen. The Rats are creating a condition of instability and distrust with their current terrorist actions," Bramis finally stated. She tilted her head slightly to the side. "They can't win this way. Every action has a reaction, Alyn Naevon. The harder the Rats push, the more obstinate the Citizens become. Tempest needs cooperation."

"Federico De Velera was suggesting that before his death."

"Yes," she said. The hardness in her face disappeared, and Alyn felt a slight chill, knowing she was about to give him something unexpected. "We should have taken his cause more seriously and worked with him before this matter got out of hand. I admit we made a mistake. We might have reached a compromise of some sort with Federico De Velera. There's not a chance of that solution with Miranda De Velera."

He had to catch his breath since the words hit him so unexpectedly. His reporter's instincts came back quickly enough though there was no doubt she had noticed.

"I've spoken with several others. Some important people suggest the only way to settle the Rat problem is to kill them all," he said. Why not? She'd given him more already than he had expected.

"Fanatics." She frowned and waved her hand in a gesture that dismissed the suggestion. "I know the people you're talking about and Jeffries is the worst of the bunch. We do not get along. I don't believe killing the Rats is the answer, Alyn. I think that's genocide, and I will not countenance it. Luckily, Commander Kalison is more level-headed."

"I believe that you originally opposed the intervention of off-world Port Guards."

"Did your homework, didn't you?" She grinned suddenly. "And you're not afraid to annoy me."

"I won't have to live with it if I do," he replied. Unexpectedly, he found himself grinning as well. Somewhere inside, he felt appalled by the thought that he was at ease with Governor Bramis Tanton.

"All right, I'll admit to another mistake. Like Federico De Velera, I made an error about Commander Kalison and the Port Guard. I wish I had invited them here long before the IWC forced them on us. If I'd brought them in a few months earlier, this trouble wouldn't have escalated beyond redemption."

"You don't think there's an answer to the problem now?"

"There is no *easy* answer. I will continue to implore peace on both sides. I'll offer gifts to the Rats for the restoration of peace and calm. If we don't achieve a truce soon, the IWC will send in a regiment of their army. After that, decisions are out of the hands of both the Citizens and the Rats."

"Do you think the IWC troops will find an answer in their own way?"

"Maybe. Some Citizens believe the arrival of IWC Whites will guarantee the chastisement of the Rats. Many thought the same would happen when the Port Guard arrived. I want to remind those people that, by IWC charter, Rats and Citizens are technically equal. Many of their soldiers have Rat origins on other worlds. The soldiers won't automatically take the side of the Citizens. Compromise now is the only assurance of saving ourselves from a new form of discomfort."

"However, you don't believe the Rats will compromise."

"I don't believe *Miranda De Velera* will compromise. There are other Rats with less personal animosity who might want peace rather than personal glory."

Alyn nodded and wished he didn't feel quite so much agreement with this woman. He had always believed that the blindness of Bramis Tanton, and others in her elite circle, had brought Tempest to this state. However, at least she was willing to open her eyes now. There were Rats, like Miranda, who wouldn't do the same.

Governor Tanton glanced at her watch. He took his cue.

"I think we've covered everything," he offered. "Unless there's more you would like to discuss?"

"I've already made my warning and my offer. I believe the only subject we haven't discussed is justice."

"Justice?" he echoed. His fingers stopped before he keyed off the cam or brought it off his shoulder.

"Destruction of property was a serious enough matter but can be repaid with credits and hard work. How do we pay for the deaths? People on both sides of this war believe the loss of a life must be repaid with the life of another. Citizens kill Rats. Rats kill Citizens. We all must make a genuine atonement for those who have lost their lives. That's the real justice we need, Alyn Naevon. When we accept that the death of any person is wrong, we'll be on our way to recovery at last."

He wanted to make a final comment about equality but refrained as he keyed off the camera. It would have sounded petty. Governor Tanton had given him honest answers with a far more open mind than he'd expected.

"Thank you for your time, Governor," he offered with a bow of his head.

She reached across the desk and held out her hand to him. He looked up in surprised shock for a single heartbeat before he offered his own. Her hand held his fingers tightly for a moment as she smiled.

"You handle yourself well. I admit -- now that the cam is off -- Janith doesn't have your style or zeal."

"Janith has her own place," he replied, drawing his hand back. "I'm not here to take it away. This is just my job."

"No, not your job; this is your crusade," she corrected. He looked back at her, startled. "That's fine. Janith has her own beliefs. Championing the Rats isn't morally reprehensible. It might be dangerous, though."

A warning. Alyn nodded and felt nearly overcome by a dozen warring emotions. He liked this woman, and he knew that she had helped create the problems on this world. Without the cam in hand, Alyn felt naked beneath her stare. He was instantly anxious to be out of her office.

"If you have more questions, contact me," she offered when he stood. "I'll try to make time for you."

"Thank you," he answered sincerely, smiling despite his tension.

He felt slightly light-headed as he left the Governor's office and headed down to the large, crowded public hall. He barely heard anything presented during the Council Meeting, grateful that he had sense enough to at least turn the cam on to record the session.

He hadn't come away as shaky from far more dangerous situations. Despite the reaction, he realized he possessed an excellent interview. He had never expected Governor Tanton to consent to his presence, let alone offer him an interview. Nor had he expected her to provide him with anything more than the standard government lines.

When the Council Meeting was over, he followed the others out. Janith glared at him as he went by, but he didn't care. She had little real power to sway influential people on this world. Even Jeffries, who admitted to trusting only her, had given Alyn an interview.

By the time he reached the ground level of the Government Building, Alyn was in an excellent mood again. He pushed his equipment into the nearest transit pod, whistling almost tunelessly as he slipped inside. The dome slid closed, and he keyed in the hotel destination, anxious to review his work and begin outlining what he needed for a full report.

As the restraints slid into place, he looked up at the passing people. Only one stared back at him; her eyes narrowed with disgust and distrust.

Beyond any doubt, she recognized him. Alyn's breath caught, and his heart pounded as the pod began to speed away. After what everyone had said, he never expected to see her here in the heart of Silver City.

Miranda De Velera.

His sister.

CHAPTER ELEVEN

The pod automatically sped away from the tall office building quickly leaving Miranda's glaring face behind. Alyn trembled. He couldn't force his hands to remain still. Alyn couldn't get his breath back. He couldn't pretend he was someone -- *something* -- different after he looked into his sister's angry face.

As the pod headed towards the hotel, he forced a thin layer of logic to overcome his panic. Miranda hadn't sent word of his identity to the authorities, or they'd have picked him up by now. He certainly wouldn't have interviewed the Governor if they knew he was a De Velera. So, if she didn't want to destroy him, what did his sister want? Miranda always wanted something.

The pod slowed, arriving too soon at the hotel, and deposited him in the crowded lobby of the Tempest Pride amid a myriad of faces and too many strangers. He wasn't confident he could trust any of them. As he rushed toward the lifts, Alyn felt the dread of Miranda De Velera's presence, as though she stood there in the shadows wherever he turned. He couldn't trust her any more than the Citizens did.

With that awful thought lodged in his mind, he sought the empty shelter of his suite, carefully locked the door, and collapsed into the nearest chair.

There was no way off Tempest without drawing attention that might be as bad as Miranda's possible actions. However, he also dared not go out to interview people without a return of the poise he'd so carefully nurtured. It would be better, he thought, to spend a few quiet hours editing his next report rather than talking with more of the local people.

The first of his daily reports was running every hour on the local Newsline. The piece he finally submitted to Kalison was a simple, innocuous five minutes with even the worst of Jeffries' statements left out. He needed cooperation to finish this work, and he had played it safe. His second report could show a little more spice now that he had established himself. Besides, Vidline had sent him here because they liked his style. Changing how he worked now was not a good idea.

Alyn hoped to lose himself in the editing work, picking short pieces for newscasts and more extended cuts for the documentary that would mark the end of his assignment. Even that work proved nerve-wracking.

"Miranda wisely doesn't come out of the Rat Maze, and we're limited in our available options to go after her."

"At least go in and drag out that bitch leader of theirs, Miranda De Velera."

"I don't believe Miranda De Velera will compromise."

This wasn't the calming work he needed. Miranda's name came up too often, and after three hours of useless exertion, he wiped the work chits clean and filed the interviews away again. In the silent emptiness that surrounded him, Alyn finally examined his situation and the choices left to him. He couldn't hide here in the hotel and ignore his work. Alyn could run away though there were risks to that action. Or he could pretend he'd never seen Miranda.

And look for her, standing there in the shadows, wherever he went.

With a single glimpse of his sister, his entire masquerade became a sham. Alyn knew he wasn't honestly doing his work if he only interviewed Citizens as though they were the only players in this drama. Murders occurred on both sides. The reactionary politics of Citizens created the initial problem, but the Rats escalated the hostilities. He wasn't Janith; he couldn't champion one side and then completely ignore the violations committed by them.

He didn't want to go into the Rat Maze where people would recognize him, dark hair and all. He wanted to confront their hostility less than he wanted to face discovery by the Citizens.

Then he realized the Rats already knew he was on-world. Miranda's face came back to him: the smug upturned nose, the familiar glaring eyes. She hadn't stood there by chance. Kalison, Bramis Tanton, Jeffries: they spoke of her in an abstract, impersonal way. He *knew* Miranda. She would find some way to use his dramatic return to her advantage, and she wouldn't let blood ties stand in the way of winning points with her people. He remembered Miranda as a vindictive and manipulative young woman who gloried in the notoriety as Federico De Velera's oldest child. She diligently resented those to whom her position didn't matter, like her brothers, who remained unimpressed by the name.

He couldn't understand why the Rats followed her. That, honestly, was the significant part of the story of Tempest that he wanted to answer. Citizens never questioned Federico's daughter assuming her father's position. Alyn knew the answer wasn't that simple.

Time to go home. Go now and face his sister and the

judgment of those companions who had stayed and fought while he left --

And lived. If they didn't understand why he'd disappeared, then they would never know why he came back now.

When Alyn looked out the window, it was nearly sunset. He'd slip home with the night -- like a good Rat careful to avoid the notice of the authorities.

CHAPTER TWELVE

Fiona was glad to see Bauer and didn't complain even though he arrived late for their date. She needed a distraction before the meeting later tonight, and dinner in the hotel's restaurant would be a welcome respite from her other clandestine worries.

More honestly, dinner with Captain Talin Bauer improved her mood on any occasion. She enjoyed his company for reasons that had nothing to do with work of any sort.

"Sorry I'm late," he quickly apologized as he climbed from the pod. His lips brushed her cheek with his usual nervous gesture of affection. The man shied away from such public displays. "Weather Satellite shows another nasty storm is blowing in and should hit in a couple hours. Looks like there could be flooding in low lying areas tonight so we took the precaution of storing all military equipment inside."

"Well, at least we shouldn't get any street fights if the rain is bad," Fiona said. She linked her arm in his and turned the Captain toward the restaurant. "I'd like to wake up tomorrow and find out no one died in another confrontation or ambush.

Are the mines closing? Bramis is usually very good about clearing them out if there's any chance of flooding."

"She closed the mines, and Kalison even canceled the night shift at the Port," Bauer supplied. He sighed softly as they paused at the doorway to the restaurant. "This storm is another mixed blessing. We don't need flooding, but if we can go a day without an incident between Rat and Citizen, it's welcome."

"True. My table's reserved for us. Let's see if we can manage a pleasant and quiet meal, shall we? And we can talk about anything but our work."

"Hard day?" he asked.

"Business isn't looking any better," she confessed.

He nodded and turned automatically toward the dining area, drawing a few surprised looks. Port Guards didn't frequent the upper-class restaurants. Commander Kalison, being of such high rank, probably wouldn't have attracted much attention, but he apparently never ate out. Fiona's face was well known, though, and that drew a different kind of look to the two.

They were both off-worlders caught up in Tempest's problems. She knew Bauer felt a considerable affinity for the locals and tended more toward sympathy with the Rats than the Citizens. Sometimes Fiona considered telling Bauer about her little secret group -- but she didn't want him to feel compromised in any way. If the choice came, she'd give up the group before she gave up him.

As they passed other tables, she savored the inviting aromas of bread, soups, and several main dishes. Fiona couldn't decide what she wanted to eat tonight. The robogate blocking her reserved table slid away at her touch, and the menus brightened even before they took their seats. The lights dimmed, and a soft whisper of music drifted around the table as the electric baffles whispered into place, dulling the noises around them. Fiona enjoyed sitting here and watching the other patrons, knowing that they came to her restaurant because it was a pleasant place amid less enjoyable realities.

"Looks like Janith has started early," Bauer said and nodded back towards the bar.

"Oh, that's great," she snarled with a touch of disgust. "She better remain calm tonight. I'm in no mood for one of her shows. If Alyn Naevon comes down for dinner, we could have that incident neither of us wants to see, especially this close."

"How's our new boy doing?" Bauer asked as he pulled a chair closer to hers. Intimacy: there was no chance anyone outside the baffles could clearly hear what they said, so he moved closer just to be with her. "I heard Bramis invited him up to her office for an interview."

"Really?" Fiona laughed, delighted. "No wonder Janith is here. She probably feels personally betrayed. Do you think she'll have the nerve to say something nasty about Governor Tanton in her next report?"

"Now there's an intriguing thought." Bauer smiled, and his eyes brightened with anticipation. "Maybe she'll annoy a few prominent Citizens, and Vidline will really send in someone to replace her. I was told I'll be watching over Naevon if he starts getting into trouble. How's Alyn doing? Any bad habits that would make him undesirable in place of Janith?"

"I like him, but I haven't seen much of him. He came in after Council this afternoon and never left as far as I can tell. At least he's smart enough to stay off the streets at night. Should I invite him down to join us for dinner?"

"Do you really want that battle with Janith?" Bauer asked. His fingers brushed along the top of her hand. "Besides, I was hoping for a few hours alone with you."

"I don't like Alyn that much," she confessed, trying to hide her own smile.

"Good." He grinned and finally looked down at the menu.

A few moments ago, she enjoyed the sounds of the people all around them. Now she wondered if slipping off to her room would be a little too obvious. She hated starting gossip among the staff. Granted, there was no secret about her relationship with Captain Bauer, but people looked for scandal. They could make any little incident or indiscretion into a significant event.

Better to eat the meal here and look forward to later, when they could spend time alone.

"This place is apparently acquiring a reputation," Bauer suddenly stated and nudged her. "You're drawing them in from the Elite. That's Ember Tanton waiting at the door."

"Ember!" she hissed the name, looking up with a start.

"Cousin to Bramis. She's a top executive at Tanton Steel."

The sight of the familiar woman waiting beside the door unnerved Fiona. None of the others ever came to the hotel outside the secret meetings. Ember's presence set a definite chill on Fiona's emotions.

"I -- I can't just let her stand there," she muttered with a quick look of apology to Bauer.

"Go ahead and get her seated. I understand about business," he said. He glanced at the menu again. "Besides, it gives me a few minutes to decide what I really want tonight -- at least for food."

She felt herself blush and he gave her another bright smile. Fiona hurried away from their table and slipped through the sound shields that made a buzzing sound and almost gave her a headache. Ember nodded as she neared, and Fiona could tell the woman appeared to be uneasy.

"Welcome to Tempest Pride, Citizen Ember," she greeted the woman with a formal little bow. "I'm Fiona Salend, the hotel manager. I'd be happy to find you a table and recommend a meal."

"Thank you," Ember replied with one quick little smile. It

probably looked normal to anyone who didn't know her. Ember followed her across the room to an excellent table not far from Fiona's own. Ember Tanton's name whispered from tables without shields in place. The woman remained polite and proper as Fiona settled her in. It wasn't until the buffers whispered into place that she finally met Fiona's eyes.

"I hoped I would see you if I came here. Sonio's dead. Someone tried to kill Wintas and barely missed. I don't know about Caden yet. Be very careful, Fiona."

"Oh damn," she whispered and put her hands on the table. "How the hell did I ever get involved in this mess?"

"The better question is why someone is trying to kill us," Ember replied. Her hand patted Fiona's in a gesture of kindness. "We were never that important, Fiona. I want to know who thinks we're so dangerous that they want us dead. Now go back to your Captain, eat your dinner. Spend the evening with him. You'll be safe with Bauer. I'm hoping that I'll have more answers by the meeting."

Fiona nodded and fought to get some mental control before she returned to Bauer. She even managed to suggest something for Ember to try from the dinner menu. They played at the game, avoiding any unnecessary suspicions. Ember stayed for the meal and left before Fiona and Bauer finished their own dinner.

And Fiona stayed very close to Captain Bauer for the remainder of the evening.

CHAPTER THIRTEEN

Alyn surveyed his equipment as he considered Miranda's petty attitudes toward anything that annoyed her. Those unpleasant memories dictated his preparations for the trip into the Maze. He pulled out his older, battered vidcam and made sure the power still worked. Then he sorted through clothing until he found plain blacks that didn't look quite as expensive as they were.

By the time Alyn finished his preparations while watching a cloudy sunset streaked reds and browns spread across his window. Lightning flashed not far off to the west. The hall outside his room remained empty, and only one other person joined him on the descent to the lobby. When he reached the bottom floor, he found small gatherings of anxious Citizens preparing for dinner at the restaurant. A quick scan showed Janith nowhere in sight, though he thought he heard her strident voice from the bar. He didn't want the rival reporter spotting him as he tried to inconspicuously slip out of the hotel. He might be able to lie about is real intentions, but if Janith somehow learned his identity, Alyn decided he would run to

Kalison and hope the man could protect him from the wrath of the locals. Alyn didn't want to fall into Jeffries's hands.

The aroma of freshly cooked foods won a protest from his stomach. Breakfast was hours behind him, and lunch had been forgotten in his panic after seeing Miranda. Alyn reluctantly turned away from the restaurant. He slid along the edges of the crowd waiting to be seated without drawing undue notice, his case held low so that no one suspected he carried a vidcam.

No line of the pod system reached into the Maze, of course, though he could take one as far as the Port. However, someone might wonder what he was doing there and why he wasn't heading into the terminal. Alyn bypassed the transportation and slipped out the side door of the building.

He quickly jogged along the narrow, dark footpaths, putting distance between himself and the hotel. Only Rats, and occasional emergency and maintenance personnel, usually traveled these dark, narrow passages between the buildings. Fading sunlight slanted low through the narrow crevices while a cold breeze, tainted with the scent of distant rain, kicked up dust and debris. The incessant noises of the city echoed around the windowless, walls. No Rats -- no *other* Rats -- walked here with the dangerous night soon coming.

Even though no Citizen knew he was a Rat, Alyn didn't pretend that made him safe. As a reporter, he had created enemies just by his arrival. Janith wasn't the least of them; others included the charming Jeffries and Lisbonne, and countless other Citizens who sided with the two. He would not trust any of those three if they found him here, unprotected. People died on this world, and he didn't pretend that his press pass was a badge of immunity.

Despite spending several years off-world, Alyn hadn't forgotten his way through the labyrinth passages linking the city to the Maze. Memorizing every path home was essential knowledge for Rats old enough to work in the city. In his youth, Alyn occasionally took such odd jobs, before family notoriety made the risk no longer worth the pay. Citizen teens were the danger when he was young, and they had gathered at corners waiting for a lone Rat to wander by. Rat packs had been the only safe way to travel in those days. He suspected the same was true today. Maybe the same Citizens gathered in the dark, older now, and murdering rather than beating. The teens had grown up on both sides of the port, and neither side grew wiser.

Alyn wasn't going to safety tonight.

However, he was going home. Miranda wasn't the only person he left behind in the Maze. Alyn's step quickened when he thought about his younger brother, Sebastian. The last time Alyn saw the then sixteen-year-old, Sebastian had been painting pretty pictures of the ugly life in the Maze. He was so unlike anyone else in the family that Miranda once insinuated he wasn't really Federico's child.

Those had been callous and unthinking words to say to the teenaged boy. Surprisingly, Federico -- who still loved a wife lost in a mining accident ten years before -- had slapped her.

Alyn remembered how they had stood there in shocked disbelief of both the words and the reaction. Miranda left and stayed with friends for the next few days. Sebastian apologized, as though he had done something wrong. For those three days, Alyn and his father worked on a handout pamphlet announcing a strike at the mine. Neither mentioned Miranda nor the incident. With Miranda out of the Hostel, an unexpected amount of calm set in. Until that time, Alyn never realized how much tension his demanding, older sister created.

As he paused to catch his breath, Alyn reluctantly recalled more of those last days he spent with his family before he fled Tempest. The strike was the last time he saw his father. The Citizen's Militia turned out to *coerce* Federico's followers back to work. Three of Alyn's friends died before his eyes, one while obviously surrendering. Alyn took a minor laser burn across the shoulder -- enough to knock him down and keep him out of the growing disorder as the strike abruptly turned into a riot.

Alyn didn't find his anger dimmed by the passage of time and other worlds. He was still Rat enough to feel the rage at the unnecessary killings. The people in the Maze weren't a threat to the city, even if they wanted to vent generations of frustration against their oppressors. The Rats didn't have many weapons, at least not back then.

He survived the battle only because Caden Paris got him out of the war zone and back into the Maze. While Caden treated his wound, the older man listened to Alyn's confession of loss and uncertainty. Though Federico's son, Alyn didn't possess Miranda's fire or Sebastian's dreams.

Caden had suggested Alyn lay his hands on some credits and buy his way off-world. The man even gave him the name of the holo shop where he could buy a new ID and tips on how to get through the Port and onto a ship without the Port Guard stopping him.

That night, while the Maze still reeled in shock at the unprovoked murders, Alyn escaped the confinement of his life as a Rat and a De Velera. He *borrowed* the needed credits from the emergency funds kept in his father's care. Alyn took only enough to get out and never come back. Alyn even intended to pay it back, but by the time he was making enough money, his father had died. He wasn't going to give the credits to Miranda. Besides, he had found a profession where he could help the Rats more than his father ever had been able to do. Citizens listened to him -- as long as they didn't know his past.

Sudden footsteps on the hard cement walkway drew Alyn away from thoughts of the past. He bolted for a shadowed corner and held his breath while ten of Jeffries's men marched by. He chided himself to pay better attention to now, and not think about the last time he walked these paths.

When the sound of the others disappeared, Alyn started out at a trot again, anxious to reach his destination and deal with Miranda and see Sebastian. And Devlin? Was she still around? He knew that answer. She was neither making trouble for Miranda nor already in charge. Alyn couldn't imagine any other options for her, and he feared to hear confirmation of her death and feel the loss of someone else he had cared deeply about at one time, though they'd grown apart in the last years before he left.

Too many dark thoughts. He wanted to turn back and not face what was bound to be a lot of unpleasantness.

Alyn kept going.

Eventually, the building-sheltered walkway deteriorated into a dirt path and scattered warehouses along the edge of the port. Alyn avoided one more set of guards before he reached the edge of the city. His timing proved perfect; the last Rat workers were leaving the Port as the guards prepared to close access to the pads. Any ship in orbit would wait till morning to land since they didn't want them caught up in the storm. There was no use dropping either merchant crews or tourists into the dangerous Tempest night.

Hugging his cam close to his body, Alyn followed in the shadow of a departing group. His unusual arrival went unnoticed since the Port Guards were only interested in making certain Rats didn't bring weapons out of the Maze and into the city. If Kalison wanted to stop the smuggling of weapons entirely, he wasn't going to do it this way. Any Rat working the Port knew several ways to slip contraband out of the enclosure. They had smuggled weapons even before Federico De Velera began organizing dissension, though nothing had been of a substantial scale or well organized.

Alyn wanted change for this world, but not that way.

His pace quickened again in the last three kilometers. The open path skirted along the edge of the Port's wireframe fence. Ahead he could see the narrow and arched entrance to the Maze.

Lightning flashed close and loud, and a cold wind swept over the outlands and across the open port. A pelting, icy rain quickly soaked him.

It was an appropriate homecoming after all.

CHAPTER FOURTEEN

People had gathered in the room below his second-floor bedroom. Sebastian heard the spreading whisper of words and an occasional anxious statement that rose above the unclear hum. He made every effort to ignore the noise, but when the Hostel's door squeaked open for the fifth time in twelve minutes, he realized Miranda had called an unannounced meeting in the hall tonight. Something important drew the crowd here: Rats usually stayed close to home during storms like this one.

As though to emphasize that point, the rain suddenly pounded loudly against the permaglass window by his desk, and the small leak at the window's upper right corner emitted a soft spray of water as the wind blew. Sebastian removed his sketches from the damp path and slid them under the protection of the bed. Settling cross-legged on the mattress, he propped his easel against his pillow and the wall. Sebastian wasn't getting much work done on his portrait of Lauren. He preferred watching the shifting pattern as droplets coalesced on the window and created braided tracks down the outer surface.

The hinge protested again, and someone cursed loud enough that he knew they were unhappy with the weather and the summons. Though he didn't like living in the old Hostel, this was the best-built building in the Maze. Unlike most Rats, he didn't worry about a sudden storm sweeping away his residence. The windows might show a little wear from more than two centuries of storms, but the roof didn't even leak.

However, the Hostel was also the seat of Rat government, which meant he had very little peace and quiet. Miranda lived here, which was why he did. She didn't let her brother too far out of reach.

If the Citizens had realized that Miranda now lived in one of the few permanent buildings in the Maze, this place wouldn't stand for long. The truth was that she didn't spend all her nights here, though.

Unfortunately, while Sebastian sought peace and solitude, Miranda thrived on chaos, which protected her power base. Neither Citizens nor Rats knew where an enemy might strike. Miranda played on those fears, rather than end them.

Sebastian had difficulty finding peace anywhere in the Maze these days. At least living in the Hostel meant he could eat a free meal now and then. It also gave him a chance to keep tabs on Miranda's latest plans and sidestep appearing at the wrong places. He diligently worked to avoid annoying her or becoming entangled in her games.

The whispering grew to sharper words again, followed by Miranda's piercing and unmusical laughter. Very little amused her these days and the sound unsettled Sebastian. He ignored the inclination to go down and find out what occasioned this gathering. Miranda never wanted him at the meetings. She didn't like him around, though she didn't trust him out on his own, either. She convinced others that her interest was a show of fraternal concern, to keep her artistic brother safe and close where she could protect him. Sebastian knew better.

She evidently thought Sebastian was blind to the real world, though he chose only to ignore any politics beyond the level that kept him alive. He cherished his art and devoted all his time to the work. In that respect, being a De Velera worked for him. By his age, anyone else would be expected to find employment in the city or in the mines but being his father's son and Miranda's brother made such outings too dangerous.

More yelling. Doors slammed this time.

Sebastian put away the painting and supplies knowing he wasn't in the mood to do any work. Instead, he laid back on the bed and watched the storm. Just as he began to relax, he heard quick footsteps on the stairs. Whispered words came from the landing, almost clear enough to understand. Then he heard the unmistakable sound of someone coming to his door.

So much for peace and quiet.

Three quick, hard pounds shook the plastic door -- as though the room was so large he might miss the sound. He knew the familiar pattern of that brusque beat but pretended ignorance. All part of the game.

"Who is it?" he asked, putting a soft whisper of exhaustion in his voice. Maybe she would take the hint and go away.

"It's Lauren, love," she answered.

Lauren pushed the door open without invitation and slipped into the room. Her smile was as false as ever, but her eyes shone brightly which meant something serious was happening downstairs. Lauren always lit up like a neon sign whenever Miranda included her in some scheme.

"Come on in, Lauren," he invited her. She didn't hear the mockery. "What's going on? You said you were heading home."

"I thought we could go for a walk, Sebastian. Come on."
Miranda wanted him out of the building.

"Go for a walk in this weather?" he replied, appalled by the suggestion. He waved a hand towards the window, where the sky obediently lit with a flash of lightning. "If you want my company, let's just stay here. I have some boards I need to sand down for a couple portraits."

"A little rain isn't going to wash you away," Lauren insisted with more bite to her words. She had never been very subtle. "We can go to my place and have some fun."

"I have work to get done," he insisted. There was more force in his words as well. That unexpected sound stopped Lauren in her march across the room to take him in charge.

"Let's go," she ordered, short on patience herself. She crossed the rest of the way to the bed, carelessly pushing aside a paint palette with her foot. "Don't tell me those boards are more important than my bed."

He would never get work done if he had to put up with her for much longer. She cared less about his art than Miranda did, which he would have thought impossible.

"Come on," she commanded and caught hold of his arm.

Sebastian suddenly decided this was the time to stop playing by her rules.

"Lauren, how the hell stupid do you think I am?" he suddenly asked, pulling free of her grip. Her eyes went wide as he stood, and she backed away two steps. "I know Miranda sent you to keep me out of her hair. I know your only job is to keep watch over me. Fine. Tonight, you can sit in that chair by the door and watch me sand boards. I'm tired of these games. Yes, my painting is more important than your bed. What I put on those boards is more honest."

She went white. Maybe Sebastian's decision went against his sister's wishes, but if he kept out of Miranda's business, she wouldn't care if he didn't bed her spy. Lauren could stay and watch over him, if she did it in silence for a change. He left her standing there in the middle of the room and busied himself with pulling the boards out from under his bed. Maybe he could bore her into leaving.

Lauren stalked across the room and settled on the chair by the door. That didn't turn out to be much better. He could feel her blue eyes on his back and wondered if she carried any weapon. Many of Miranda's people did. Lauren's anger continued unabated by the silence or the passage of time. Several minutes later, her breath still came in little gasps of rage.

The noises suddenly rose downstairs. Sebastian could hear several excited people make a sudden entrance. He tried to ignore the distracting noise, but Miranda's laughter came again, disturbing him.

Sebastian dared a look at Lauren. She glared back.

"You made a mistake," she hissed, the anger gnawing at her. Her face had gone pale, her eyes were large and glaring. "You should have kept playing dumb. I'm sure Miranda will deal with you when she finishes with your traitor brother."

"Brother!" he yelped and came to his feet so fast that the boards went flying. "Alonso is alive? He's here?"

She glared back at him, clamping her mouth tightly shut -- but a little too late now that she'd given away Miranda's secret. He realized why his sister didn't want him around, and he wasn't going to abandon Alonso to her mercy. He started toward the door, but Lauren leapt up and slid in front of him.

"You really don't think you can stop me, do you?" he asked.

"I don't have to play sweet anymore," she warned, a feral smile replacing the less honest one he usually saw.

"I guess neither of us does," he agreed.

She still underestimated him. Lauren grabbed his wrist and

tried for a knee in his groin. Side-stepping, he used her momentum and unbalanced position to toss her on top of the bed. She held tight to his arm, and Sebastian came down hard on top of her. He had no trouble keeping her pinned. Lauren gasped out several unflattering remarks as he pried his wrist free.

"Everyone forgets that I was raised by Federico De Velera," he said. Those words stilled Lauren, her bright eyes blinking. "Do you think he let me wander around, even just in the Maze, without being able to defend myself? Of course, I know how to fight. I just choose not to. Beating each other senseless never won any wars, especially when the fighting is in the ranks, rather than against the enemy. I left Miranda to her games. However, I won't leave Alonso to her perverted sense of justice."

Lauren, remembering why they fought, managed to unsettle him and work free. She got to her knees, ready to fight again. Sebastian dissuaded her with an open-handed blow to the cheek. She fell backward, hitting her head on the bed, sending her unfinished portrait flying. He winced, seeing the work smeared and ruined. Even a portrait of her was part of the art he loved.

Sebastian held her down while trying to decide what to do next. A glance to the right reminded him that he stored some of his painting supplies in old cloth bags beside the bed. H used one hand to untangle a rope that held one bag closed. As Lauren started to earnestly struggle again, he wrapped the line quickly around her wrists and secured the end to the bedpost. That left Lauren stranded with her arms uncomfortably raised over her shoulders. Her eyes glared again, and she ineffectually kicked at him.

"You bastard," she hissed. "You better let me go or Niel will --"

He stuffed an old paint rag in her mouth. It probably tasted awful. Then he tied her legs together and wrapped the rope around the bottom of the bed.

"When I finish downstairs, I'll send your brother up to get you lose," he promised. Part of him enjoyed the scene, after all the humiliation she'd put him through. "Just relax, Lauren, *love*. This won't take long."

Lauren scowled, but Sebastian saw a hint of worry in her narrowed eyes. She had failed Miranda De Velera, and Lauren's rage was giving way to worry. Sebastian blew her a kiss before he turned off the room's only light and closed the door behind him. If anyone came by, they'd assume Lauren had done her job.

He carefully made his way down the dark stairs. A large crowd had gathered for Miranda's latest show, though he spotted only her devoted supporters. Ino even stood with the group, which showed the boy had come up in status. Sebastian didn't trust him.

Whatever she intended, Miranda didn't want witnesses she couldn't control. Well, he didn't expect her to greet their brother with open arms.

Sebastian remained unnoticed in the shadows near the stairs. Miranda stayed by the far wall, anxiously looking towards the door. Around him, people mumbled with a mixture of worry and anger, though except for her most ardent followers, they seemed uncertain. Alonso would walk straight into this hostility. Sebastian hoped they both survived the reunion.

CHAPTER FIFTEEN

The storm muted the sounds and smells of the Maze, though bright flashes of lightning illuminated the **squalor.** Abandoned and decaying shacks lay in disrepair just within the fenced-in boundary. Rubbish washed up by the storm now littered the narrow alley with slick, dangerous debris and ankle-deep streams. Alyn's good boots proved a hindrance here, where he needed to carefully feel out each step.

Whoever was on guard on the Rat side of the arch never stopped him, so he knew Miranda wanted him here. He didn't expect it was for any good reason.

Some port workers turned off towards the bachelor's quarters, a solid row of buildings at the eastern edge of the Maze. They formed the first line of defense in times of trouble. Ten years ago, Federico De Velera moved all families closer to the heart of the Maze. There the children had some protection from occasional random violence by Citizens.

The narrow pathway leading between the temporary buildings suddenly gave way to an open stone-paved lot of nearly 30 square meters. This place represented safety to a Rat.

Citizens never came this far without an invitation.

Alyn Naevon didn't feel very safe here now.

Pausing at the edge of the square, he looked for any obvious trap. He didn't trust Miranda. He wanted to reach the Hostel before she reached him. He wanted witnesses.

He stood still through several flashes of lightning, none of which showed anyone lurking ominously at the edges of the wet, shabby buildings. Only a single figure jogged down a side pathway, hurrying before the fury of the storm. That might have been a spy watching for him. If so, it only meant Miranda still wanted him to come farther into her territory. It didn't matter: There was no turning back now.

Alyn started across the square, then stopped again when the lightning momentarily illuminated something that caught his immediate interest. He quickly keyed on his cam, punching up the night mode and shot by feel, forgoing the eyepiece.

He wished he had brought the new cam. The bright, multihued colors of the mosaic were delightful, and sparkling layers of tinted glass brightened at each surge of the storm. The picture showed Rats living in a mythical, happier time. Pretty artwork transformed the hovels of the Maze into colorful, well-kept houses any Citizen might envy. Children held comps as they sat outside a school. Well-dressed, happy adults smiled as they greeted each other.

Alyn recognized the delightful, bright style, and was glad Sebastian hadn't given up his art. The Rats needed dreamers to remind them of the ultimate prize for which they fought. He feared most of his people buried those hopes in self-perpetuating anger that would never bring the needed change. They had to want, as well as fight for, a different future.

Alyn left the vidcam on as he headed out of the square, holding it unobtrusively under his arm. Footage from within the Maze would help fill out his reports.

Pretending that he was going to file more news after this.

Alyn chose the alley leading directly to the Hostel, a path he knew very well. He even felt comfortable walking here, which he hadn't felt anywhere in the City; he couldn't deny that this was his home.

As he negotiated the narrow, winding tracks, he thought about Kalison's problems of coming in to capture Miranda. Every roof could -- and would -- shelter a sniper and simple buildings would harbor deadly traps. The alleys twisted and turned in confusing circles and those who didn't know the way would easily get lost. Vids from above ground proved less than helpful; buildings often bridged both sides of a path, and some of those paths even changed direction from one week to another as a makeshift structure disappeared, and another grew somewhere else. Even knowing the direction, he needed to go didn't mean a person would get there without a few backtracks.

Attacking from the air and indiscriminately was the only hope of winning here -- but most of the Citizens knew they didn't want the kind of war that would bring ruin to the world. The Port Guard certainly wouldn't want it. News would spread to other planets, and the minor trouble on Tempest would become a rebellion across many worlds.

At a point nearly a kilometer along the walkway, Alyn instinctively leapt a shallow stream of water which had always rushed across this intersection whenever it rained very hard. A Citizen Committee even investigated the problem, several years ago. Their final report stated the system wasn't inadequate but that the Rats overused it.

The wording fooled no one on either side of the Port. Reworking the sewer system would have entailed rebuilding much of the Maze, and the Citizens weren't going to put their money into the project. The Rats hadn't the income to finance the construction themselves. Though the report automatically went to the IWC, nothing more came of it.

At the time Alyn believed, like all Rats, that the IWC just sided with the Citizens. However, having left the Maze and Tempest, Alyn was wiser now. The Citizens buried the report among others, carefully worded to draw the least attention. IWC clerks couldn't ferret out every hidden account of trouble and Citizens who feared they might be taxed for the work were very good at that type of deception. They guarded their riches and didn't care --

He remembered his interview with Governor Bramis Tanton and that he liked her. He could no longer dump all Citizens into one category.

Alyn pushed aside the thoughts of past problems and concentrated on where he was going, though that didn't help his state of mind. The smell of filth washed up by the rain made his nose itch and his eyes water. The sounds of people behind the thin, composite walls made his heart pound, though he was unsure if the reaction was fear or longing. Though he'd run away, this place still represented family and friends to him.

He took the last familiar turn at a hasty jog and found himself in the very heart of the Maze. He stopped again and stared at the brightly lit building before him. Built in the days when Rats were still well-paid wayfarers, the tall building personified the Rat's better past when colonies were under-populated, and workers prized. Without buildings and other trappings of their former lives, most colonists couldn't survive the strain of relocation. The new settlements needed extra hands in the early years, and itinerant workers had been glad to visit and move on until it became economically prohibitive to ship the people to even newer colonies.

Some Rats still hoped for an opportunity to move out into the new Fringe colonies. Damn few ever saved the funds needed to emigrate, though. Some governments on the more crowded colonies -- and even Earth -- sponsored the relocation of a section of their Rats, but that was never likely to happen on Tempest. Someone had to do the dangerous work at the mines, clean the streets after storms, and unload ships. The Citizens collected family stipends from the mines and worked in the mostly-automated factories and shops. The Citizens wouldn't do Rat work. Rats couldn't accept employment in Citizen occupations. The Government called it job assurance for both sides. Alyn thought of it as a form of slavery.

He couldn't stand out here in the rain all night.

Federico De Velera had made his family's residence in the old Hostel when they moved in from the outer edge of the Maze even though it was the most easily targeted building in the area. He knew Miranda would still live here because nothing else was good enough. Besides, the building also housed the Rat government and the local school. Most Citizens didn't even realize the Rats governed themselves. They assumed the laws that kept them safe in their cement and steel homes were good enough for Rats in their flimsy world.

Alyn took one quick shot of the building before he turned the cam off. Whatever greeted him inside, he didn't want it on record. He didn't slow as he crossed the last open space and pushed the ancient metal door forward. It still squeaked. He didn't slow as he entered the room.

"I really didn't think you'd have the guts to show up here, Alonso," a familiar voice spoke as everyone else went silent.

He smiled at Miranda, but that was only for the benefit of the others gathered in the wide entry hall. She'd changed, and not for the better. Her hair was a velvety, brown stubble, shaved in a style that was years out of fashion on any of the Inner Worlds. Her dark eyes looked enormous in her thin, pale face. She pursed her lips tightly together in a look that promised anger at the first chance.

"Hello, Randa," he greeted her. He came halfway across the foyer, ignoring the other stern and worried faces. He recognized most as long-time friends of Miranda. Alyn wondered where his father's advisors had gone. "So, why wouldn't I come home?"

"Home," she snorted and stalked toward him. Fury: he could see it in the sharp movements she made and heard the hardly hidden rage in her fierce, short words. "You don't have a home anymore, traitor."

The others made slight, apprehensive sounds and some nervously shifted their stances. Miranda put on this show for them, and surely the others knew this was a demonstration to reinforce her power. No one could live long with this woman and not realize she acted, rather than felt, any emotions.

Maybe he misjudged her, though. The glare in her eyes looked real enough this time.

"I've betrayed nothing and no one," Alyn replied calmly. Anger was her tool; he wouldn't give her that weapon. "I'm only fighting the war in a different way, Randa."

"You ran away."

"I walked away. I'm not the first, and I won't be the last. I looked for an alternative to dealing directly with unconcerned Citizens. I found it in my work. And I came back."

"What good is your new work?" she demanded. Had she expected her brother to sound contrite? To fall down and beg her forgiveness and mercy? "What battles have you won with your vidcam?"

"No battles," he conceded, "but I haven't gotten anyone killed with it, either."

"People die in war, Alonso De Velera," she answered. She took another step closer. He held his place. "They fight if it's important enough to them."

Those words won sounds of approval. The reaction annoyed Alyn at the way that they accepted Miranda's trite little pronouncements as though they were words of enlightenment. He wondered if all her friends were so shallow. Maybe those eager to watch her entertainment were the only ones she allowed into her presence. He wondered why the hell the rest of the Maze followed this illusion. Was it just her father's name that kept Miranda De Velera in power?

So many questions he wanted to ask, at least as a reporter, but he knew better under these circumstances. Alyn realized there was no use being subtle with her. Even as a child, Miranda refused to see anything beyond her own limited and possessive reasoning.

"What are you fighting for, Miranda?" Alyn demanded, his own voice growing louder. "Do you really think this is a war you can fight hand-to-hand against the Citizens? How many more do you intend to push from Kalison's side and into Jeffries' camp? How long before they come in here looking for you?"

"Oh, I want them to come here," she replied. Her eyes brightened. "I want them to come into the Maze and fight us."

"A few weapons won't make you invincible," he answered, feeling a slight chill. "Miranda, if you provoke them enough, they'll come for you. People will die --"

"People die in war." She cut him short with a wave of her long-fingered hand. "If they come for me, that means they think I am too important to leave among my people. They know my name, Alonso. They know my *real* name, and they respect what I am."

"So, you don't care about who dies for your precious name," he replied, drawing another genuine glare. He refused to acquiesce to the simple answers she gave him. He wanted someone here to think. "You don't care who dies, as long as it isn't you. What are you really fighting for Miranda? For the Rats or just for the personal glory?"

Her cheeks reddened, and her eyes went wide. Alyn held her look, knowing he'd stepped into hazardous territory.

"You don't have the right to judge me, *Alyn*. You ran away and gave up the war. The glory I've gained, I earned, brother. I've planned ways to make the Citizen's take notice of us --"

"They notice, all right," he replied. She didn't like the interruption, but he wasn't willing to listen to the propaganda. "Even Governor Bramis Tanton admitted that they made a mistake in not dealing with our father. They think there's no hope of dealing with you."

"Dealing with me?" she snorted. "What kind of deal could they possibly offer me?"

"What if they offer you peace?"

"Peace? We've had peace on their terms for generations. You really have forgotten life in the Maze, haven't you? I don't want their peace, *Alyn Naevon*. I intend to win."

"Win!" he repeated and felt a start of true fear. The others listened, but he wasn't certain they heard what his sister truly said. Were they this blind? "Win *what*? Do you really think you can beat them? Do you think the IWC will stand by you if you prove to be the aggressor?"

"I don't need the IWC."

Her lack of sense finally drove him beyond any self-control.

"What do you think keeps Jeffries from blowing the hell out of the Maze, you fool? Do you think anything other than IWC sanctions holds the Citizen's back when you keep provoking them? If the IWC hadn't sent Kalison in, there wouldn't be a building standing in here by now. Miranda, our father was fighting the war too -- but he never took it so far that he endangered those for whom he fought. He believed the Rats should have a better future. I suspect you don't care if the Rat's lives change at all. You just want to stay in charge."

She went white at his untimely judgment. Alyn knew he'd gone too far, but there was no way to back out gracefully now. Well, to be honest, Miranda had made her judgment of him long before he showed up here. He lost nothing by maintaining his own self-esteem.

"So, as usual, we disagree." He forced a smile and reminded himself that this really wasn't home anymore. Disagreeing with Miranda was more than a family quarrel he could walk away from this time. "We never agreed before, Randa; I don't know why it should be different now. And it doesn't mean we can't each work in our own way."

"No," she replied, voice hard and cold. The onlookers shifted position again. They plainly knew her moods. "No, Alonso. You walked out on us, and I don't see any reason to let you continue this charade --"

"Why not?" another voice asked. Someone pushed his way through the thin line of spectators. "You have no reason to prevent him, Miranda. He hasn't done anything to harm us."

Alyn was glad for the support. Then he felt a new shock as he recognized the tall, thin young man with long dark hair.

"Sebastian? Damn! Four years changed you!" He stepped forward, laughing as they embraced.

"Glad to see you, Alonso," Sebastian whispered as he leaned closer. Then he spoke more softly, "Be careful."

The warning was wise. Alyn looked over Sebastian's shoulder to Miranda. She was even less pleased now, and he suspected Sebastian had just put himself out of her favor to help him. However, there were better changes in the looks of some people surrounding them. Maybe Sebastian's greeting reminded them that their prey really wasn't an outsider.

Sebastian pulled away, a hand staying on Alyn's shoulder as he faced Miranda. Alyn felt a little odd, as though he stood between two strangers. Sebastian was almost a head taller than him now, no longer a lanky, nervous sixteen-year-old. He faced Miranda without a hint of worry. Even Sebastian's smile stayed remarkably steady before her glare.

"He hasn't come back here to oppose you, Miranda," Sebastian offered softly. His fingers tightened on Alyn's shoulder, as though to warn him not to dispute that point. "He's here to show the Citizens that they're blind to our problems."

"How can he show them if he never comes here to look?" she asked. Her voice stayed hard, her eyes darting from one brother to another.

"I wasn't certain of my welcome. I thought I'd do my prelim work out in the City and wait for an invitation," he offered, half-truths, but calming ones. "I'm here now, if you want to tell your story, Miranda. I only ask you keep our personal problems out of it."

"Protect your secret." She grinned, which wasn't a friendly look.

"Let him do his work for us," Sebastian corrected. He spread his free hand in a gesture of peace. "I've never known you to throw away any advantage before. Maybe you're letting old family squabbles get in the way of your judgment."

People shifted uneasily again. Sebastian apparently stood on thin ground, though Alyn wasn't sure what he did wrong. Was Miranda's power so absolute that no one ever questioned her? His sister, who threw tantrums well into her teens if she didn't get her way? Were these people blind?

He was grateful for his brother's guidance.

"Get your cam," Miranda suddenly ordered. She acted as though the threats of a moment before had never been spoken. "I'll do an interview. Let's see if you can get it on the Citizen's Vidline. I doubt they'll let you do it. And if they don't, we'll know just how important your work is, won't we?"

Maybe this was a fair test, though Alyn could tell Miranda

never expected to see the vid aired. She wanted him to fail, and she would do her best to make certain of it. An interview with Miranda wasn't going to win him any friends in Silver City, even if she smiled and played nice -- which he knew she would not.

Nevertheless, he picked up his vidcam and keyed it on before he slipped on the eyepiece -- reminding himself that he worked for an Interstellar news agency and this might well prove a noteworthy achievement if he came through the interview unscathed. He didn't trust Miranda.

Miranda leaned against the nearest wall in a deceptively casual pose. She waved everyone else away from her. He thought that gesture was to protect their identities but then decided it was only to keep them from stealing her glory.

"Go ahead," Alyn stated. "Say whatever you think ... wise."

She glared for a moment at the statement then looked back at the vidcam. Alyn narrowed in on her face. Her brown velvet hair and dark eyes were all that distinguished her pale face from the white wall behind. Looking this closely at her, he saw changes he'd missed or misunderstood. He could see the pure fire of a fanatic in those dark eyes that stared out at the world. It made her look inhuman. Something alien.

"I am Miranda De Velera," she suddenly stated. She lifted her head and gave a smile that didn't make her look any more human. "I've decided to offer my insight on this trouble to the rest of Tempest. You'd be wise to listen to me this time. You'll know soon enough that I am not someone to ignore."

I, me, my, I. Alyn felt a sense of dismay inching its way up his spine again. This woman had only one vision, and it didn't include her people or their future.

"I will not settle for any compromise in my policies," Miranda stated. "Compromise won nothing in the past. This time you will give me what I demand, or you will pay for it with what you love most. Someone recently told me that I can't win against the Citizens. Maybe all I need do is bring you down to my level. And you'll learn I can do that."

If he played this on the local Newsline, it would incite the Citizens against the unquestionably aggressive Rats. Miranda was doing this purposely and putting him in an untenable situation. To save himself, Alyn must submit the interview and get it aired. If he did, he provoked more adversity. Alyn had never thought Miranda was clever. He began to revise his opinion.

"I am the leader of my people because you didn't give us what we need." She tilted her head. "I want equality. And if I can't be equal to you, I'll make you equal to me."

She waved her hand in a gesture that was a sign of ending.

"That's all, *Alyn Naevon*. Take your vidcam and go back to the Citizens. If I want you back here, you'll know."

Alyn turned the cam off. His fingers tingled as he nervously pulled off the eyepiece and shoved it back into his pocket. He tried to look professional while his heart pounded with fear.

"So, am I free to go, Randa?" he asked, testing her.

"Certainly. Sebastian thinks you won't hurt us. We'll see how good his judgment of people really is."

Sebastian grinned; either trusting Alyn or taunting Miranda, he wasn't sure. Alyn put a hand on his brother's arm and didn't like the idea of leaving him here. Sebastian patted his hand, smiled and gave him a nudge toward the door. He had to believe that Miranda would find no reason to hurt their artist brother. He had, after all, survived this long.

Alyn tucked his cam back under his arm and walked away with as much outward calm as when he'd walked in. The storm nearly blew the door out of his hand, and it slammed shut again, so he only heard the first whisper of sounds from the others. Would they protest Miranda's handling of the matter now that he -- now that the *outsider* was no longer among them? He wanted to believe there was still some sanity left in the Maze.

Later, when he found himself skirting the Port Tower, he finally believed Miranda didn't intend to kill him -- at least not right away. He still hurried on as a strong, gusty wind howled across the open cement field of the port. It was a cold, miserable night but Alyn felt a chill for a different reason. The guard looked startled when he showed his Vidline News credentials. He went on past without any trouble and headed for the Port Tower's front entrance hoping Kalison was still there this late, though this was another confrontation he wasn't looking forward to.

CHAPTER SIXTEEN

The empty chair drew covert, worried glances; so did the bandage around Wintas's arm. The four sat in strained silence while Ember Tanton shuffled through the little stack of papers before her. Fiona wondered what the note cards said and where they came from. Ember had connections through her family that none of the others could touch. They relied on her to find the answers this time.

"From all I can learn, the two attacks were not related," Ember suddenly stated. She shuffled the papers back together and stuffed them into her pocket. Then she looked up at the staring faces and shrugged. "That's all I can tell you."

"You found no connection to us?" Caden asked, still suspicious of the answer.

"I haven't *found* any," Ember replied and shrugged again. That was an uncommon reaction from the woman and made this seem all the stranger. "How about it, Wintas? Any suggestion that we are all in danger?"

"No," he replied as he cast a nervous glance around the room. Fiona thought she saw a whisper of mistrust mingled with the edge of panic in his pale face.

The man didn't want to be here with them. Well, after what happened today, maybe he had a right to doubt everyone. Especially since Caden gave him a wary, mistrusting look of his own.

That was it, then. With the trust gone, they could do nothing more. Fiona tried not to feel relief, especially when the release came at the death of a friend. She just wanted out. Fiona wanted to devote all her worries to running a hotel in a city under siege. She didn't want responsibility beyond that work.

"What can you tell us about your attacker, Wintas?" Ember asked. He looked at her as though startled by the question. "It might help if we have misread this incident."

"It was Rats," he suddenly said.

The glare he gave Caden surprised even Fiona despite the accusation. She never expected him to turn so quickly on one of their own. Maybe she wasn't the only one feeling pressure of even such a harmless act as these secret meetings, and perhaps the tension proved worse for someone working in the government.

Caden met the man's hard look, surprised, and more distrusting as well. Fiona wondered if she should order them all out of the building before this went to blows.

"You're certain that Rats attacked you?" Ember asked.

Wintas even dared turn the glare on her but must have remembered what power this woman represented. The look changed to a barely civilized frown.

"Who else would it be? Rats trying to disrupt work in the government!"

"I never heard even a hint that Miranda was going to make a move of that type," Caden began. At Wintas's new scowl of rage, Caden lifted his hand in a gesture of peace. "But there's a lot I haven't heard, isn't there? Odd, though, because I was in the Maze when the word came about the death and Miranda looked surprised. She was apparently calling a meeting of the faithful tonight. When I get back, I'll try to learn what it was about."

"You do that," Wintas growled with such a sneer that Fiona almost took him to task for it.

"We might as well call this a night, and get out of here," Ember suggested, managing to keep her head when Fiona was ready to snap back at Wintas. "Caden, take care getting back to the Maze."

That ended their very short meeting. Fiona hurried to her feet and unlocked the door. Wintas rushed out, stopped in the hall to look back at them, and then hurried on. Caden came next, pausing when Ember touched his arm. He gave her an uncertain look. She glanced down the hall, bit at her lip, and shrugged again.

"Remember to be careful, Caden. Be damned careful."

"You think there's something more going on," Caden replied. It wasn't a question. "So do I."

Ember nodded, patted Caden's arm, and let him go. Wintas had already disappeared around the end of the hall. Fiona stepped out of the room, Ember following her. The Citizen woman stared down the hall, still not leaving. Fiona suspected she didn't even notice they stood exposed to any passerby.

"Ember, what's going on?"

"I don't know," she admitted with a deeper frown. "After our last meeting, Sonio told me that he thought he was on to something and he'd let me know. He said he didn't want to start us worrying if he was wrong. And now he's dead. And Wintas is acting peculiar."

"He acts as though he suddenly hates all Rats," Fiona agreed. She sealed the door behind her. "Nothing is right. Rats targeting minor government clerks? Why? They could go for anyone in government, and neither Sonio or Wintas are irreplaceable. If they were going to kill someone, I'd think they'd concentrate on a person whose death would really disrupt the Citizens."

"True." She nodded thoughtfully but then looked up and down the hall, still frowning. "I don't want to distrust Wintas. He might simply feel shaken after his brush with death. However, if Wintas is wrong about why someone attacked Sonio and him, that leaves only one other item they have in common. Which means, you and I must be very careful now, too."

"Bauer is in my rooms," Fiona told her. "I said I had some hotel work to do, and I'd come back soon. I can't imagine any safer place than next to him."

"Damn mess," Ember whispered. That was the closest Fiona ever saw Ember Tanton come to admitting this was more than even she could handle. "See you later, Fiona."

Fiona watched Ember head towards the delivery entrance, and she turned away, heading for the lifts. The unease she felt during the meeting grew. Mistrust Wintas? Mistrust Caden? She didn't like the touch of paranoia this madness created. And she now realized that she forgot to tell them not to come back for the next meeting. She didn't want to go through this strain again tomorrow.

Fiona only felt safe when the door to the lift slid closed, protecting her. That wouldn't last long. She couldn't hide in here, drifting indefinitely through the interior of her hotel. Nor could she go back to her room and face Bauer while in this state of mind. Instead, she decided to spend a few minutes in her office, doing that work she mentioned to Bauer. That would calm her down. She didn't want to make him suspicious.

Arriving in the lobby, Fiona found a crowd gathered by the large front windows overlooking the city. The storm raged with an intensity that astonished her as lightning brightened the dark with startling flashes of illumination and the wind pounded against the permaglass, sometimes startling the people with the vigor of the rain-splattered attacks.

"Fiona!"

She leapt at the sound of her name and then gave Bauer a nervous wave as he moved his way through the growing crowd to her.

"Where the hell were you?" he demanded. The hand on her arm softened the harshness with a show of concern. "I spent the last fifteen minutes looking for you!"

"I was downstairs taking care of some filing," she answered with a calmness that surprised her. "What's going on?"

"The storm's worse than predicted," he said with a wave toward the window. "Damn, I wish they could get the weather data right on this world. There's flooding around the Port and probably in the Maze, too, though no one has word from there yet. The water might rise high even in the City. People are beginning to panic. Commander Kalison wants me to come in and help coordinate emergency operations. I'll come back when I can."

Fiona didn't want him to leave her here, alone. She didn't trust ... Wintas? Caden? She still couldn't decide which if either. She wanted to confess everything to Talin Bauer. She refrained from speaking, knowing he had business elsewhere tonight. Fiona gave him one quick hug, then watched Bauer dart away. He paused by the pods and waved once more. Fiona Salend returned the gesture and suddenly felt very much alone and vulnerable, standing there in the lobby of her perfect hotel.

"Damn," she whispered, pushing fingers through her hair.

Bauer's pod pulled away, slipping on the track that led directly back to the Port terminal. Maybe she should have gone with him.

"Fiona?"

She spun on the person who slid up to her side. Too damned jumpy! Orlon, her night manager, didn't notice. He looked worried and harassed.

"What's wrong?"

"We have some panicked guests," Orlon reported. He waved towards the reservation's desk. Guest stood around, demanding attention from two beleaguered clerks. The room lights flashed in growing numbers on the wall behind them. "I'm glad you're here. I can't handle this."

She was grateful for the work.

CHAPTER SEVENTEEN

Kalison looked up from his work-strewn desk and offered Shanley a weary smile. She stood at the edge of his doorway and didn't return it.

Trouble.

"Alyn Naevon is here to see you," she reported. Her voice remained neutral, but a slight nervousness showed in the movement of her hands. Kalison wondered what the reporter did to prompt this reaction out of the normally stoic Shanley. "He says he just came out of the Maze and he has an interview you should see."

"The Maze?" Kalison repeated, stunned by the unexpected statement. "That boy went into the Maze and came back out again? In one piece? Damn! It must be the luck of fools and idiots!"

"Yes, sir," she said and nodded emphatically. Her hands brushed at her jacket.

"Show the *fool* in," Kalison finally ordered.

He shoved aside paperwork on the flooding that no longer

held his interest despite the pounding storm outside. He prepared to berate Alyn and probably kick him off-world. Kalison didn't need hotshot reporters upsetting this uneasy balance by trying to dig up a sensational story. He felt annoyed because, for some reason, he had expected better of Alyn Naevon.

Then he suddenly wondered why Naevon came running straight to him with this one. Granted, Kalison was supposed to pass any sensational reports before they could be aired, but the reporter's employer was a powerful agency that seldom felt compelled to cooperate with local authorities. If Alyn wanted to, he could send his report straight off world and Kalison would have no control if Vidline even aired it on Tempest, not until official sanctions were in place. Neither he nor Governor Tanton had pushed for those controls which would have unsettled the population.

Nothing in the law said Alyn Naevon had to come with anything except the knowledge of a preventable crime. No Rat would be stupid enough to confess to something on vid before it happened.

By the time the soaked and worried reporter came into the office, Kalison felt far calmer and a little intrigued. Alyn Naevon stood there at the doorway, looking wet and uncomfortable. In fact, he looked as though he expected Kalison to reprimand him. Or just shoot him.

Lightning flashed outside the building, and thunder shook the walls. If the storm continued at this force much longer, they'd face flooding all the way uptown. Looking at drenched Alyn only reminded him of those problems he had pushed aside. Nothing cooperated on this world.

"What kind of idiot do you think you are?" Kalison sighed.

"They expected me to come in or else I wouldn't have gotten far." He spread his free hand, the other holding tight to a battered cam. "I have something you'll want to see. Miranda De Velera graced me with an interview, and you're not going to like it."

Kalison made one disgusted sound and slapped at his desk in frustration. Then he waved his hand toward the comp.

"Go ahead, load it in. I'm beginning to think you're too damned much trouble, Naevon."

"No one else could have brought you this," he replied softly. Alyn crossed to the desk, still looking worried and uncomfortable. And wet. He ineffectually wiped damp hands against wet clothes before he popped open the chit slot on his cam. His fingers shook, and Kalison thought it might be from more than the cold.

"Shanley!" Kalison shouted into the comm -- loud enough that she probably heard without the equipment.

"Yes sir?" her voice came back, calm and serene.

"Bring Naevon something to dry off with before he floods my office, will you?"

"Certainly."

"Thanks," Alyn offered with a nervous little smile. He held the chit out. "I have a little footage from inside the Maze if you'd like to see it. Nothing that's likely to help you find your way, though."

"I haven't gotten past the front gate," Kalison admitted, slipping from his chair to get out of the way. "I would like to see what it looks like in there. Line it up."

The reporter didn't sit. He keyed up the chit and fidgeted with the controls, explaining that he'd used the old cam, afraid to take the new one in. Before he had the picture fully aligned, Shanley showed up with a towel and a dry shirt requisitioned from supply. She apparently liked the boy. Shanley was hell on clerks who gave away Government Issue.

"Change," Kalison ordered.

Alyn nodded gratefully and stepped away from the comp. He quickly slipped out of his soggy shirt. Kalison felt a surge of surprise when he saw the reporter's bare back. The long, burn scar looked suspiciously like a laser wound. It had healed naturally, too, without regen treatments, and was surrounded by minor blemishes that didn't come from a comfortable life.

Kalison said nothing as he took the towel while Alyn pulled on the other shirt. Until now he hadn't considered that Alyn Naevon might have personal justification in campaigning for the Rats. Maybe there was a reason the Rats invited him into their sanctuary, and let him out again, unharmed. Kindred spirits.

Kalison didn't ask. He had trouble enough here without dragging Naevon's past into it. He let Alyn line up the vids and watched the unedited report in silence.

The shots from within the Maze drew his immediate interest, but it was Miranda's interview that troubled him. Naevon played that section three times before Kalison finally signaled a stop. He forced the tight muscles in his shoulders to relax, but acid still churned in the pit of his stomach. This was as close to Miranda De Velera as he had ever been, and though he didn't like what he saw, he was uncertain why her statements so severely unsettled him.

"What do you see here?" Alyn asked. His fingers abruptly retrieved the chit. He stared at the small cube as though he could still see the images trapped within.

"What do I see? She makes me more nervous than before. I always knew she was trouble, but there's something more here that I can't put my finger on."

"I see a woman obsessed with power," Alyn replied. He looked up, his eyes narrowed. "*I, me, mine.* She doesn't really give a damn about the people who follow her, Commander Kalison. She's in this only for the personal glory -- and that means you can't offer her *anything*. She doesn't want the war to end because if it does, she loses what she holds most precious: her own power."

Kalison felt his mouth go dry as he stared at Alyn. He had listened to her promise of trouble to come and hadn't heard the insinuations behind the words. Everything Alyn said made sense, but he didn't like this new revelation. He didn't want to believe there was little chance at peace between the Citizens and the Rats.

"If we play this on Newsline it's going to incite the Citizens," Alyn continued. His fingers tightened on the little chit. The reporter looked at Kalison and shook his head. "And if we don't, it's going to incite the Rats. It'll prove to them that no one's interested in their side."

"Which side is more dangerous to provoke?" Kalison wondered aloud. He suddenly glared at Naevon, as though this situation was really his fault. "If you hadn't gone in there --"

"It wouldn't change who she is. She would have found another way to provoke trouble," he answered with a slight shrug. He had stopped trembling. Maybe it had only been the cold, though Kalison doubted the reporter could dismiss danger that easily. Despite everything that happened, Alyn Naevon wasn't that stupid. "It's just as well I went. I can guarantee this is legit. Whether it gets on Vidline or not, you had a chance to look at Miranda De Velera."

Kalison nodded. He had the interview, and damn few options now.

Lightning brightened the sky once, shook the building with a new force. The storm wasn't abating. One more problem added to this mess.

"Is there anything else you can tell me that might help us -- "

Shanley arrived at his door and came in without an

invitation. Her face was pale, her eyes wide.

"Explosion, mid-city," she gasped as she crossed towards his rain-splattered window. "It sounds as though this one was bad."

Alyn headed straight to the window, reaching it before Shanley or Kalison got there. The reporter quickly keyed on his cam and shoved the chit back into place. Kalison looked over Naevon's shoulder, watching as errant lights flashed from somewhere behind tall buildings as power lines arced with unconfined power. Those lines had torn loose from buried conduits, which meant the explosion probably came from somewhere underground. His guess, from the apparent location, was the central transit station.

Alarms began ringing throughout the Port terminal, alerting emergency crews. As Kalison continued to watch, lights flickered in the entire northern section of the city and then went dark. He could almost feel the panic growing, like something wild and untamable. He didn't want to see it unleashed.

"Damn her!" Alyn suddenly growled as he lowered the cam and keyed it off. One fist unexpectedly pounded the glass in anger. "She warned us it was going to get worse, didn't she? *You'll know soon enough that I am not someone to ignore. Maybe all I need do is bring you down to my level. And you'll learn I can do that.* I better get down there."

"Hold on. You can go in with me," Kalison told him. He wasn't certain why he offered except leaving Naevon on his own was apparently dangerous. "Shanley, call up all the crews and get them moving. Put the Maze under guard. The Citizens are going to try to go in again."

"What if Jeffries and his men show up?" she asked, crossing to his desk to use his computer.

"I want you in charge there. If Jeffries makes trouble, I want a senior officer on hand to do -- whatever is necessary.

But, for God's sake, don't be the first to fire!"

Alyn Naevon stood waiting at the doorway, looking as though he didn't want to be privy to even this much knowledge. Strange reaction in a reporter. Kalison grabbed his jacket from the rack and pushed the reporter out of the room. This was going to be a damn hard long night.

Chapter Eighteen

Alyn dutifully followed Kalison from his office and through the busy terminal halls as alarms continued a cacophonic ring of disaster. Shanley's voice sometimes rose over the blare to give cryptic, number-encoded orders to the gathering squads. Port Guards moved with quick ease that showed they had prepared for emergencies, though Alyn saw that many of the faces were pale with shock.

No one looked at Alyn, and after traversing a few crowded hallways, Alyn realized the shirt he now wore gave him unexpected camouflage. The soldiers saw half a uniform and didn't look any farther. This gave him a chance to study an aspect of this war he hadn't much considered until now. These men came from off-world, dropped into a class struggle to which they didn't really belong on either side. He wondered what they thought about this stupid, useless hostilities. Maybe he could get a few interviews after the current crisis was past.

In the crowded lift, the men muttered about the damn natives, making no distinction between Rat and Citizen. Kalison only looked at Alyn and sighed. There was no doubt the

Commander felt much of the same frustration as his men.

When they reached the roof, Kalison stopped to give orders to a few waiting men. One of them was Captain Bauer, who looked at Alyn and then looked again in surprise. Alyn felt a weak moment of amusement.

"Come on, Naevon," Kalison ordered. He caught hold of Alyn's arm and led him across the wet, busy roof. "Let's get out of this damn rain. You're soaked again. You'll have pneumonia out of this if you're not careful."

As though it mattered to the man.

The aircar was a small, battered two-seater with the IWC emblem painted on the side. Kalison waved away the man who was probably his usual pilot and took the controls himself as he keyed the machine on. He received instant clearance from control, and in a moment, they lifted into the windy, rainy night.

Alyn looked beyond the port toward the Maze. Several aircars already sat outside the arch, and he hoped they were IWC vehicles. He couldn't see much more than their indistinct shapes in the rain.

Shanley was either on her way or already there. Strangely, he thought he could trust the woman to keep the Rats safe, even from Jeffries and his people. If Alyn hadn't trusted her, he might have been tempted to go there himself. Despite his disagreement with Miranda, there were still people in the Maze that he would want to help protect.

Kalison didn't ask what Alyn thought, and he forced himself to look away from his old home.

The rain made viewing the ground difficult, though the occasional lightning gave brief glimpses of the city. Walkways generally emptied in the pouring rain now overflowed with panicked people who must have been working late in the city and who now rushed to get away from the dangerous area. Were there other bombs planted out there? Numb shock and trembling anger began to take hold of Alyn in turns. The closer they came to the center of the explosion, the more signs of destruction they found. Alyn barely had the sense left to take shots from the air.

"The transit system is out," Kalison finally observed. "That looks like smoke coming from the mid-city terminal."

"She didn't strike at the rush hour," Alyn mumbled. "That surprises me."

"Yeah," Kalison said and nodded. "Maybe, in a few days, I'll feel grateful for that consideration. Right now, it doesn't make a damn bit of difference. Take care down there, Alyn. Janith is spreading rumors that you're in league with the Rats. You're lucky that interview with Miranda De Velera hasn't aired yet."

"The last nail in my coffin, huh?" he said. He carefully adjusted the older cam as Kalison brought the aircar closer to the chaos.

"If we do air her interview I can guarantee that you won't be safe."

"If we don't show it, I won't be safe."

"You could leave the world."

"I have my job to do."

"Huh. Only as long as I let you stay and do it."

The round of useless words helped to settle Alyn's nerves. Kalison didn't appear to take the conversation seriously. The Commander flew them circling the explosion site, swinging in close enough to see the superficial damage done to buildings nearby. Two other buildings showed cracks in their surface, running for several floors. Windows were broken all around. These were mostly office buildings, and nearly empty this late at night. Strange that Miranda had that much concern for human life.

"Maybe she couldn't hide it earlier," Alyn suddenly stated,

drawing Commander Kalison's attention for a moment. The man circled around the area again, while Alyn spoke. "This bomb had to be fairly large unless it was some type of nuclear device. I assume we wouldn't head to ground zero if it were. Could something that size go undetected during the busy part of the day?"

"Maybe not," he agreed. "If you get a chance to interview her again, be sure and ask."

"If I get a chance to interview her again, I'll bring you her head instead of a vid."

Kalison looked at him with surprise. The words probably sounded too angry. Too personal. Damn, maybe it was time to make confessions --

Not now. Kalison had a real crisis on his hands, and he didn't need Alyn to complicate the matter, so Alyn didn't even offer any further insights into Miranda's behavior.

Kalison angled the aircar towards the heart of the trouble. Intense, flashing lights in blue and green marked the official barricade to the explosion site. The aircar went over the lights, slipped through a small, dense cloud of smoke and landed in an area of pandemonium.

The smoke still billowed fitfully from the terminal entrance. There didn't appear to be an inferno below the surface. People staggered from that opening, dazed and many injured. A few slipped and collapsed on the rain-slicked walkway where emergency workers descended on them with med bags in hand. Kalison had landed the aircar with a blare of his siren and turned a bright light on that opening. The commander popped the door open and passed in the cam's view, dashing into the smoky opening to the Transit system.

"Damn her," Alyn whispered.

He climbed out and slapped the aircar door closed after him. One quick video scan of the area showed guards in grey uniformed Militia moving at random among the gathering people, though not trying to contain the populace or help with the injured as the Port Guards were. The sight angered him more. He turned away with the cam held under his arm and followed the Commander.

As he neared the opening, guilt rushed through his mind with the force of a blow. Alyn slipped on the rain-drenched ramp, landing on knees, gasping.

A man stumbled past, making soft sounds of panic and pain. More vehicles arrived, the blare of emergency sirens filling the night. Damaged power lines sent a shower of sparks into the air, while the storm raged with anger all its own. This was a scene from hell: his own, personal hell as much as that of anyone caught in this trouble.

Alyn got back to his feet and rushed into the dark, smoky opening.

Scattered movement surged around him as more people limped out of the manmade tunnel. Coughs and cries echoed from the eerie, red-tinted dark leading down into the terminal. His eyes already stung from the smoke and he tried not to choke at the smell of human fear mingled with burning plastic.

After a few more steps, he entered the midst of pure chaos. Massive metal beams lay in twisted, unnatural piles and electrical conduits, torn open by the blast, flashed with menacing power. A water main -- split in half in half and ripped from the wall -- created a new hazard around the open power lines. Someone in a city-worker uniform was already surveying that situation and shouting into his communicator. Hopefully, they'd soon cut off the power to this area.

As his eyes adjusted to the dim, flickering light, Alyn realized confusion lay everywhere he turned. Destruction and devastation littered an area at least a quarter of a kilometer square. Walls stood bereft of their supports, one visibly teetering. Vast chunks of the cement ceiling had dropped in broken pieces across the area, mingled with comp terminals, water fountains and other innocuous fragments of normality.

Kalison was only a meter ahead of him, kneeling beside a travel pod that rested more than a dozen meters from the track. A massive metal girder rested in a twisted pile across the cracked dome. Kalison tried lifting the beam with little success. Alyn could barely see movement within the pod.

Alyn turned the cam to full wide view and shoved it into a sturdy looking crevice by the exit. He couldn't stand by and watch while people remained trapped in this deadly chaos.

This wasn't his fault. He wasn't responsible for Miranda De Velera's behavior.

How could the rest of the Rats let her lead them to this madness?

Kalison nodded grim thanks when Alyn caught hold of the jagged metal and helped shove it free. Together, they peeled away a layer of fractured permaglass and uncovered an older woman inside the wreckage. By then the meds arrived and took over.

The two of them went on, deeper into the heart of the trouble. Alyn wasn't sure when they separated, and he lost track of how long he had been down in the wreckage. He cut his hand on jagged metal or glass while helping a med pull a sobbing child from the far corner of a pile of debris. His eyes ran with tears long after the smoke dissipated.

Sometimes fires flared unexpectedly. Several sections of the plastic covering from the ceiling collapsed followed by a more dangerous layer of cement. Alyn saw an emergency worker crushed beneath a falling wall. Rainwater seeped through the floodgates that no longer had the power to operate, and they had to work harder to get to people trapped who might now face drowning.

The hellish images were all that remained to him: dead everywhere in the convoluted wreckage of metal and cement; wires, still sparking with sporadic life, swaying dangerously around them creating shifting shadows and occasional clarity when he would rather have not seen so well. Rain, smoke, fire, destruction, and death ... this wasn't a scene he would ever forget. Alyn was glad he hadn't brought the cam beyond the opening. He didn't want to recall this horror so clearly again. He didn't care if it would have made an excellent report.

He remembered Governor Bramis Tanton's words: When they accepted that the death of any person was wrong, they'd be on their way to recovery. This bombing ended all hope of peace in the immediate future.

Alyn considered going back into the Maze, dragging Miranda out and throwing her -- and himself -- to the Citizens as a salve. That would be a useless gesture because even her death wouldn't calm them, but the idea suited his mind right then.

Until now, the disagreement between Citizen and Rat consisted only of skirmishes. Some of those encounters resulted in deaths but didn't lead to war. This was irrevocable. Kalison might not have the resources to hold the Citizens back this time.

These poor people weren't going to be the only dead before long.

CHAPTER NINETEEN

Sebastian watched the disaster unfold from the window in his second-story room and no longer felt the little spray of rain from the leak. His view cut across the top of the Maze to where lights flashed, and emergency aircars darted everywhere. He only felt numb -- and an underlying guilty relief that he couldn't see the tragedy clearly. He silently observed the distant flash of bright lights reflected on steel and glass buildings without allowing himself to feel the human loss. He knew people had died in that explosion and he knew that Miranda was responsible. However, tonight the rain diffused and diffracted the multitude of flashing lights making them almost unreal, much like the sudden sound of his sister's giddy laughter.

The size of the crowd downstairs grew larger than usual after the explosion. Some came in a panic, but Miranda's people kept everything in hand. Sebastian had retreated upstairs after Lauren had left with Niels. He remained in his room with the light off, hoping to escape the madness and survive the aftermath. He didn't want anyone to ask what he thought of this action. He wouldn't lie.

Lauren had trashed everything in sight before she left. Luckily, he kept most of his artwork under the bed and in the closet. She hadn't been that thorough. He very much wanted out of this life and away from the insanity. Sebastian didn't want to hear his name coupled with Miranda's. He wanted to sit in some quiet corner of the world and paint pictures and dream. Maybe that was a coward's way out, but he didn't care.

Sebastian didn't think there would be any quiet corner in the world tonight as word of this evil spread even to the smaller towns and single farms. Perhaps he should take Alonso's way out and find some way to leave the world. Sebastian wondered where his brother was tonight and if Alonso realized Miranda's part in the bombing. Of course, he did: she had all but admitted to it during that interview.

Someone knocked on the door, and the sound startled him. Sebastian hadn't heard anyone coming upstairs this time. He glared once at the door, then ignored it. Turning back to the window, Sebastian wondered if he could paint that scene? Could he capture the distant colors, spread and brightened by the layer of rainwater on his window? He could almost make it look pretty.

No, this was not a night he wanted to look upon again, even on canvas. Nothing could make this ... acceptable. Those diffuse lights marked the end of any illusion of peace on this world.

The person pounded again, insistent this time. The door suddenly opened, bright hall light flooding the room. He turned with a curse --

"What a mess, Sebastian," Miranda stated. "You really should take better care of your room."

Sebastian bit back every ill-worded statement that came to his mind, both about Miranda and about Lauren. He couldn't hide his glare as easily, so he turned back to the window instead.

"I didn't realize you could see so far from in here," Miranda mused.

She moved beside him, staring at those horrible lights. He saw the whisper of a smile on her lips and turned away before she provoked him to his own madness. He wondered if he could kill her. She was a better fighter. Then he realized, with a startlingly clear thought, that someone would have to do it.

"Why didn't you answer the door?"

"I didn't feel like it," he answered, his voice very cold and hard. "And I didn't know it was you. You don't make a habit of visiting my room."

"True."

He didn't like having her here, invading his little sanctuary. He schooled his face and changed his tone. Play the game. That allowed him peace the rest of the time.

"What did bring you up here?" he finally asked.

"I have a task I'd like you to do for me, Sebastian. Something important."

Damn. He knew by her tone that he'd already stepped beyond the bounds she allowed. He had drawn her attention when he came to Alonso's aid, and she wasn't going to let him walk away unscathed. Now he had to face the consequences for crossing her. Fine. He didn't regret his decision.

"What can I possibly do for you, Miranda?" he asked with a hint of mockery in his voice. She wasn't Lauren: she caught the tone and frowned.

"I'm sending Niel Taress into the city to look over the situation. I want you to go with him."

"Me?" he replied, stunned by her decision. "Go into the city, *tonight?*"

"Niel is a good advisor, but he doesn't have your eye for detail. I want to know the extent of the damage. The Port

Guard isn't going to come in here and make reports to us about it, you know. In fact, they have the entrance under guard, as though that would stop us from getting out."

"More likely they're trying to keep others from coming in."

She glared again.

"We have enemies, Miranda," he reminded her, for once undaunted by her look. This had gone far beyond family squabbles. "We have more enemies tonight than the Rats ever had before."

"I want the report before dawn, Sebastian. Niel is waiting downstairs."

She turned and stalked back out of the room, slamming the door behind her. Sebastian briefly considered what would happen if he didn't go. None of the outcomes sounded good. Living in the Maze while out of Miranda's favor was always difficult, but more so in his case. People couldn't pretend they didn't know she was mad at him.

Go look for her: the job was dangerous, but at least she didn't ask him to go out and have a word with the Port Guard at the front gate. That would be suicidal.

He took a well-worn jacket from the closet and pulled it on. It was Alonso's old coat, and that felt appropriate, under the circumstances.

Niel waited impatiently at the bottom of the stairs with Lauren. She gave her brother a quick hug goodbye and grinned maliciously at Sebastian. Maybe this little excursion was as much her revenge as Miranda's and that made going into the city with Niel even less appealing. He kept those worries to himself. No one else was in the foyer, and he wondered if any of the others knew he was leaving with Niel. He heard Miranda speaking in the main meeting hall a loud rush of words about standing together now that they faced real adversity.

The fools might not even blame her.

He and Niels headed out into the uninviting, wet night. While the fury of the storm was less, the rain still fell incessantly. Most of the Maze was already ankle-deep in running water. Niel navigated the dangerous streams with a constant flow of curses. Apparently, despite the importance of this mission, Miranda's counselor didn't want to be out here tonight and the glares he directed at Sebastian laid the blame on him. Niel was probably right, given Miranda's state of mind.

Sebastian was more surefooted than Niel, and that probably annoyed the man as well. He followed Miranda's advisor without any comment, ready to do the work and get back to the relative warmth of his room.

Most Rats knew at least a dozen secret passages out of the Maze. Niel led him to the one in the northwest corner, near the port grounds. Along that edge ran rows of sturdy orange trees, an adapted hybrid that thrived on Tempest. The owner of the orchard ran an electrified barb-wire fence on the Maze side, but that didn't stop the Rats from tunneling under it and stealing oranges. The Citizens never remembered that many Rats were the descendants of itinerant engineers. A little tunneling and a camouflaged exit were hardly a challenge at all.

Tonight the tunnel was half full of muck, and Niel cursed it and Sebastian in endless rounds.

"You think this was my idea?" Sebastian finally growled in return. He was tired of the tirade. "Let's just get Miranda's work done, and get back home, all right?"

Niel didn't answer. Sebastian began to suspect taking Miranda's little brother with him annoyed the man. Maybe he didn't see this as punishment for Sebastian but a slur on his own abilities. Great. He didn't want Niel as an enemy -- any more than Lauren made of him, anyway. Maybe, if he proved himself on this little jaunt, Miranda might come to respect him, which meant something to him, in an odd way. He didn't like Miranda, but she still represented a whisper of the authority his father once held. Sebastian still wanted to impress a man long dead.

The orchard sat empty on this dark, stormy night, and even the automatic feeders remained still at the end of each row of trees. Everyone in the city was probably crowded around what working comps they could find, watching the news and waiting for the next attack.

And here he was, the brother of Tempest's most infamous Rat, out wandering the streets with her chief advisor. He quietly whispered his own curse as he realized what Citizens would think if the two were spotted. He hadn't considered more than keeping Miranda happy.

Port Guards walked the inner perimeter of the Port. Niel took them farther to the east and had stopped mumbling now that they were into enemy territory. Sebastian felt his heart thump at every unexpected sound. He never spent much time in the city, and he didn't know his way around. Sebastian could only follow Niel, farther and farther into the city until he was lost and feared that he must depend entirely on Niel to get home again.

Miranda's respect wasn't worth this.

Niel stopped. Somewhere very close, lights flashed in a bright profusion of colors, and he realized they'd reached the site of the explosion and the sounds of angry people echoed around the edges of the buildings. Niel looked around the corner of his wall and quickly pulled back, nodding.

"This about as far as we go," he growled. Those were the first words he said directly to Sebastian since they'd left the Hostel, hours before. Sebastian nodded and inched his way closer to the building edge, ready to take a quick look.

"Get this right, boy," Niel ordered as he slid aside.

"I will," he replied coolly. They had enough trouble, standing here in the city, without Niel trying to provoke him.

Ah well, he didn't expect better from Miranda's new favorite.

Sebastian took a deep breath and peered around the edge of the building. The brightness of the direct lights blinded him for a moment, and he saw only shadowy movement and heard the constant hum of many voices. He blinked and felt a sudden shiver at the sight. At least a thousand citizens crowded into the area in front of the Transit Station.

Sebastian -- *Sebastian De Velera* -- didn't want to be here with so many angry people hardly more than a dozen meters away. What if someone came this way? Was there anywhere they could take cover?

He turned to search out any shelter --

Niel was driving a knife at him.

With a yelp, Sebastian ducked and shoved at Niel. The knife caught at the shoulder of his jacket but didn't reach flesh. Niel tumbled backward under Sebastian's unexpected attack, but he grabbed Sebastian's arm in a tight grip. Both went down, Sebastian fighting to keep the knife away. He hadn't the breath to ask Niel what the hell he was doing.

Knew anyway. Niel never would try to kill him without Miranda's order, not even for Lauren's honor. Miranda never meant for her brother to come back from the city. He stood beside Alonso and faced her down, and that annoyed her. That was enough provocation.

No one except Miranda and Lauren knew he was out here with Niel. He would be just another of the many dead Rats and without even friends or family to mourn his death.

Alonso might --

He fought for his life, but Niel was more experienced than his younger sister. Federico De Velera taught him the fundamentals of self-defense but then left his son to his art. Despite the lack of extensive training, he did have at least one advantage. The man had counted on stabbing Sebastian in the back. He didn't want to fight here.

If Sebastian was going down, he was taking Niel with him.

Sebastian heard approaching steps, echoing voices growing louder. Niel panicked. He jerked free of Sebastian and scrambled to his feet, frantic. Sebastian grabbed for his leg and missed. Niel took the time to deliver one solid kick to the right side of Sebastian's head. Then Niel took off at a quick, loping run.

The voices drew nearer. Panicked, and muddled by the last blow, Sebastian could only roll until he pressed himself against the wall and held his breath.

Four people rushed around the corner. With their hoods pulled tight against the rain, they never spotted him. He lay there on the ground, frozen in terror, while they sped past, talking about destruction and vengeance against the Rats. They saw Niel running and pursued, though Sebastian didn't think they would catch him.

When they disappeared around the next corner, he scrambled to his feet and took off in the direction Niel had run. He didn't know his way around of the city. However, if he could get clear of these tall buildings, he could spot the port tower and head for it and the Maze beyond. That gave him a vague direction to run. Staying in the city was out of the question, even if the Maze wasn't entirely safe. If he could get among witnesses, Miranda dare not move directly against him again. That was his only hope.

He had no luck this night. Coming around the next corner, he found himself face to face with a dozen citizens. One woman held a vidcam. She gave a shout, and he turned and fled. They came after him.

CHAPTER TWENTY

"Alyn."

A hand dropped heavily on his shoulder. Alyn spun on Kalison, ready to bolt or swing -- he wasn't sure which he had intended. Indecision kept him from doing either.

Dark streaks smudged Kalison's face, his reddened eyes squinting between the marks. It looked like the war paint from the ancient Earther vids that Alyn sometimes found so fascinating.

"Come on," Kalison ordered. The hand tightened on Alyn's shoulder. "The meds and troops will clean up. We've done all we can here."

Alyn barely nodded, allowing the numbness to sweep over him again. Kalison released Alyn's shoulder and caught his elbow instead, steering him upward along the path. As they neared the Terminal entrance, Alyn heard the pounding roar of thunder above them. Before they reached the exit, a cold wind, laden with rain, rushed past him. He gasped at the clean air, coughing as it slipped past his raw throat.

They stepped aside from the entrance in the shadow and

safety of a wall that showed some cracks in the façade but still seemed steady. Both men took a moment to breathe in the fresh, cold air. There was chaos out here, but it wasn't the same as the nightmare on the other side of that entrance.

"You did all right, Naevon. I didn't expect you to come in and help. Where's your cam?"

"Set on a wide angle back in a crevice by the opening," he answered. The words left him gasping for more fresh air. Icy rainwater seeped through his sweat-dampened clothing, and he began shivering.

"Better get you out of this rain," Kalison decided. "When did you cut your hand?"

"Don't know." He looked down at the nasty gash across his right palm. Blood stained his fingers. "Can't be too bad."

"You'll need it closed," Kalison disagreed. He again pulled at Alyn's elbow. "The meds are --"

"The meds are busy. They have real emergencies," he interrupted. Looking at the wound made it sting. Looking at the chaos of lights and unmoving bodies laid out in the rain made him ill. He wanted away from here. "I can get by with it wrapped. I'll do it back at the hotel."

"They want my aircar to take victims back to the hospital. I'll get you to the hotel first --"

"Stop worrying about me," he replied with a surge of exasperation. "I am on my feet and walking. It's only a couple kilometers from the hotel. I can manage that far. It'll help clear my head."

"Might not be safe out there on the streets tonight," Kalison quietly replied. His eyes moved towards the crowd watching beyond the lighted perimeter. Alyn didn't want to see those faces. "I'll get your cam and walk with you. It's the direction I'm heading, and an aircar can pick me up easier away from this mess. Wait here."

Alyn nodded and watched the Commander dash away, noting that the man limped, favoring his left side. No one left this scene unscathed, either in body or soul.

When Kalison disappeared into the Terminal, Alyn considered walking away, but a logical part of his brain kicked in before he moved. Leaving would only annoy Kalison, who would still catch up with him. There was no use in needlessly provoking the Port Commander.

Kalison returned a moment later, the cam under his arm, and a medpad in his hand. Alyn let him push the white pad against the dirty wound and medications quickly eased an ache he hadn't noticed until it disappeared. While Alyn leaned against the wall, carefully flexing his fingers, Kalison mumbled a few orders to one of his men. Then they began to walk away.

Behind them, the sirens, red lights, and black smoke filled the night with the spectacle of catastrophe. Drenched crowds encircled the area, held back by a line of port guards. They parted unwillingly, questions shouted at Kalison as he passed. The guards kept anyone from following.

There was no gray-uniformed Militia in the area, and surprisingly no sign of Janith. The woman couldn't ignore the biggest disaster her world had suffered in years, and especially when this would paint the Rats as the evil aggressors. Maybe Janith spent too much time at the Tempest Pride's bar tonight, and just couldn't quite make it here.

"They aren't happy," Alyn whispered as he looked back. He felt very uncomfortable in the midst of angry, sullen Citizens.

"This time they have a reason for their anger, Naevon," Kalison quietly admitted. "This time there are no easy answers."

Within a few meters of the site, another crowd surrounded them. Alyn realized he was lucky Kalison insisted on escorting him. However, even the Commander didn't appear much of a deterrent to this hostility. Several bolder Citizens encircled them in a hostile trap, baring their way. Kalison quietly handed Alyn his cam, and he surreptitiously made sure it was still on.

"This has gone too far, Kalison," someone growled.

"It went too far long before this," Commander Kalison replied, remaining even-tempered in the face of this open hostility. His hand brushed against his jacket, activating a key on his pocketed commlink. No one else noticed.

Help on the way. Alyn felt some of his anxiety ease since that call from the Commander of the Port would draw a swift response. He tried to distance himself and remember he was a reporter, not a Rat caught in an infuriated Citizen crowd. When he brought the cam up, it startled the nearest antagonists. Some backed away in haste, faces averted from the lens. These were not people used to making trouble, but only victims looking for somewhere to vent their rage.

"Would you care to elaborate on this situation?" he asked, scanning the crowd at random.

They backed farther away. Then a band of ten tan-clad soldiers pushed through and the people scattered. Bauer was in the lead, looking grim and angry.

"Sir." He saluted, glared at the shadowy figures, and looked back again. "Can we escort you and Alyn somewhere?"

"Back to the hotel and then I'll go on to the Maze," he said. "We won't need all ten. Two with laser rifles will suffice."

"Are you implying you're in danger from the Citizens?" a dark-haired woman demanded. She stepped forward, the fire in her eyes showing a very honest rage.

"This isn't a very friendly confrontation," Kalison replied softly. "Would you feel safe if you stood beside me without the guards present?"

Bauer and another guard fell in beside the two. The shadowed crowd parted with unsettled and angry whispers. They finally rounded the nearest corner before Alyn breathed easily again.

"That makes you nervous?" Kalison asked. A hint of amusement touched his face as he rubbed the sleeve of his wet jacket across his face, though that didn't remove much of the grime. "I'd think you were used to it. Anyone who can walk in and out of the Maze shouldn't find a few irate Citizens very disturbing."

"He went into the Maze?" Bauer looked at him in shock. Alyn feared for his reputation if this went much further.

"People always assume Rats have no laws, no ethics," Alyn replied. He finally keyed off the cam, dropping it down under his arm once more. The building, night and rain slipped between them, and the disaster and the empty walkways settled his nerves this time. "I think the Citizens are more dangerous because they often don't think the laws really apply to them. Is there trouble at the Maze?"

"Some. We were right. Jeffries showed up with his Militia to *protect* the area. Shanley is holding him off, but he's pushing. I have more troops heading in, and I'm going as added authority. I suppose you think you want to go there too."

He felt leaden and tired, but he gave a little shrug.

"It's my job, Kalison."

"I'll probably order you off Tempest, boy. I hate writing death certificates on off-worlders, and I don't need any added paperwork. I get the feeling you're looking for the kind of trouble you won't always be able to walk away from."

"I'll just stick with you for now, since you clearly aren't looking for trouble," he said and grinned. Bauer made a slight sound of amusement, though his eyes never stopped scanning the area. The Port Guard did take protecting their Commander seriously. Alyn wondered if they worried as much about Rat assassins as Citizen mobs.

Except for the rumble of thunder, the night grew quieter

away from the bombing site. Quiet enough that they could hear trouble coming this time.

Angry shouts, running feet -- at the next corner, a dozen shadows crossed their path. Someone sprawled at the edge of the walkway, and then the others were on him.

"Damn! Must have caught some Rat in the city!" Kalison hissed and started forward at a quick jog.

Alyn was only a step behind him. Bauer, with his rifle in hand, pushed ahead while shouting a warning to back off, and finally firing a shot that scorched the wall above the heads of the attackers. Half the group backed off, slinking into the shadows. The others never noticed.

The faint light illuminated the nearby corner, and Alyn clearly saw Janith with her own cam in hand. She taped the scene of a single Rat beaten by the mob. He doubted it ever occurred to her to attempt stopping the attack. For her, this would be nothing more than a few minutes of good footage.

Bauer and Kalison waded into the group, pulling the closest Citizens away while the last guard kept his rifle up and ready. There was a moment when the group still seethed with anger and rage -- but seeing tan uniforms and laser rifles finally drove them off. Janith glared at Alyn, as though he interrupted her story, rather than saving a life. She spun and walked off with the last of the marauders.

The victim remained a huddled mass on the cement.

"Can you walk?" Kalison asked softly. "We can't leave you here."

A face looked up from under his protective arm. Dark blood ran in a trickle down the side of an ashen face.

"God! Sebastian! What the hell are you doing out here?!"

Kalison looked back at Alyn with a start. However, the boy looked up at him with hope replacing the fear. Alyn nearly cursed for giving away even that much of Sebastian's identity, though.

"Alyn Naevon," he his brother said, quietly reminding Alyn to guard himself. "Thank you --"

"Sebastian?" Kalison looked back at the young man and offered a hand to pull him to his feet.

"Sebastian De Velera," Sebastian stated.

Silence. Kalison glanced around with a start, as though he feared someone close by might hear. The guard's pulled their weapons up again, but none of them looked at Sebastian as though he represented the enemy.

"Are you crazy?" Kalison finally demanded. He kept his voice very soft. "What are you doing out here?"

"Miranda said she wanted to know what was going on in the city," he replied. Bitterness touched the words, but Alyn dared not ask for the story. Sebastian finally allowed Kalison pull him to his feet. His torn shirt showed a stain of blood on his right side. "She ordered me out here."

"And you couldn't argue with her?" Kalison softly hissed, still nervous.

"No."

"No," Alyn agreed and met Kalison's worried look. "You saw the interview. Did she sound like a woman open to any disagreement?"

"No," Kalison finally agreed. "Damn, this is another mess. I should pull you in for questioning. Miranda De Velera's brother is surely worth something to us."

Sebastian gave Alyn one quick, amused look, but only shrugged at the suggestion.

"You might be safer with Kalison if this is what Miranda thinks you're worth," Alyn suggested.

"I'll go wherever the Commander thinks best. However, if you hold me, she'll have another point against you," he offered with open honesty. He winced as he took one step with

Kalison's help. "I don't know anything about her activities, Commander. Everyone in the Maze knows she keeps me out of her business. But I annoyed her tonight, and she finally realized she could use me as a martyr. I was never meant to get back to the Maze."

"We heard she's jealous of her power," Kalison agreed. "And you're lucky you remained out of the spotlight. That group only knew you were a Rat, nothing more."

"I don't have any record on which you can hold me," Sebastian added. "Unlike the rest of my family, I have been very careful to stay out of trouble."

Thank God for the rain, and the night, Alyn thought, as he blushed. Sebastian looked amused, knowing he made his older brother ever so slightly uncomfortable.

"You must know something about what happened here," Kalison finally replied. The man wanted answers, and Sebastian must look like a prize to anyone who didn't know how Miranda despised him.

"I suspect Miranda had her hand in the bombing. I don't know anything more."

Kalison made an annoyed sound but signaled the soldiers around them. They started away at a slow walk, Sebastian trying to keep his balance on the slick cement. Alyn hoped he was only shaken and not really hurt.

"Sebastian De Velera is an artist," Alyn offered. "He did that mosaic I showed you on the vidchit."

"Really? Then why did Miranda send you out here?" Kalison demanded, taking more of his weight.

"A whim. Miranda doesn't have much use for artists," he replied.

"Disappointment to your family, are you?" Kalison asked. The Commander's arm went around Sebastian's waist, helping to steady him better.

"My *father* liked my work," he answered softly.

They traveled in silence for nearly a quarter kilometer. Alyn wanted to say something. He even considered confessing his own real name and heritage. He held back though not from fear this time; Alyn Naevon had work left to do, and he might help Sebastian and other friends caught in Miranda's trap. Some of them, like Kalison and Bauer, weren't even Rats.

Maybe he even did this for Miranda, the sister who taught him to read. The sister who often played jokes and sang with friends in the square, and laughed --

"Alyn?" Bauer softly spoke his name.

"Keep him going, Captain," Kalison ordered. "This was a hard night for him too. We're going to walk the rest of the way to the Maze. Calling an aircar now would draw more attention to Sebastian. Alyn, if I order you out of the line of fire at the Maze, I do expect you to obey me."

"Are we still going to the Maze?" he asked. "What about Sebastian?"

"The Maze is the only place Sebastian will be safe," Kalison replied. The night shadowed his face, but Alyn heard resignation and determination in his words. "I don't see any reason to take him to the Tower. If the Citizens found out, they'd storm the place, and I don't need another flashpoint for trouble. Besides, Miranda would use holding him against me. We don't want to instigate riots on either side."

"You can stay at the hotel with me, Sebastian," Alyn offered. The words drew a curious look from Kalison. "You shouldn't go where your sister can find you."

"I'm grateful for the offer, but it wouldn't be safe for either of us," Sebastian replied. "I can stay with friends in the Maze. Caden Paris won't turn me over to Miranda."

"You going to have a problem with this Alyn? Bauer? Mattei?" Kalison asked. "If any of you make a fuss over this incident later, it'll cause me trouble. However, I guarantee you'll have more trouble than me."

The three professed that they'd say nothing. Alyn trusted Bauer, and Mattei sounded sincere. If there were trouble later, he'd live with it. Right now, getting Sebastian to safety was more important and at least the dark night and heavy rain would help.

"That group had no idea who you are, did they?" Alyn asked.

"None." Sebastian shook his head so emphatically that he nearly lost his footing again. "I'd be dead if they knew."

"You were lucky. Did you see Janith there with her cam?"

"Saw someone when they first came after me." He looked back at Alyn, wide-eyed with sudden fear.

"Janith wouldn't recognize any Rat by name," Bauer replied. "You're beneath her attention."

"Damn lucky she's so unprofessional," Kalison added, then shot his own warning look back at Alyn. "If you have that vidcam on and play that statement anywhere --"

"She'd shoot us both," Alyn replied. Both grinned at what was almost a joke. "Don't worry, I'm not suicidal."

Sebastian gave him a quick look of disbelief, as did Kalison and Bauer.

They said little else as they traversed the four kilometers back to the Maze. The cold, black night enveloped them in some anonymity and if anyone looked, they likely only saw more Port Guards heading toward the Maze. Alyn would have liked an aircar, but he consigned himself to walking without complaint, knowing they would have missed Sebastian if they had already been in the air. Alyn knew Sebastian's presence in the city was a result of their earlier encounter in the Maze. Miranda's little revenge almost got her brother killed.

The area around the entrance to the Rat's area was awash in rain-streaked light. Though the storm still raged, it wasn't dissuading either side to back down from this encounter. Tension ran high between the line of tan-uniformed port guards and gray-clothed militia. Hands rested on weapons on both sides. The Rats were well back and wary of watching this unusual confrontation.

Kalison's group stopped at the edge of a half dozen aircars abandoned haphazardly when the two forces came face-to-face. The commander listened to some quiet reports on his commlink and then turned back to Alyn.

"There is no trouble at any of the other entrances. Jeffries is focusing everything here. We'll never walk Sebastian through there," Kalison softly growled. "Janith may be stupid, but I suspect Jeffries will recognize our boy, or at least wonder why we brought him home, instead of in for questioning."

"Can you reach another way in, Sebastian?" Alyn asked. He could have given himself away with that question. Sebastian looked at him with worry and warning --

"Jeffries's Militia is covering the entire perimeter of the Maze," Bauer offered. He shook his head, glaring at the scene. "They know there's more than one secret entrance and our friend here isn't very steady on his feet. Sebastian's safer with us than turned out to find his own way in."

"And that's not very safe at all," Kalison admitted.

"We need a distraction." Alyn brought his cam to his shoulder, ignoring the pain in his hand. "Commander, can you make certain your people don't stop me? I can draw Jeffries's attention for a while, and his men will follow his lead."

Kalison looked at him, glanced at Sebastian, and finally nodded. Sebastian gave him a different look that hinted at worry, gratitude, and a slight whisper of amusement.

"Here. Put this on, Sebastian." Kalison slipped out of his tan jacket. It still smelled of smoke and disaster. "That's a bit of disguise. When I say go, walk behind the line of Port Guards, and head as quickly as you can into the Maze. Bauer get over to Shanley and tell her to let Sebastian through. I'll make an entrance with Mattei if I think it needs a little more distraction. Go on Naevon. Just remember, my people won't shoot you, but Jeffries isn't under my command."

Alyn gave his brother one quick nod, wishing ... but this wasn't any better time for personal feelings than when they stood before Miranda.

Sebastian smiled. That was enough.

Alyn went out into the heart of the trouble. He stood there in the rain and harassed Jeffries with stupid and trivial questions about his intentions. From the corner of his eye, he saw a figure slipping among the tan soldiers. Sebastian finally jogged through the gate to safety. Jeffries never noticed and if any of his people saw they probably thought it wise not to say anything and draw their commander's wrath.

Sebastian was safe, at least from the hands of irate Citizens. They could count this as one victory on a night of loss.

CHAPTER TWENTY-ONE

S ebastian slid around the edge of the narrow arch and
snaked toward the dark inner wall and nearest
crevasse. He prayed to all the Rat Gods in the universe that
whoever watched the gate for Miranda found Alonso's act as
riveting as Jeffries did.

Sebastian knew he wasn't safe in the Maze. Miranda all too
obviously wanted him dead. Unfortunately, he was equally
unsafe in the city because he was a Rat, let alone her brother.
He had been tempted to Alonso's offer of safety, but that had
been an illusion. The moment he went with his brother he
would have put them both in danger from Miranda. Some
Citizen might also wonder why the reporter offered to help him
and figure out Alonso's past. There could be no safety in the
city.

So far, no alarm had sounded. Sebastian stayed in the
narrow opening between arch and wall for several terrifying
moments, expecting someone to catch him. All he heard was
the continued pounding of rain and the lessening thunder. The
confrontation at the gate had quieted as well.

Sebastian carefully glided along the wet shadows, edging silently away from the arch. The continual splatter of falling rain covered the noises he made but the rushing water, more than ankle-deep in some places, made travel difficult. He wasn't as surefooted as when he had left with Niel.

Had Miranda's henchman made it back into the Maze? Maybe he found it difficult to return with the entire city looking for Rat prey. Maybe Miranda didn't yet know that her brother was still alive. He'd go to Caden if he could make it that far. There was no one else he could trust.

He sometimes heard voices as he traversed the narrow area between the outer wall and the first row of Rat buildings. Sebastian wished he could just knock on some door and find shelter. He continued toward the bachelor's quarters with one weary step after another. Unfortunately, there were damn few people, in the Maze or out, who might feel comfortable hiding Miranda's brother from her wrath.

Sebastian stumbled in the ankle-deep water and went down on his hands, hitting the hard surface with a bruising force. Needles of pain lanced through both his hands, but he was too drained to even get back to his feet again. Sebastian ached and shivered and feared he hadn't the strength left to go much farther. If he laid down here in the water, maybe he would drown before Miranda found him.

Let her win?

He could crawl a little farther. Caden's hut was only around the next corner --

The row of huts suddenly looked frighteningly alike in the rain. With his head pounding, he couldn't remember which one was Caden's home. Stunned at the sight, he sat in the rain-washed alley and let the flood water rush over his lap. Sebastian lowered his head and desperately reminded himself that he wanted to survive. He didn't want to let Miranda win.

And he didn't want Alonso to feel any guilt about letting his brother return to the Maze. He believed in Alonso and the power of Vidline to sway the opinion of people who were off-world. Those people could help the Rats of Tempest, but only if people like Alonso told them the truth of what happened here. Sebastian purposely avoided telling Alonso and Kalison that Miranda ordered his murder. They believed she sent him into the city on a whim, nothing more.

Too tired to move --

Someone sloshed through the water a meter away. Sebastian sat very still, his eyes straining as he tried to make out the shape. If he couldn't reach Caden, maybe there was someone else --

Distant lightning flashed, and he clearly saw the man. Sebastian thanked those Rat Gods that his luck was changing again.

"C-Caden!"

Caden Paris spun, his hand raised ready to fend off an attack. He apparently didn't see Sebastian, sitting at his feet.

"Caden," he whispered. "Me. Sebastian. I need -- help."

"Sebastian?" Caden knelt, looking worriedly from side to side.

"Alone. No one else -- not out here, at least. Caden, Miranda is -- unhappy with me. Sent me off with Niel. He tried to kill me --"

"Oh damn," Caden replied softly. "Well, we better get you in my place, hadn't we?"

Caden began pulling Sebastian up on his feet. Sebastian swayed and tried to get his breath before they started away again.

"We have to go, Sebastian. The storm is finally passing. People will come out to check on damage. And I hope none of them are counting on aid from the city this time, not after that explosion. We need to get you inside before someone spots you."

"You don't have to take me in."

"No, I don't."

With that understood, Sebastian let Caden drag him down the pathway. He quickly lost track of where they were going, trusting Caden to know his own place. The other end of the huts -- that was right. Was the rain ending? He felt far too wet and cold to tell. Less lightning though -- less chance of someone seeing them. It couldn't be far, and yet the walk took forever --

Caden opened a door and shoved him inside. He tumbled to his knees, gasping with surprise and new pain.

"What brings you out in the rain, Caden?" someone asked.

Sebastian caught his breath and held it, staying very, very still.

"Damn mess of a night," Caden replied. His voice stayed calm as he stepped away from the doorway. "The storm, the bombing, the Militia at the gate. I went to have a look."

"Miranda doesn't like people wandering around when there's a crisis," the voice replied, a little coolly. One of her people.

"I figure Miranda can handle things without me!" Caden laughed and leaned casually against the doorjamb. "Besides, if there were trouble, we'd go to the gate. I really hoped -- I really thought she'd call us out, this time."

"Yeah," the voice answered, mollified by the answer. "Miranda has her own agenda. Jeffries won't dictate what we do."

"Wiser than me," Caden said and sighed. Damn good actor. "It's too cold. I'm going to warm up a bit before we go out for damage control."

"Yeah. Talk to you later."

Caden stepped into his hut, neatly avoiding Sebastian's outstretched legs. He pushed the door closed.

"Bastard little spy," Caden snarled. "Lay there, Sebastian. I'm going to light a couple cubes, then close the window."

"OK."

Resting on the floor was very comfortable considering some other places he been tonight. He could smell fresh paint on the wall and knew his work was near. He closed his eyes, let the world drift away.

Tugging at his shoes, pulling at his pants --

"Lauren, I told you to leave me the hell alone!" he growled.

"Did you really tell her that?" Caden laughed. "Good for you!"

Sebastian awoke with a start. When he quickly sat up, the world spun around him. Sebastian didn't even know where he was until his eyes fell on the wall painting. He put both hands firmly on the floor and hoped everything would stop moving.

"Oh God, she's going to kill me," Sebastian whispered.

"Lauren or Miranda?" Caden mused.

"Either. Both. Hell, the two of them already turned Niel loose on me. He was probably as glad to attack me for Miranda as for his sister. I tied Lauren up in my bedroom. She wasn't happy."

Caden watched him for a long, long moment.

"Ember was right about you."

"Pardon?" Sebastian asked, leaning back on an elbow. "Ember?"

"Ember Tanton."

The world took another of those strange, twisting leaps. Sebastian fell back against a pillow, staring back at Caden Paris. Treason. No -- just someone who was not following Miranda's Agenda. Someone he could trust.

"I made the right choice, coming to you," he finally said.

"The De Velera instinct for survival finally kicks in. I was beginning to think I was the only one of the children who hadn't acquired it. I knew you didn't care much for Miranda. You showed that by hiring me to do your silly wall --"

"I like your art."

The statement was so unexpected that it almost brought tears to his eyes. He really hadn't thought anyone cared much about what he did. He had always thought he was only a pawn in some game his sister played.

"Sebastian?"

"Sorry. Damn long night."

"Looks like it got the worst of you. Did Niel do this?"

"Some. Then I got caught by a mob of Citizens." He shivered at the memory. "If Kalison and Alonso hadn't come along --"

"Commander Kalison saved you? And got you back to the Maze?" he asked. Then he looked shocked. "Alonso? Your brother, *Alonso De Velera*? Alive? Here, on Tempest?"

"Going by the name of Alyn Naevon --"

"Naevon? The reporter staying at the Tempest Pride? Thank God we didn't run into each other there."

"You were in the city?"

"Nearly every night, including tonight. I was halfway home when the explosion hit. Where's Niel?"

"Probably back to Miranda by now. Caden, Alonso was at the arch talking to Jeffries while I slipped in."

"Yes?"

"You told someone you went to look at Jeffries. They would know Alonso was there. If you didn't know --"

Caden's gray eyes went a little wide as he nodded. He took a deep breath.

"We did each other a good turn tonight. I would have used that excuse, even if you hadn't come along. And word would get back to Miranda, eventually."

"Why don't you move against her?" Sebastian asked.

"She still has too large a following. You know that." Caden settled on the gray chair in front of Sebastian. And for the first time since his father died, someone discussed politics with him. "Maybe you or I could kill her, but that's not the answer we want. Miranda dead isn't much better than alive. Her people would keep control, and neither of us would survive long enough to make a difference. I don't want to make her a martyr. Does Miranda know your brother is back?"

"Oh, yes. Miranda let him into the Maze, gave him an inflammatory interview, and sent him off again. She thought about killing him, but I talked some sense into her. I think. She tried to kill me for far less than what Alonso is doing. I don't understand her, Caden."

"None of us do. Miranda didn't learn her politics from your father. Let's get you out of these wet clothes. You just stay here and sleep for a while. I'm going out to work on damage control. Just keep quiet, OK?"

"Certainly," he agreed. He was grateful for the chance to rest and get his wits back before he faced any more trouble.

Still trembling, Sebastian drew off his shirt and let Caden help him with the pants. He hardly noticed as Caden wrapped bandages around his left side and covered him with a blanket. Sebastian began to slip back into sleep long before Caden finished. Not strangely, he felt safer here than he had ever been at the Hostel.

CHAPTER TWENTY-TWO

The cavernous public hall held far more people than it had during the Council Meeting Alyn had last attended here when he first arrived. Was that only yesterday? How could a world change so much overnight? He barely remembered that other meeting. Today most of the audience looked harassed, frightened, restless, and worried. They suddenly found themselves victims and didn't like the reversal of roles.

Alyn nervously adjusted the lens on his cam, focusing carefully on the dais. He fidgeted with the eye patch, then put it back away and barely kept from resetting the tripod again. Too anxious, Alyn realized. He felt just as uneasy as everyone else. After the excitement of last night, he wasn't ready for this dawn meeting. However, this was the first official word on the explosion, and he needed the footage. Otherwise, he would have gladly stayed in bed --

Well, maybe not. Kalison personally called and asked him to attend. He wasn't certain why the Port Commander wanted him here, but he didn't risk annoying the man. Alyn knew he already walked a precarious line after his trip into the Maze.

This morning the hall held mostly government workers called in for the emergency. The rest of the population would watch through the Vidline services, which were running both of their feeds. That was another reason he had to be here. If he left this reporting to Janith, there was no telling what riots she would incite before the day ended.

He happened to look towards the door as Janith arrived. Her eyes swept the room with a haughty and unpleasant scowl. She probably didn't like mornings any better than he did. When she spotted Alyn already here and ready, her face predictably darkened. She came across the room with her cam case swinging like a weapon ready to strike.

"Not this morning, Janith." The growl of his sharp words stopped her barely within striking range. "I'm not in any better mood than you. Cover the conference from one side of the room, and I'll stay on this side. We don't even have to look at each other."

She didn't take the hint to get clear of him. Instead, her hazel eyes narrowed, her pale lips parted in a snarl. Alyn half expected to see fangs. She wanted blood.

"I don't know what the hell your game is, Naevon, but I saw you last night! You helped that Rat!"

"You probably didn't notice he was about to get murdered, right there in front of your cam!" he snarled in reply. *My brother is just an artist, not a damn terrorist like --!* He barely held those thoughts back from his lips. "Would have made great airplay, right?"

They were drawing attention, and he didn't appreciate it, but she wasn't going to back away.

"I was doing my job."

"I was doing more."

"Janith, Alyn," a soft voice interrupted. "You weren't called here to entertain the crowd. We would like to get the conference called to order."

Governor Tanton stood beside them, her somber black suit a reminder of the solemn occasion. Alyn instantly bowed his head in apology, but Janith glared. She wasn't winning any friends, and possibly losing old ones. Alyn didn't want to be in the middle of this show, but he couldn't leave since Kalison invited him here.

"Take your equipment, and go set up somewhere else, Naevon," Janith ordered. "This is my place."

The Governor's weary face showed distaste mingling with a more profound weariness. Alyn grabbed his cam and reached for the bag, only to find the Governor of Tempest retrieving it for him.

"Come with me. I know just the place for you," the governor offered.

Stunned, he followed her without comment. He didn't dare look at Janith. Governor Tanton led him to the area reserved for top government officials and nodded to a place beside Kalison. This was an excellent location with a full view of the podium and clear shots of the crowd as well. He quickly repositioned the equipment.

"I don't approve of Janith's behavior, Alyn," Bramis Tanton suddenly said.

"Maybe she just has a hangover this morning," he offered.

"That's no excuse, *especially* today. I intend to file a complaint with Vidline News."

"Do me a favor? Wait until I leave Tempest?"

She offered him the very ghost of a smile and nodded. Alyn felt an odd little flutter, realizing again how he felt at ease with the Governor of Tempest. He turned his full attention back to refocusing the cam and steadying his nerves.

Kalison stood and patted his arm, drawing Alyn's attention

away from the work.

"Ready?" Kalison asked, as though Alyn's setting up was somehow crucial. "This isn't going to be pleasant."

"You made a decision about the interview." He now understood why Kalison called him here. He wasn't sure this was where he wanted to stand when Miranda spoke to the crowd.

"I discussed the matter with Governor Tanton. We'll show the clip here before release the footage to the Newsline and people outside Silver City and off-world see it. We hope to contain some of the initial reaction this way. However, you're going to keep company with Captain Bauer for a while."

"Pardon?"

"He won't stop you in your work. He will only make certain you remain unbothered by less understanding segments of the population. You knew this wasn't going to make you popular. I intend to make sure it doesn't also make you dead. We're going to try to deflect the focus of the interview away from you and straight at Miranda De Velera. Are you going to argue with me on any of this?"

"No. Why show the interview at all?"

"We're hoping to put pressure on Miranda. Make her unpopular within the Maze. Any hope of that?"

"Damned if I know."

Kalison nodded and slipped past, heading for the well-lit dais. Jeffries, sitting several chairs away, glared at Alyn. He reminded himself that he hadn't come to Tempest to make friends.

Considering the situation, Alyn wasn't entirely certain why he came home. *Career* sounded like a like an abstract conception in the face of all this madness. However, since he was here, he had a job to do. He slipped the eye patch into place again and focused the equipment on Kalison. The meeting would soon begin. If he concentrated on the work, he could forget the personal problems intertwined with this mess.

"May I have your attention?" Kalison asked. The room went instantly silent. "I'm going to ask you to hold all your comments until all three speakers finish their presentations. You will receive separate paperwork on the statistics I give you. We will also discuss the emergency procedure for the remainder of this crisis. The vid of this meeting will repeat several times on the Newsline feeds. Let's try to act like professionals, shall we?"

Though Commander Kalison didn't direct the words at him, Alyn felt himself redden at the memory of his recent encounter with Janith. This was only going to get worse once Miranda's vid aired.

"We also have three vids to show at the end of the meeting, and none are pleasant. I'll start with the worse news from the bombing. Twenty-seven people died at the blast site. Fourteen more died during the night. Ten are still listed in critical condition, despite extensive regen treatments. The transit line lost 43% of its function, and repairs will probably take months. Besides that, the rains last night caused extensive flooding in several areas of the city, and we have at least a hundred families living in shelters today. I checked the weather satellite, and another storm will hit later today."

That won sounds of dismay from everyone. Insult to injury, Alyn thought. On the other hand, maybe the weather would keep the amount of new violence at a minimum. If people feared for their possessions in a flood, they were less likely to go looking for trouble elsewhere.

Kalison continued with data about the damage. He gave a long list of buildings around the site that now needed substantial repairs. Strangely, the Commander's litany calmed much of the nervous crowd. He told the worst of the news at the beginning and then bored the group afterward, which proved an excellent ploy with this emotional crowd. Alyn dared a couple shots of the audience, including Port Guards, and several members of the Militia. Could they keep the population calm over the next few days? He suspected some weren't even inclined to try.

Kalison finally turned the podium over to Governor Tanton. An expectant hush returned to the crowd. They waited to hear from the woman who brought them through so many crises in the past. This time she stood there with her head bowed for a moment, looking worn and very sad. Alyn felt strange; something was wrong.

"I have an unrelated death to report this morning," she suddenly stated. She looked up, and her face steadied. The black of her clothing took on a more ominous, personal aspect. "Sometime after the explosion, my dear friend and cousin, Ember Tanton, was murdered outside her apartment building. Before any of you begin making assumptions, I have personal information that does not implicate any Rat in this killing."

The beginning of discord as quickly ended, this time in confusion. Alyn Naevon wondered what the hell was going on with this case.

"As you all know, Ember was a member of Tanton Steel's executive branch," Bramis stated. The words sounded empty. Not emotionless, just a loss too deep to speak. "Ember worked on several projects for me, covering at Tanton Steel during my years as Governor. I cannot begin to tell you how much this is going to affect the future of the Tantons on Tempest."

She stopped and sighed. Alyn kept the cam focused on the woman though he felt he should look away. Governor Bramis Tanton deserved a moment of peace to regain her composure. He doubted she had ever appeared in public without her emotions held in check.

"Tomorrow at sunset we will hold a Memorial Service for

Ember Tanton at the estate. It is open to the public. Thank you."

Not a single word about the bombing or the floods. Had the death hit her that hard? Or was she allowing others to handle those sensitive situations, avoiding further provocation by people who would take anything she said to heart? He believed in the political abilities of Bramis Tanton, and the woman wouldn't think about filing a protest about Janith and forget more pressing trouble.

Whispers spread quickly through the room, hinting at new distress. Kalison stood as the Governor neared, rested his hand on her arm, and nodded. Though never political allies, apparently they were friends.

Jeffries stalked past them heading for the podium. Unlike Kalison, he showed no sign of commiseration for Governor Tanton's personal loss. Alyn felt a combination of relief at how poorly the man handled the situation and distaste that they let the man talk at all. A few people watched the head of the Militia with anticipation, expecting a show. It was a shame that wasn't all he was -- just a bit of entertainment to keep the people's minds engaged. Jeffries had too much power.

Alyn considered keying off his vidcam, but then he remembered he was a Vidline reporter, and this was still news and not a private vendetta. He didn't have to make Jeffries look pretty, however. Alyn focused tight on the man's corpulent and flushed face; his light blue eyes glared out at the shifting crowd. He took a moment to glare directly at Alyn and then purposely gave Janith a showy smile.

One fleshy hand suddenly pounded the podium, startling even Commander Kalison, and Governor Tanton. Both scowled back at him, but the man never noticed.

"This has gone too far. It's time we act, instead of react!"

A scattering of applause swept through the room. Alyn

noted that most came from Militia-uniformed guards placed strategically throughout the crowd and Alyn intended to say so when he edited this report for airing. He didn't need to play any more games after this meeting, not after Miranda's interview aired.

They would show the vid when Jeffries finished his speech. That left Alyn half hoping the man whipped the crowd into a frenzy and they left without getting to the final presentations.

"The Rats are trying to take over our world. Rats murder us with impunity, while our so-called Guard protects them. They destroy our city while the Guard protects the Maze. It is time we take back control of our own destiny. It is time we demand that the Rats receive punishment for their crimes, or else we shall take justice into our own hands --"

"Enough," Kalison suddenly spoke.

Everyone in the room went silent and still. Alyn drew the focus back from the podium and put it on the widest shot he could manage. The image in his patch showed the two military heads, Governor Tanton, and half the crowd. Jeffries turned to the Commander of the Port Guard, and his fat chin lifted in a gesture of defiance.

"I did not interrupt your speech, Commander. I expect the same courtesy."

"I don't give courtesy to people who are trying to get others killed."

"You don't give courtesy to anyone who speaks out against the Rats, you mean."

Dangerous whispers ran through the room. Did this crowd symbolize the rest of the Citizen population or did their positions in government make them more reactionary? Would the rest of the community automatically feel inclined to follow Jeffries, one of their own, rather than Kalison? This was an unexpectedly dangerous confrontation.

"Jeffries, do you really want the IWC to send in regular troops?" Kalison asked. His voice sounded tight and hard with control.

"We could handle this problem ourselves if the Port Guard didn't stand in our way," Jeffries replied. "Or are you afraid that you'll lose your job, Kalison?"

"You damn fool," Kalison growled. "Do you really think I enjoy sitting here and watching this world tear itself apart? The people of Tempest deserve better than the destruction you crave. And yes, I mean Citizens and Rats. I believe in the equality of all people, Jeffries. What do you believe?"

"I stand for the rights of the hard worker over the rabble, Kalison."

"Sounds very proper," Kalison replied. He took two steps closer to the dais. Governor Tanton backed away, leaving the battle to the two military leaders. She didn't side with Jeffries. That wouldn't go unnoticed and hinted at a drastic change in policy. "I spend time at the Port watching Rats work at jobs considered demeaning for Citizens. Whatever other problems you have with Rats you can't claim that they don't work." Kalison reminded the man. The statement didn't make an impression on Jeffries. "Do you really want to help the people of the city, Captain Jeffries? The flooding last night has clogged several sewers and drains throughout the city. When the rains come again, they're going to add to the problem. Why don't you take some of the Militia out and do something constructive like help clean them?"

"That's not our job!"

"No, it isn't. It's a *Rat job*. However, they aren't coming into the city today. Except for the high-ranking city engineers, there aren't any sanitation workers. And you're the people who will suffer for it. I have as many Port Guards out as I can spare. We could use help, Jeffries. Or does saving the city from damage mean less to you than your vendetta against the Rats?"

Jeffries stood caught in a confrontation he didn't want, facing a question he apparently couldn't answer with any grace. His bulbous nose flared, his eyes glaring at Kalison.

"I don't have to put up with this bull shit," he growled. "You can stand here and talk, Kalison. My people and I don't have to play your games anymore."

Kalison had won this round. Jeffries abandoned the dais amid less than friendly looks from most of the crowd.

"Don't cause trouble, Jeffries," Kalison ordered. "If you try to force your way into the Maze, you'll face more than angry words this time."

The man stalked towards the closest exit. Alyn found himself staring at Kalison, wondering why the hell the man antagonized Jeffries into such a show. Maybe he hoped to win a few more Citizens over to the side of sanity --

Or perhaps he just wanted Jeffries and his people gone before they showed the vids. Alyn saw Commander Kalison give Governor Tanton a single nod. Jeffries's people followed their leader out, but so did Shanley and a few other Port Guards. They couldn't hope to keep Jeffries from learning what was on the vids but perhaps they averted the instantaneous, and dangerous, explosion of anger the man would show.

"My apologies," Kalison offered as he again took the podium. "We're all uneasy in this situation. Nonetheless, this doesn't give anyone the right to incite mindless violence. Let's use our heads rather than weapons! Let us go on to the next segment of the meeting. We still have three vids to show, and then I'll answer questions."

A full wall screen lighted to a pale blue behind the Commander. Alyn steadied his pounding heart and his trembling hands. He didn't want to see these vids again, for reasons that had nothing to do with how the rest of the people would react. Alyn could remember the chaos of the Central Terminal too well. And he didn't need a reminder of Miranda's madness, either.

"This first vid comes from inside the Terminal, taken by security cams. It shows the moment of detonation. We've edited together several views in succession. All the cams went offline within 15 seconds of the blast when the power failed. Please run the first vid."

He slipped aside. Alyn held his breath as the screen came to life. People walked past a cam while several pods moved in and out of view. Someone made a mumbling comment about the damn rain --

Lightning struck within the room, and thunder shook the air, deafening even in vid reproduction. On that screen, people screamed, and alarms wailed. Alyn hadn't seen the source of the explosion and found himself recoiling in shocked surprise.

And then they relived the disaster from another cam.

And another.

"The explosion apparently came from this pod." Kalison used a handheld comp to draw a circle on the now still screen where they saw the moment before the disaster, frozen forever. "Several people standing nearest to it were immediately engulfed in the initial discharge. None survived. The force of the blast sent a shock wave through the entire building. Walls toppled in its path for a full 70 meters. Closer to the source, a ball of fire expanded for ten meters. We have samples from the area and are analyzing them to learn all we can about the device used. Our initial results show the same compounds used in some local mining work. They were readily available and therefore harder to trace. Let's move on to the second vid. This was taken several minutes after the explosion when I arrived on the scene."

Alyn decided to take the chance to watch the crowd rather

than the screen. He could edit in cuts from his own copy, later. That saved him from watching the horror again. Concentrate on crowd reaction --

"I arrived on the scene within ten minutes of the initial blast --"

"That's Naevon!" Janith shouted, suddenly interrupting the Commander. Alyn knew he should have considered that reaction. "This is his vid, isn't it? I'll file a protest! They wouldn't let me inside the area, even this morning!"

"Yes, this is Alyn's vid," Kalison agreed. The vid froze on the view of Alyn and Kalison trying to free that first victim. Alyn looked away again. "He was with me at the time of the explosion. However, you will notice the cam is stationary while Alyn is helping me with the injured. I had to go back in and get the cam later. He forgot he even brought it with him. This was not an intentional slight to you, Janith. Most of us weren't considering anything so petty at the time."

Janith stared. The crowd whispered but still not with an open attack against the Commander. Kalison spent only a couple more minutes showing the few details they could see from his cam's limited view. On the vast screen, injured and med teams moved with frantic haste. Alyn and Kalison disappeared further into the smoky darkness. Kalison only showed the first five minutes of vid while he pointed out damage and injured.

When the screen went blue again Kalison looked toward Governor Tanton, and then Alyn. Both nodded, though Alyn felt his pulse race. Janith was unhappy with that last vid. More than Janith would protest the next one.

"Alyn Naevon brought me this last piece only minutes before the explosion. It is not pleasant in its own way. It is an interview with Miranda De Velera."

"How the hell --!" Janith hissed. This time she showed

equal shock with anger.

"I was invited into the Maze," he explained, more for the crowd than her. He remembered Miranda, standing there in the city and his final realization that he had to go *home*. Had she just planted bombs? If he had known ... but he couldn't have. "I had the feeling it wouldn't be wise to ignore it. I wasn't even certain I would come back out again."

"But you did, didn't you? And you got yourself a real story, right? Did it ever occur to you to do something to stop that woman?"

"Hold on," Kalison interrupted. He looked annoyed and tired, and on the verge of losing any patience he had left. "Janith, let's remember that Miranda De Velera isn't accused of any crime. We may all suspect her of any number of evils. However, she's no more personally responsible for what her people do than Jeffries is for how the Citizens react. They both incite the emotions of others, but so far neither personally steps over the line. And remember that this interview came *before* the explosion."

Janith didn't like that one and Jeffries would have fits when he heard he was put in the same league as the leader of the Rats.

"Shall we watch the vid and then get back to our own squabbles?" Kalison asked. He won a sullen nod from Janith. "Thank you."

Miranda's pale face suddenly filled the screen. It was a good shot, steady and effective. Alyn felt surprised, remembering how damn worried he felt at the time.

"I am Miranda De Velera." Her chin lifted. Her brief smile was all teeth and predatory. "I've decided to offer my wisdom to the rest of Tempest. You'd be wise to listen to me this time. You'll know soon enough that I am not someone to ignore."

People around him shifted uneasily, though the room remained very quiet. This was the first time they saw the face of the enemy and heard her talk. He suspected they never realized she was human, or powerful. Perhaps, without the explosion of the night before, they wouldn't have taken this as seriously.

"I will not settle for any compromise in my policies," Miranda told them. "Compromise won nothing in the past. This time you will give me what I ask, or you will pay for it with what you love most. Someone recently told me that I can't win against the Citizens. Maybe all I need do is bring you down to my level. And you'll learn I can do that"

She was safe in her Maze today. Did she really think the IWC soldiers wouldn't tear that place down, wall-by-wall if they wanted to get her? The regular troops only came in when all other approaches failed, and they didn't leave until they solved the problem.

"I am the leader of my people because you didn't give us what we need." She tilted her head. "I want equality. And if I can't be equal to you, I'll make you equal to me."

She waved her hand in that gesture of dismissal. A queen in her castle, regal and commanding. No one could watch this vid and doubt her power.

"That's all, Alyn Naevon. Take your vidcam and go back to the Citizens. If I want you back here, you'll know."

The screen dulled to black this time. Alyn heard worried words filling the shocked silence.

Janith crossed the room charging at him. He narrowly avoided her swinging hand. This woman wanted an enemy. Maybe he could arrange an interview between the two. Might settle both his problems.

"She admitted --!" Janith gasped.

"This was before the explosion," Alyn quickly explained. "Do you think I like that woman any more than you do?"

"Are you going to tell us you don't side with the Rats?" Janith angrily challenged him.

"I won't lie about it. I believe the Rats suffer under unreasonable restrictions and prejudices on this world. However, I also believe Miranda De Velera is doing them more harm than Jeffries ever could. I don't like her, Janith. And my siding with the Rats is only a counterpoint to your blatant favoritism of the Citizens. Why the hell do you think Vidline sent me here? They wanted the *entire* story."

Fewer people glared at him, which was a surprise since he hadn't expected to win anyone over.

"And again, let me remind everyone that Miranda De Velera is only suspected of involvement in the bombing," Kalison offered. He raised a hand to silence the instant protests. "That doesn't mean I won't do my best to bring her in for questioning. That's my job, at least until the IWC decides otherwise. You face a different challenge as government workers. The frightened and reactionary public will look to you for guidance. I hope that our precautions will eliminate any more bombings. However, since we can't stop the rain, we could face worse flooding tonight. Let's discuss how best to avoid any preventable disasters. I am open to any *reasonable* suggestions."

CHAPTER TWENTY-THREE

The damned long night had seemed to stretch endlessly behind her like a nightmare from which Fiona thought she'd never awaken. Floods and the bombing brought panic to her guests and sent refugees to her lobby. Fiona Salend didn't think she could face another hysterical off-worlder who couldn't book passage off-world since the port was closed. Perhaps Commander Kalison could arrange for some shuttles to take people off world before the next storms arrived. She suspected he might agree that the fewer panicked off-worlders in the city, the better. She'd suggest that to Bauer as soon as he showed up.

She leaned against the reservations counter and surveyed the crowded lobby with a total lack of emotion that only exhaustion can bring. Though she offered rooms to all the Citizens displaced by the night's disasters, many elected to stay down here where they could watch the world through the large windows.

The initially bright morning began to give way to scattered clouds. More rain was on the way, according to the weather report.

Could she book passage on the next ship?

"Hey, Fiona!" a friendly voice called out. "You look a bit frayed around the edges."

She looked up and offered a weary smile to Talin. Alyn was with him. They looked as tired as she felt and even more worried, which didn't settle her nerves. Captain Talin Bauer carried Alyn's vidcam case and often glanced uneasily over his shoulder at the crowd. Alyn kept his head down as though he feared to draw anyone's attention.

"What's wrong now?" Fiona asked. She couldn't put much emotion into the question, though.

"Turns out our boy here is suicidal," Talin answered with a quick glance at his companion. His voice lowered to a near whisper. "He went into the Maze last night and got an interview with Miranda De Velera. It hasn't made him any new friends."

"Are you crazy?" she demanded.

"It was before the explosion," Alyn replied as he leaned against the counter. He, apparently, had a long night as well.

"I'm keeping watch on him for a while. Make certain no one shows their displeasure. They're showing the vid with the rest of the report from this morning's meeting. Should be on again in a couple minutes."

"I'll pass," Fiona decided. She stood straighter and patted Alyn on the arm. "Come on. Let's all go get something to eat."

"I don't --"

"Talin looks hungry. And he can't eat if you don't, right?"

The ploy won a bright, brief smile from the reporter, who agreed with a polite bow. He walked beside her towards the dining room and Capt. Bauer followed behind. Fiona was glad he always took his work seriously. Even she felt safer.

The restaurant wasn't open to the public yet though employees could take an early meal. People waiting outside the door scowled when Naevon went by. No one here had likely even seen that interview yet. The reporter needed a guard.

Sounds of growing panic came from the kitchens as her chefs prepared to cook on a larger scale than they usually did. The food smelled good, though. Fiona refused to count the credits lost by housing and feeding these people.

"Damn long night," Fiona said. They settled around a table midway to the kitchen. She didn't bother with the sound screens since there was no one else here. "How did Commander Kalison's meeting go?"

"Well, Kalison had it out with Jeffries, right there in front of God and the Vidline reporters." Bauer grinned with delight at the memory. "And Janith had a couple goes at Alyn here, but she kept getting knocked back down."

"That going to be in the news report? Good. That will give me something to look forward to when I have enough energy to care again."

"No one will have the nerve to edit the broadcast since it was such an important meeting," Alyn replied. He leaned back in his chair, ignoring the lighted menu before him. Fiona suspected that he really wasn't ready to eat. "The only real surprise was Governor Tanton's announcement."

"I felt sorry for her," Bauer said. The humor disappeared from his face. "I knew something was wrong when she arrived -- she had a look I'd never seen before -- but Kalison kept a tight lid on the news. I wonder why they think Rats didn't commit the murder."

"Murder?" Fiona asked. She automatically keyed in the orders for all three of them since neither of the men looked in any hurry. Something with lots of sugar, extra energy.

"Her cousin died last night," Bauer explained. "She took it very hard --"

"Cousin?" Fiona whispered. Her hand caught at the table,

drawing their attention. "Not Ember."

"Yes, Ember Tanton." Bauer quietly confirmed. He laid a hand on her fingers, offering reassurance even if he didn't understand why the news upset her. "Killed outside her apartment building sometime after the bombing."

"Did -- did they mention any others?" she asked. Panic reached toward her heart. She trembled and paled. "Wintas? Caden?"

"Caden?" Alyn repeated the name with sudden interest. "Caden Paris, the Rat?"

"Yes. Oh damn, Talin. I need to talk to Kalison right away. I need to know. First Sonio, and now Ember -- and Ember said she didn't think it was Rats --"

"You really knew her." Talin looked intrigued and very surprised.

"We met here in the basement, the five of us," she whispered.

She was afraid to say more. Many people out in the lobby might not appreciate anyone associating with Rats right now. Did one of them kill her friends? Talin's fingers tightened on her hand when she began to panic again. She couldn't hide the secret from him now.

"You met?" Alyn asked softly. For an off-worlder, he seemed to understand the problems here and the need to be careful.

"We just talked, attempting to keep some line open between the Maze and the Citizens. Recently, Sonio told Ember that he suspected Wintas of something. And then he died. And Ember suspected, and now she's dead --" She stopped and took a deep breath, holding both hands together. Alyn looked at her with more than a little interest. Reporter. They had joked about him, yesterday. "Talin -- we were never that important. There's no reason for anyone to kill us!"

They sat in silence, Bauer, and Alyn staring at her as though she suddenly turned into some alien creature. She canceled the food. The scent from the kitchen suddenly made her ill as the hunger of a few moments before changed to a lead ball sitting in her stomach. She looked helplessly from Alyn back to Bauer and wondered if there was any hope of recovering his trust.

"I never asked you anything, Talin," she reminded him. He looked startled by the words, then nodded, as though the thought never occurred to him. "Whatever I offered was from my own experience. I want to go to Kalison -- but I'm afraid to go out alone."

"I can't leave Alyn," he replied. Bauer lifted a hand when Alyn began to protest. "No. It's my assignment, and I can't abandon it, even for the woman I love."

She blushed but felt hope and relief at the words. Fiona took his hand tightly in her own and Alyn made a show of not noticing, allowing them this little moment of privacy.

"I'll call in, get you an escort," Talin offered.

"No," Alyn replied. Talin frowned. "If Governor Tanton is right, and it wasn't a Rat job, who do you trust? Let's all go see Commander Kalison."

"I didn't mean to drag you back out," Fiona protested.

"Hell, it's a story." He stood and shrugged. "If it turns out that these deaths are more than coincidental, I have another scoop on Janith."

"You really are suicidal if you want to annoy her any more today," Bauer repeated.

That briefly brought some of her humor back until she remembered that two of her friends were dead. *Murdered.* Even if she wasn't on the same death list, the loss was enough to unsettle her again. She would miss Ember Tanton.

With the transportation system suffering from last night's

explosion, they had to wait several minutes before a pod answered their call. Naevon nervously watched the crowd of refugees. So did she. Fiona had never felt like just another outsider until now.

The journey into town took uncommonly long. The pod made several unexpected pauses, each time bringing Fiona's heart into her throat. Overuse and damage, Talin quietly explained. The diminished system resources couldn't sustain even the limited runs made today. Still, traveling by pod was preferable to walking where anyone could see her. She sat between two friends and suspected even Alyn Naevon would come to her aid if she needed him.

Not friendless on this damn world.

Commander Kalison had set up a temporary office in the Government Building where he could be closer to the rest of the officials during this crisis. She would have preferred going to the nearby port to see him, but with everything there closed, it made more sense for him to be in the city.

A steady stream of traffic moved through the guarded door and a dozen more people leaned against the long walls of the outer hall. Captain Bauer's uniform got them to the front of the line, and a few whispered words got them inside very quickly, though doing so won more glares from those they bypassed, primarily directed at Naevon. She was glad when the door sealed shut behind them.

Kalison sat behind a cluttered desk. He gave them a quick nod of greeting.

"I thought you might come to see me soon, Fiona," he stated with a wave toward the chairs scattered around his desk.

"You knew? About Ember and me and the others?"

"Bramis told me this morning."

"The Governor knows? How did she find out?" Fiona asked. Relief that she needn't make a confession left her giddy.

She dropped into a chair while Alyn and Talin stood behind her.

"Governor Tanton always knew," he answered. He sat back, pushing aside a pile of papers as though talking to her was more important. "Ember was Bramis Tanton's closest confidant. She helped form your group because they wanted a connection with Caden Paris. You getting all of this, Alyn?"

"Yes, thank you." Alyn grinned though he didn't have the vidcam on. Fiona realized how much she trusted this reporter not to repeat anything which could make enemies or put her in danger. "Why did they want Caden?"

"I don't know. We didn't have time to go into details about that part of the matter. Our immediate concern is with the murder, not your group or what you were doing, except that I know it was benign work. We suspect there is a connection, but we could be wrong. The Tanton's are a powerful family and have enemies of their own, though. I sent someone to watch the hotel when I learned of your association with Sonio and Ember. I just couldn't spare Bauer for the job."

She blushed again. They had made no secret about their relationship but realizing even the Port Commander knew unsettled her.

"We're working on the case. I intended to call you in for questioning later this afternoon but now is not a good time. The Governor and I agree that getting the problems of riots and flooding settled must take precedence over the investigation of even Ember's murder. I'm glad you came to me. You can trust us."

"We never did anything that would hurt this world."

"I know. Bramis told me as much."

"What about Wintas and Caden? Any word?"

"Wintas came through the night unscathed. We're watching him." Something in the Commander's eyes flickered, and she wondered if he, too, mistrusted the clerk. "We have no direct word on Caden Paris."

"I could --" Alyn began.

"Don't even consider going back into the Maze to find out," Kalison ordered. "Bauer would feel obligated to go in with you, and I'd hate to lose him."

"Good point," Alyn conceded.

"Why don't the three of you go back to the hotel and spend some quiet time together?" Kalison suggested. He glanced at his comp, frowning over other work. "Captain, if Alyn must go out on business, call in and ask a guard to cover Fiona. Is that acceptable? I'll choose the person myself."

"Yes," the three chorused.

"Good. We'll talk again soon. Fiona, Governor Tanton stated at the meeting that this wasn't the work of Rats. I trust you know enough to be careful around anyone else."

"I'm so damn scared, even Talin makes me nervous."

The Commander grinned as he keyed the door open again and let them leave. Fiona felt steadier, even under the unfriendly stares of those forced to wait through their short meeting.

The trip back to the hotel was as long but less anxious. With Talin and Alyn running interference, not even her desk clerk dared get too close. The hired help could handle the work for a few hours. She needed rest.

"I have a penthouse suite with a guest room, Alyn. Why don't you come up there with Talin and me? We can all do with some rest. Otherwise, I don't know how Captain Bauer will keep watch on both of us."

"True," Alyn said, looking as though he was trying to hide a smile. They reached the lift and hurried in the first empty one, sealing the door before anyone else could join them. "Can we stop by my rooms first? I need some editing equipment."

"Aren't you tired?" Talin asked.

"Exhausted," he admitted. Fiona keyed the number to his floor, and Alyn leaned against the wall as the lift began to move. "I just need to wind down before I can sleep, and work usually helps. Do you mind?"

"Of course not," Fiona replied. She gladly leaned back into Captain Bauer's arms.

"You can wait here," Alyn offered as the door slid open again. "I'll only take a minute."

"The walk won't kill us," Bauer replied. He put his arm around Fiona's waist and led her out into the hall. "I do take my work seriously."

Alyn only sighed and shrugged. Fiona wondered how long he would put up with Captain Bauer's presence because it would, eventually, interfere with his work. Alyn Naevon had the look of someone who would take his job more seriously than protecting his own life.

Hell, he'd gone into the Maze. He must not think much of his life at all.

Fiona frowned as she looked down at the floor.

"Look at that! Mud all the way down the hall!" she growled. The randomly scattered spots of dirt almost blended into the brown carpet but it still annoyed her. "Damn sightseers out looking at the floods! The robos cleaned this floor once this morning already. I'll have to call them out again."

"Ah, now there's my Fiona!" Talin laughed. "Back to business again!"

"I should follow the trail and find out who --"

She saw that the trail led to Alyn Naevon's door.

So did Talin.

"Alyn!"

Bauer shoved Fiona aside and tackled the reporter whose hand had barely touched the palmlock--

And the door exploded.

The deafening sound made the floor tremble. Fiona only had time to make one little sound of fear before the worst was over. Talin and Alyn sprawled on the other side of the opening. Pieces of the door lay scattered in an arc across the floor with two large pieces embedded in the wall.

"I'll pass on the equipment for now," Alyn stated, his voice dead calm. He sat up and peered carefully around the corner of the shattered door. "I don't think I'm going to sleep, though. And never again assume a little walk isn't going to kill me."

Talin made a slight sound of amusement. "Both of you are all right? Fiona?"

"All right," Fiona said. She didn't try to stand.

"Good." Talin drew a commlink out and thumbed it on, putting the earpiece in place with shaky hands. "Connect me with Commander Kalison. Yes, an emergency. Commander? Someone trapped Naevon's door and just about got us all killed. We're fine. I want a team here immediately to check the debris and examine the rest of the room. I'm taking Alyn and Fiona somewhere -- safe."

She stared at the debris. It would take more than the robos to clean this mess up.

People began emerging from their rooms, looking with frightened dismay at the catastrophe. Fiona wearily picked herself up off the floor and went to help settle nerves. Talin and Alyn scrambled back to their feet to stay with her. Somehow, she suspected none of them felt safer for it.

She also intended to have her door checked before they took refuge there.

Captain Bauer kept dangerous company these days.

CHAPTER TWENTY-FOUR

Sebastian sat by the wall and squinted at the painting.
The shielded blue cube to his right provided barely enough
illumination to see the outlines of his previous work, but that
proved enough. When he closed his eyes, Sebastian could
clearly recall the picture: greens of the land and pale blues of an
alien sky. He carefully wetted the ghosts of paints from two
abandoned palettes and used the colors judiciously, his fingers
moving lightly across the sky again.

How long could he live like this? Caden couldn't keep him
hidden much longer without risking both their lives. The older
man said he had friends who would help, but Sebastian, who
knew his sister far too well, remained skeptical of their ability to
outwit her for much longer. He had survived the day, but that
was only because Miranda had more important matters at hand.

Maybe Alonso could help him. Now, with the bleak night
behind him and a full day to think through his actions,
Sebastian thought he was probably a fool to have run home to
the Maze. As a reporter, his brother had outside help that was
neither Rat nor Citizen. Sebastian, in the insanity of what had

happened, had never considered that there might be help elsewhere. Alonso had escaped, and perhaps Sebastian might even escape off-world, as his brother had. He wondered what it was like to go places where people didn't give a damn that your name was *De Velera*. Those places plainly hadn't hurt Alonso any.

Another storm ravaged the night beyond the little hut. Each flash of lightning and roll of thunder felt like an explosion in the city or some high-tech weapon aimed at the Rats. His hand trembled, and he drew away from the painting in haste, fearing what he would do to the work. Closing his eyes, Sebastian listened until the sounds became only the force of nature once more.

Someone walked quickly along the alley outside. Sebastian killed the light with a tap of his hand. He sat in the darkness, barely daring breathe.

A hand touched the door latch, and Sebastian finally retrieved the knife Caden provided for him. The hilt felt cold in his hand. He didn't like weapons.

"Careful, Sebastian," a voice whispered as the door eased open.

Caden.

"You scared the hell out of me," he said, laughing softly to make it a joke. Sebastian laid the knife aside and brushed his damp hand against his pant leg as Caden slipped in and quickly snapped the door shut again. Sebastian illuminated the cube, and unshielded its light, glad to have company again. He stayed in the corner, away from anywhere that a second shadow might draw attention.

"Sorry I scared you," Caden apologized.

"Well, the storm scared the hell out of me already," he confessed. "I keep thinking something else is going on out there."

Caden gave him a halfhearted nod of agreement.

"What's wrong?" His heart began beating harder.

"Trouble," he said softly. The man settled onto the chair by the door. "Ember Tanton is dead."

"Damn," Sebastian whispered. The death of that woman might well mean the destruction of the Maze. "Did they catch who killed her? Was it done on Miranda's orders?"

Caden looked back at him, startled.

"It isn't that serious." Caden ran his hand through his hair, dislodging a small trickle of water down the side of his face. "This is more personal trouble. Ember and I knew each other, and we worked together. Governor Tanton says this was not a Rat assassination. Another of our friends is already dead."

"Damn, Caden --" He wanted to ask what the man was into, but he was Miranda's brother and didn't think it wise for him to know.

"How are you feeling?" Caden suddenly asked.

"Sore," he admitted. The change of conversation felt awkward but welcome. "Worried. Miranda tried to have me killed. I'm not safe, and neither are you for keeping me. Did Niel make it back from our foray into the city?"

"Afraid so," Caden said. He went to the cupboard and pulled two cups and a tin of powdered tea. "And he isn't talking about you. Neither is Lauren. However, today Miranda announced open worry that you are missing."

"Yeah, I bet she is worried, given the circumstances."

"Don't move while I get some water for the tea."

He obeyed feeling a chill that came from more than the cold when Caden opened the door and held the cups out into the rain. The man blocked most of the opening and inconspicuously balanced one cup below the other. Someone shouted from across the alley. Caden gave a standard, and rude, answer about the weather before he closed the door again.

"Miranda must wonder if you ever made it out of the City. Maybe the Port Guard got hold of you or even the Militia. She probably doesn't give you enough credit for staying free on your own."

Sebastian felt a whisper of annoyance at the statement, though it was accurate enough. No one thought he was competent enough to find his way home, let alone take care of himself when in danger.

Both heard footsteps outside in the water-slick alley. More than one person. Sebastian's fingers hovered over the light.

"No," Caden whispered. "Too obvious. Slide away. Get out of the light."

No time to get to one of the back rooms. The footsteps stopped outside the door. Sebastian quietly slid toward the darker corner --

And the door flew open to darkness and the shadows of people.

He knew Miranda before she spoke.

"Caden." She said the name with open contempt. "I just learned you have friends you never told me about. Friends in the city."

Sebastian held his breath, uncertain what to do next. She really hadn't come here for him? Could this have to do with Ember Tanton?

"Maybe I do," Caden answered her coolly. One of the other three shadows was Niel, and the third was Briss. Lightning briefly illuminated them all -- and the laser in Niel's hand. "Someone in the Maze had to show a little discretion."

"Wrong answer. Niel?"

If Sebastian stayed here in the dark, he might go unnoticed. He didn't want Miranda to find him--

He didn't want to see Caden killed, either.

As Niel stepped forward, Sebastian reached for the cube to

throw it. He grabbed the cube went dark at his touch, but at the same time a flash, duller than the lightning, lit the room. Caden tumbled backward, sprawled on the floor beside Sebastian.

"What the hell?" Miranda took a step closer, her eyes narrowed against the dark. Then she laughed. "Wonderful! Sebastian, you don't know how much I worried about you!"

"So I heard." He slowly stood, drawing all her attention to him.

"Is he dead Niel?" she asked with a bright smile.

This was a good night for her. Sebastian let her play the game, providing a distraction of another sort.

"He's dead, Miranda," Sebastian replied after he made a show of nudging Caden's leg. He dared a step closer to her, hoping that in the dull light she couldn't see the little flicker of movement in Caden's fingers. "Why? Are you that afraid of competition? Finally, realize the Rats would drop you in a moment if someone *sane* came along?"

Niel growled, took two steps forward, and slugged him with the laser pistol. Sebastian fell back against the chair and pushed away to launch himself back at his attacker.

His momentum carried them out into the alley. He didn't stop struggling until Miranda's two companions held him, face down, in the mud. They only pulled him up when he went very still.

"Get him. Let's go! I don't want any witnesses, you fool!"

Sebastian gave up struggling as they pulled him back to his feet. Miranda slapped him once across the face, ostensibly to get his attention. It was unnecessary.

"You're more trouble than I ever expected," she said with a hiss of annoyance. "You are the most uncooperative little martyr, I've ever known. Let's go!"

Sebastian never dared a glance back at Caden's home. Niel didn't check on the body. Even under these circumstances,

Miranda didn't expect him to lie.

Sebastian hoped Caden's friends found him quickly. One of them might survive this night.

CHAPTER TWENTY-FIVE

Kalison tapped notes into his handheld comp all the way to Governor Bramis Tanton's penthouse office. He noted new rain predictions, flood potentials, supply estimates, and new trouble spots. For once, no one bothered him on the long walk. The building was nearly empty except for those few people with too much work to dare go anywhere else. Like him. Like the Governor.

Perhaps she wanted to work right now. Kalison had never seen the Governor as shaken as she was at the loss of her cousin. Governor Tanton had aged decades overnight.

He finally reached her reception area and pushed the comp back into his pocket. One lone clerk remained on call, and a single guard lingered at the edge of the hall. The clerk nervously nodded a greeting and led him straight to the Governor's private office.

Bramis sat behind her desk, greeting him with only a solemn nod. Her black jacket contrasted with the bright, empty white of the room. Kalison remembered the office back at her estate and the last meeting there. He wished for that day again when they had unexpectedly found common ground and laughed together. Governor Tanton didn't look likely to laugh much again.

This damn world took too much from everyone.

"Don't stand there, Kalison." She waved a hand toward the two chairs by the desk. "Nedra is on her way. You look tired."

"So do you."

She shrugged, shuffled a few sheets of paper, and looked up again.

"How is it on the streets tonight?"

Maybe that was a question Bramis thought was expected of her. She didn't sound very interested.

"Quiet enough. The storm is again holding down the incidental trouble. However, those determined to provoke another bloodletting won't let the weather deter them much longer."

"You mean the Militia is out in force and looking for trouble . . . or creating it when they can't find enough to keep them busy."

"I was trying to be more politic about it."

That won him a brief smile and a moment's reprieve from the dark world. The look passed when the door opened again.

Kalison didn't know Nedra very well since their work seldom overlapped. Citizen children didn't often get into the type of trouble that required Port Guard intervention; it was their parents he had to watch. Alyn Naevon's interview with the head of the Education Department had portrayed Nedra as unexpectedly open-minded. He knew about her letter of resignation and regretted not knowing her better.

"Thank you for coming, Nedra," Bramis greeted the woman. She also wore black and looked as worn by the day as the two of them. Bramis waved her in. "I know it's late --"

"I don't mind," she replied. Nedra settled into the empty

chair and gave Kalison a worried look. "How can I help you?"

"By giving us information about one of your employees," Kalison answered. No use dragging this out: they all wanted to be somewhere else. Or maybe Bramis didn't, but she should go home anyway. "He's a clerk in your division. Wintas."

"Wintas?" she repeated the name with a sound of surprise and brushed at her short hair with a nervous little twitch of her fingers. "Wintas doesn't work in my department. I fired him well over a year ago."

That took a moment to digest.

"The files we checked still show him on your payroll, Nedie," Bramis spoke at last. She leaned forward, intrigued again. A little life came back to her eyes.

"I let Wintas go because we became far too antagonistic over personal politics. It became impossible to work with him. He's not getting money from my department."

"He has a high-priced apartment," Kalison spoke again. Bramis nodded, pulling a paper from the stack before her. "And he has expensive tastes in companions. Someone is keeping him on the payroll."

There was a touch of fire growing in Governor Tanton's eyes. Perhaps she only needed an enemy to focus on.

"Wintas and I disagreed over my pro-Rat policies," Nedra explained. She looked from Bramis to Kalison. "This man is not in league with the Rats."

"We didn't suspect him of it," Kalison admitted. He watched her eyes narrow, and then go wide again. She looked back at Bramis and paled a little. This one wasn't stupid. If Wintas didn't work with the Rats, there was only one other crime that would draw both the Commander and the Governor's attention right now.

"Thank you for your help, Nedra," Bramis offered. She even smiled though it looked strained. "Again, I apologize for calling you so late --"

"I'll do anything I can to help. You know that." Nedra reached across and took hold of the Governor's hand. "Take care of yourself Bramis. We can't afford to lose you. This world has far too little stability right now. Don't let Miranda De Velera -- *or anyone else* -- win."

"Thank you," Bramis said. She sounded sincere. "Go home. And be discreet about our meeting."

"I understand. I'll say I came because my department opened three schools to take in refugees from the storm. You and Commander Kalison wanted to know if they were safe from other trouble. I'll upload their plans into your comps before I go home."

"Damn," Kalison whispered, impressed by the suggestion. "Probably something I should look into anyway. You're right."

Nedra gave him a brighter smile as she stood. She bowed her head to both and hurried back out. Kalison leaned back in his chair, feeling some tension ease. They were finally gaining answers.

"Don't let that woman resign," Kalison advised. "We all need people who can think that clearly under pressure."

"Very true. I'll see if I can persuade her to stay a while longer. It may take a bribe. A school out in the Maze might do the trick."

"Will the Council let you get away with that?"

"It won't be their choice if I do it with Tanton Steel funds. I've wanted to build and staff one before and always let public sentiment hold me back. Many women in my family were Evites, you know. First Teachers. I'm sorry we lost that link to our past." Bramis appeared more animated now. She looked around, pausing at the sight of the window. "The storm tonight isn't as bad as last night, but the flooding is still serious."

"And we can only count on storms for one more night

before they slack off. Tomorrow is my next big worry. I already have my people out. What do you suggest we do about Wintas?"

"I want to know who's paying him," she replied, her voice cold with anger that she had managed not to show until now. She stared at the window where lightning brightened the night again. "And I want to be certain of our suspicions. We have the real enemy almost in sight. We must move carefully, Commander."

The woman was a marvel. He was too used to dealing with excitable fanatics.

"I'll put Wintas under surveillance, and I suggest we both start sifting through the files and see what we can learn."

"Carefully," Bramis said as she looked back at him. "Someone has already doctored the comp files to make certain even Ember thought Wintas still worked with Nedra. Someone with powerful private codes did that work, and not everyone can manipulate government employment records."

"Good point. This isn't my usual line of work."

"Just move carefully, Commander. I want this bastard, but I also want both of us to survive to see it."

CHAPTER TWENTY-SIX

Flames filled the sky to the north with a sudden red glare and then died back down as quickly. Lights flickered even this far away. Alyn tried to gauge the distance to the new disaster. There had been several others tonight, and he suspected this wasn't another act of terrorism, either. The flooding had started shorting power stations and created problems of their own.

Or maybe that was just wishful thinking on his part. He didn't want his people to do more wrong.

"What now?" Bauer asked stopping to look out the window with him.

"Trouble," he answered. "At least the fire isn't far enough to be in the suburbs, so that's probably warehouses along the route to the mines."

"Yeah, could be." Sirens wailed so close that they could hear them even in the penthouse as aircars darted past the hotel, heading towards the new trouble.

Alyn couldn't see the Maze from here, and he didn't ask how matters were going there, even though he knew Bauer had constant reports. He would need to know facts for his reports, but for now, he only stared and tried to make sense of a world where people fought each other for rights and nature knocked them both down with impunity.

"Damn bad night out there," Bauer said. He leaned back against the wall. "When do you want to go out?"

Alyn turned to the Captain with considerable trepidation. He did want to go out. He was a reporter, and there was a story to cover. However, he didn't want to drag this man into danger with him. After all, Bauer and Fiona nearly faced death once tonight just because they kept company with him.

"We can't go, Bauer," he finally announced. Alyn started to step away from the window. Captain Bauer frowned and blocked the way.

"Kalison told me to let you do your job, and I get the feeling you think you can't go out because of me."

"I will not risk your life. And what about Fiona?"

"She's staying here in her rooms," Bauer answered and completely ignored the first half of the statement. "I called a guard to stand watch outside the door."

"We can't --"

Bauer again ignored him. He walked back to the sofa, gathered up Alyn's cam case and moved to the door. He stood there, waiting.

Anxious. Captain Bauer didn't like being in here anymore than Alyn, and that was because both had jobs that normally took them out among the public in times of danger. Both knew they were ignoring their work, the guard and guarded.

"I'll carry the vidcam," Alyn relented. "You make certain you're free to protect us. Remember, I haven't made any friends today."

"Oh, I remember!" Bauer nodded emphatically, and his hand rubbed against his shoulder which had been bruised by the exploding door.

Alyn felt his own aches and pains, but he took the case and removed the old vidcam. The better equipment still sat down in his room, but the Port Guard hadn't finished their examination, and he wasn't in any hurry to get it back. He wanted to make certain no one had messed with it. Knowing they could face danger anywhere, including in the hotel, he keyed the vidcam on and nodded to Bauer to open the door, ready for whatever they might encounter on the other side. Anything beyond this door might be a story.

"Be careful," Fiona advised. She stood at the doorway to her bedroom, dressed in a long robe and looking worn and disheveled. "Both of you, be careful. These people are crazy. They don't even have to be your enemies to come after you."

"We'll remember," Bauer promised. "Get some sleep, Fiona. We'll come back soon."

"I don't intend to go very far," Alyn offered. He hoped to reassure her by pointing out that he wasn't entirely insane. "I just want a couple shots outside the building, and maybe an interview with someone on the street. Then we'll come back."

"Thank you." She smiled and gave them a wave to go on their way. Fiona looked so tired that it made Alyn wish he'd lingered in that lovely, soft bed in the guest room.

A guard already stood outside the door to Fiona's apartment and saluted Bauer in a half-hearted, joking way.

"Thanks for coming, Delin," Bauer greeted him. They shook hands. "Fiona feels safer with someone I know and trust standing guard out here."

"Don't mind doing the work," Delin said and grinned. The dark-skinned, tall man looked competent and formidable. "Better than out on the streets tonight."

"Look, if you know Delin, why can't he go with me?" Alyn asked. "You can stay with Fiona --"

"Guarding you is not *his* assignment," Bauer replied.

Delin smiled with a look that bordered suspiciously on relief. He could hardly blame the man for showing some sanity.

By the time they reached the lobby, Alyn only felt anxious to get on with his work. Too many people had gathered at the windows to watch the storm and worse. He heard the whisper of dismay everywhere he passed along with some disparaging words about his work. Alyn ignored them, though he saw Bauer give a quick glare at the crowd.

"Don't take everything so personally, Bauer. You know it doesn't mean anything. They need someone to blame. You've seen how this works; the Port Guard isn't any more popular than I am."

"I don't like impolite people," he replied evenly.

"Must make life hard. We both know there are impolite people everywhere, and most of them aren't bad humans."

Bauer shrugged, glared at the people again, and took his place at Alyn's back. Having a Port Guard to protect him was supposed to make Alyn feel safe, but instead, it only made him feel conspicuous.

The first spattering of anger had passed by the time he reached the far side of the lobby. No one possessed the energy left to sustain the useless tirade against him. Most even knew that while Alyn Naevon might look like a convenient target, he was *not* the real enemy.

Alyn looked back and took a lingering shot of the crowd. He saw only restless people, eyes dulled by days of pressure. Stunned, frightened ... and everywhere the whisper of the same question: Why here?

Here, because when mankind left Earth for better places, they still brought all her problems with them.

Alyn panned to the window where reflections of distant fires gave a hellish glow to the world outside. He couldn't see the Maze from here and again wondered if trouble had broken out there as well. Alyn really wanted to know if Sebastian was all right, but he had no way to tell without going to find his brother, and he wasn't going to drag Bauer into the Maze for something that crazy.

"Damn mess," Bauer said with a soft sigh. He looked out the window, shaking his head in dismay.

"The vidcam is on," Alyn warned.

Bauer made a little sound of amusement. "I don't mind saying the truth, Alyn. And really, nothing either of us does will make much difference now."

That unexpectedly stung although he realized that Bauer was right. The war would rage out of control, and neither a member of the Port Guard nor a single reporter could arrest the progress of destruction. He almost keyed off the cam and went back to Fiona's suite. Maybe they could all get drunk together tonight and forget the war beyond the opaqued windows.

Then he remembered that Vidline hadn't sent him here to prevent the war, only to report on the troubles. He was not personally responsible for this war no matter what his relationship was with either side.

"I want to go out and get a clearer shot of those fires." He waved his hand vaguely toward the north. "Maybe we'll find someone on the street willing to talk. I don't intend to go looking far for anyone, and we won't go more than a block from the door."

"Wise," Bauer agreed. "Looking out there, I suddenly realized that I don't want to die on this world."

"Good. Sanity at last. I feared staying with me was adversely affecting your survival instincts." He patted the man on the shoulder, brought the vidcam up again, and started toward the side door away from the massive front window and the unused pod landing. More people stood between him and the doorway, but they moved out of his path. He caught glimpses of their hard eyes in the vidcam, the moment preserved forever.

When he and Bauer reached the far side of the lobby, he palmed open the door and stepped through the opening, grateful for the chilly and damp night. Dark out here --

"I suggest you get your hands off me," Bauer growled.

Alyn turned, surprised by the vehemence in his friend's voice. Bauer was still inside the hotel.

Someone came between Alyn and the view of the city.

"What the hell is Kalison pulling?" a harsh voice demanded. "He lets our city burn, but gives a guard to that perverted, Rat-loving reporter!"

Alyn started back into the building.

"Don't move," a man's voice whispered. Something hard pressed into his back. "If you move, I'll open fire and take you and anyone else in range. Understand?"

"Yes."

"You're coming with us."

Alyn nodded, wondering how many he faced. The night was too dark and the noises of the city too loud for him to get a clear indication. Two pairs of hands grabbed him. He didn't pull away as the enemy maneuvered him a step from the door. At the last moment, Alyn swung the vidcam inside. The door snapped shut, sealing it out of reach.

"Why the hell did he do that?" another voice demanded. This one stood somewhere off to the right, which meant there were three people, at the very least.

"You can have me, but not my work," Alyn replied. He turned but could only see shadows moving around him.

"Let's go!" yet another voice hissed. "I don't want to stick around here!"

He wasn't going to surrender that easily. Bauer would get

free of his own entanglements, and when he saw the vidcam sitting there, he would know --

Alyn slowed, and someone tried to force him forward. Alyn took advantage of the slick cement to jerk the guy off balance and pull one arm free. A swift jab of his left hand connected with soft flesh, followed by a whoosh of surprise and pain and the other one let go as well.

Something hit him hard on the side of the head. Pain and shock were followed by the realization that they were dragging him away. His fingers clutched at a signpost and held tight. They kicked, and he caught one foot bringing the person down and forcing the others to back off when that one nearly fell on them. Bauer wouldn't be long now. Alyn could see the edge of the hotel window, and surely the Captain wouldn't have trouble finding him this close.

The attackers landed multiple blows, and Alyn couldn't defend himself and hold to the pole. They kicked him, grunting like mindless animals intent on their prey. He remembered Sebastian waylaid by a mob like this without any hope that his own personal Port Guard would come and rescue him. Hands pounded his fingers, and his hold began to weaken. Couldn't hold on and if they took him, Alyn knew he wasn't coming back.

He wanted Bauer!

I don't want to die on this world.

Bauer arrived before he realized the attackers were scattering. The Captain shouted, but Alyn couldn't follow the words. Laser fire momentarily brightened the little area before Bauer dropped to his knees beside Alyn, his hand fumbling in his pocket.

"Oh damn, Alyn. I'm sorry --"

"Both set up," Alyn whispered. The words came with a slur, almost unintelligible. He could hardly breathe, let alone move. He couldn't even convince his fingers to let go of the pole. The pain began to edge in over panic.

"Stay still," Bauer ordered. The man pulled out his commlink and thumbed it on. "Bauer to Tower. Emergency! We need a med team --"

"Captain?" a tinny voice answered. Shanley, Alyn thought. Hard to tell above all that ringing noise that began filling the night.

"Fell into a trap. Alyn's hurt. We're just outside the hotel, northeast side."

"We'll get help there as fast as we can, Captain Bauer."

Alyn somehow grabbed Bauer's arm, drawing his attention. For a moment, he still couldn't talk.

"Come ... quiet. Scare the hell out of F-Fiona, otherwise," he whispered. "Don't want her out here, too."

"Our boy sounds coherent enough," Shanley replied from the link. "We'll come quietly. Squad on the way to keep you company."

"Thanks, Shanley," Bauer said. Alyn could see him looking from side-to-side, waiting for the enemy to return. The dark, wet night looked even more ominous. "Let me know if there's any delay."

He pushed the commlink back into his pocket and looked down at Alyn. His hand reached out, but Alyn only saw a whisper of the movement before everything went very black.

Later, when he opened his eyes, the world had turned all white. Sterile smells, hissing equipment.

Hospital. Bauer and Fiona sat by his bed. He felt numb everywhere and knew from unpleasant experience that meant it was going to hurt very much, later.

"Hey," he said.

"Damn you scared us, Alyn," Fiona whispered. Tired again. Worried.

"S-Sorry."

"The meds say you'll be fine. They put you through one regen to repair broken ribs and mend a lung," Bauer explained. "You need to stay down for a couple days, though."

"Where's my vidcam?" he asked.

"Right here," Bauer answered. He lifted it from the floor and balanced the case on the edge of the bed. "You take your work way too seriously if that's your first concern."

"Not entirely. Take the chit out."

Alyn paused, catching his breath. The med equipment beeped in protest, and Alyn knew it was already pumping in drugs to make him sleep again. Bauer fumbled with the machine, uncertain of functions. When he finally held the small chit in his hand, Alyn nodded. Not much. Even his neck ached.

"Have them on it. Voices, at least. Didn't dare purposely focus on them. Left it inside the hotel for you and Kalison."

Captain Bauer looked down at him and blinked several times. Then he grinned.

"I'll personally deliver this to Commander Kalison right away." He slipped the chit into his pocket as he stood. "Fiona, do you mind keeping Alyn company while I take care of this? Delin is still right outside the door, and I won't be more than an hour."

"Be careful," she ordered. "Be damn careful. And take another guard with you."

Bauer started to protest. Then his hand brushed against the pocket of his beige jacket, and he nodded.

"Don't do anything silly. Remember that you don't want to die on this world," Alyn offered.

"No reason for any of us to," Bauer nodded. "It isn't our world, anyway."

The words stung again. Alyn wanted to confess, but the drug-induced sleep came first, robbing him of everything but dark dreams.

CHAPTER TWENTY-SEVEN

Fiona nervously tugged at her dark blue jacket as she stepped from the aircar behind Bauer. A half-dozen people headed into the tree-lined path a few yards away, disappearing into the canopy of green. Strangers, all of them. She had received a personal invitation to attend by Governor Tanton, and Bauer would not let her go alone, of course. All three of them went to the estate because Alyn was Bauer's charge and couldn't be left behind. In fact, he insisted on coming with them to the Memorial Service for Ember Tanton. Bauer feared he would slip out of the hospital and come alone if they didn't take him. So here they were. Alyn admitted he never met Ember, but he liked Governor Tanton. He came in respect for her.

Alyn began struggling out of the vehicle and Fiona belatedly offered her hand. Bandages covered wounds to his neck, and above his left eye. Bruises still showed on his hands although most of the injuries lay hidden under his plain black suit. He swayed slightly as he came to his feet. The reporter shouldn't even be out of the hospital, let alone wandering around the world.

However, Talin gave his own dress uniform a nervous sweep of his hands as he glanced anxiously around the pad, clearly expecting trouble at every corner. The day felt cooler with a hint of dampness to the air, though no rain had fallen and only a few clouds dotted the sky. They might get lucky tonight and not have another round of storms.

"Let's get inside the grounds," Bauer suggested. "They'll have good security in there."

"Probably an understatement," Alyn replied.

Naevon took one limping step forward as though testing his ability to walk. His words sounded slightly slurred from drugs, and he looked unsteady enough that Fiona took his arm. The touch startled him. She saw Talin's worried look; Alyn might not even have sense enough to look out for trouble.

People wandered everywhere in the well-tended garden beside the mansion. Gentle, Old-Earth music drifted across the grounds from unseen speakers. Or maybe the Tanton's had a real orchestra hidden away somewhere. They were rich enough.

Fiona could not make herself associate Ember with this place and the old-line politics it represented. Could she place Bramis Tanton in that category with the conservatives who drove this planet to the brink of war? Not if Governor Tanton was the one who sent Ember to her group.

Though by the end she had hated their clandestine meetings, she never wished or imagined things would end this way. Sonio and Ember were dead, and there was nothing the better for their sacrifices. She wished Sonio could have received an honor like this, but his death was less significant, at least by the way people judged their world. There would be no public memorial where she could go and bid farewell.

As they neared the center of the garden, the three newcomers immediately drew stares from the crowd. Alyn wasn't the most popular person on Tempest right now, especially since he insisted his attackers last night were not Rats, and the voices on the chits seemed to confirm his claim. The sight of bandages and bruises couldn't make the people any more comfortable with his presence.

Fiona decided not to stay long. She didn't like the angry stares directed at her companions, especially Alyn Naevon. Petty people, afraid to look too closely at their own world and afraid to see their willing complicity in the lies that brought them to this state of war. She had so hated to see it happening that Fiona had worked with Ember and the others to stop the evil from spreading.

Nothing more she could do.

Governor Tanton came down the stone-paved path between rows of pretty flowers. People moved out of her way, making polite sounds. They looked distressed as she walked past them.

"Alyn," she greeted the reporter. She took his hand in her own and looked honestly worried. "I just heard about the incident last night. What are you doing here?"

"I -- wanted to." He looked uncertain, but she nodded as though she understood.

"It is kind of you, Alyn," she said and let go of his hand, frowning at the bruises. "And to you, Fiona. Ember often spoke about you. She said I should try to lure you away from the hotel industry and offer you employment in Tanton Industries. She liked working with you."

"Then you always knew what she was doing?" Fiona asked very softly.

"Yes," Governor Tanton answered. Her eyes narrowed as she glanced cautiously around. No one else dared come near. "I couldn't attend, you understand. Where's your vidcam, Alyn?"

"Didn't come here for sensationalism," he mumbled.

"Damn drugs. Can't think straight yet."

"Janith brought her vidcam."

"That's her choice."

"Come and sit down," Governor Tanton offered. "Or leave now, if you prefer. I'm grateful you attended, but you really look as though you need rest."

"Captain Bauer's my guard, and Fiona was attending as well." Alyn frowned, knowing he wasn't tracking right "Am I making any sort of sense?"

That won a brief smile from the Governor. The woman looked more like Ember than Fiona had realized. Bramis Tanton took Alyn's arm and carefully led him towards the long rows of chairs. That was a show of concern on her part and a sign of her favor that did not go unnoticed among her other guests.

"Can you tell me -- why you had an interest in Fiona's group?" Alyn softly asked.

"Head clearing, is it?" she asked and almost smiled again. She paused at the edge of the seats. Her voice lowered, careful of their secret. "My interest in Fiona's group was primarily Caden Paris. You do realize he's the only Rat with a following even remotely comparable to Miranda De Velera's, right?"

"I didn't know," Alyn answered. For some reason, he sounded amused. "What did you want with him?"

"We just wanted . . . contact," Governor Tanton replied and put a hand on the back of a chair, looking weary for her own reasons. "You were doing good work for this world, Fiona. We hoped Caden's following would grow large enough to attempt wresting power from Miranda. If it went that far, I would even have offered aid."

"He wouldn't have taken it," Fiona replied.

"That's what Ember -- Ember thought," she said. The moment of animation left her face again. She looked older. "Ah damn, this is all such a mess. Alyn, I didn't want to own Caden. I only wanted to know someone in the Maze with whom I could work."

"You don't believe Miranda is behind Ember's death?" Fiona asked.

"No. We have other suspects. Miranda is far from the only one who doesn't like the idea of Rats and Citizens working together. And here comes Commander Kalison."

Fiona glanced over her shoulder, catching a glimpse of staring faces and angry eyes that betrayed the feelings of other guests. She'd never spent much time among the elite of Tempest. Few ate at the restaurant, and none had reason to stay at the hotel. She realized she was still just another off-worlder to most of them. However, Governor Tanton had greeted Fiona, and her two unpopular companions, with a warmth that bordered on friendship. She apparently liked Alyn Naevon.

"Governor Tanton." Commander Kalison formally bowed his head when he reached the little cluster of people. "My condolences -- and apologies for arriving so late. I went to the hospital to see how Alyn was doing. How did he talk you into this, Bauer?"

"You told me to guard him, not hold him captive," Talin said and shrugged. "And he thought it was important to be here."

"Where's your vidcam?" Kalison frowned.

"In the aircar. That's not why I came."

"Good boy." Kalison nodded approval and laid a gentle hand on his shoulder. "And you will stay out of dark alleys for a while, won't you?"

Alyn only shrugged. That didn't settle anyone's nerves

"Thank you all for attending," Governor Tanton said. "It does mean something to me, to know that politics isn't the only reason someone has come here."

"I liked Ember," Fiona offered. "She was a good friend."

"Thank you. Try the food."

She wandered off. Fiona realized this was the first time she had ever spoken with the Governor and yet the conversation had felt natural and comfortable, despite the circumstances. Very much like talking to Ember Tanton.

"Not a friendly crowd," Talin stated. His eyes roamed from one end of the chairs to the other. People stood at both ends, most of them glaring. Alyn looked at one group and quickly turned away again. "Don't worry, Alyn. If anyone tries to detain me again, they'll get a laser up their ass."

Kalison made a little coughing noise but didn't reprimand his subordinate. Instead, he put a hand on Alyn's shoulder and directed him towards the food. That left Talin to take Fiona's arm. She didn't care if people stared, if he was there to protect her.

"We're running the chit through analysis again," Kalison told Alyn. "So far, we haven't found anything definite."

"Don't you have other work to do?" Alyn asked. He sounded less woozy.

"All the random violence on Tempest appears interrelated to a larger problem. We both know Rats didn't attack you and me, at least, suspect that someone planned the incident. They waited for you outside the hotel. Your chit may give us the key we need to find answers to the larger picture."

Alyn nodded, and Fiona was glad to see he seemed more coherent again. He didn't look very interested in the food. Kalison pushed a plate into his hands and dropped a few odds and ends on it. Fiona felt a little relief to see someone else take the reporter in hand.

With plates full, they turned back and finally reached an empty stretch of chairs. Kalison gently pushed Alyn down into one and sat beside him. Talin escorted her to the other side of the reporter before he settled beside her. People still watched them, but Fiona cared far less than when she first arrived. Governor Bramis Tanton was glad she came. Nothing else was important.

They ate in silence for a few minutes. Alyn even nibbled at a roll.

"Have you heard anything about Wintas or Caden yet?" Fiona dared ask.

"We have Wintas under careful watch," Kalison replied. "We can't get any word on Caden, but there's a rumor he's in serious danger. We heard a rumor that Sebastian De Velera is also missing," he said and didn't add more. "Can I get you something else Naevon? Like an ambulance back to the hospital? You don't look well at all."

It was true, Fiona noted. However, it was the word from the Maze that apparently upset him so badly. He took this war too much to heart. A reporter shouldn't get so involved in his assignment.

"Naevon?" Talin whispered.

"I'm fine," Alyn finally offered. When he lifted his head, he looked both alert and steadier. "I just need to relax for a few minutes. And you can stop hovering around me. No one would dare make a scene here. Even Janith is keeping her distance. I need time to think."

Fiona noted the local reporter a couple meters away, her vidcam in hand and running. Why didn't someone tell her it was bad form? Maybe they just wanted to keep the woman occupied.

"Alyn's right," Kalison said. "He's safe here. Let's give our reporter some space. There's nowhere else on-world we would dare leave him alone. Which brings up another subject, Alyn --"

"I'm not leaving Tempest now," he replied. He gave a slight wave of his hand. "They've made this very personal,

Commander."

"That's no reason to stay."

"Then why haven't you resigned?"

Talin grinned and took Fiona by the arm, leading her away from the two.

"He's too bright for his own good," Talin decided. He moved slowly along the garden paths, careful not to intrude on others. "At least Kalison isn't going to kill me for bringing him here. This is turning out to be a far harder assignment than I expected."

"Why do you think someone attacked him?" Fiona asked.

"Alyn's unpopular and an easy target. I don't care which side did the work. It was cowardly. And it's worse to be angry with Naevon because you don't like his reports."

"Talin," she whispered.

"I don't have to be politic, Fiona," he replied. He even glared at someone nearby. "I like this world. I just don't think much of the people, sometimes. And that's Citizens and Rats. Too damn many fanatics, and not enough reason."

Fiona hoped Governor Tanton didn't regret their arrival. She suspected the woman would probably welcome the honesty, though perhaps not here and now. Talin didn't mind wandering through the garden, admiring the pretty colors and unusual plants. Fiona began planning some type of indoor garden for the lobby. They needed a change.

Then Kalison came around the corner, looked at the two, and shook his head.

"He's not with you."

"No," Bauer replied. "What happened now?"

"Bramis said she last saw him heading toward the landing pad. Let's go see if his equipment's still in your aircar."

"Damn! What the hell would make him take off like this?" Talin demanded. The three hurried through the crowd, drawing looks of worry more than distrust this time. "He knows he's not safe out there --"

"He was very upset about the news from the Maze," Fiona offered. She skipped along beside them. "Though maybe he just wasn't feeling well and didn't want to disturb us. I know he feels like he's intruding."

"And maybe it's drug-related madness, and he doesn't know what he's doing," Kalison added as they reached the pad.

"Aircar's gone!" Talin hissed. "I gave the codes to Alyn and Fiona in case something delayed me, and they needed to get out. Sorry --"

"It was a good idea," Kalison replied. He ran his fingers through his graying hair. "Neither of us thought Alyn was crazy."

"Should we put a report out to look for the vehicle?"

"No. Too dangerous for Naevon. I'm going to pack that boy up and ship him back to his home office before he gives me an ulcer. These days, he's causing me as much grief as Miranda herself."

"He'll be fine," Fiona offered. They looked at her, surprised. "He was coherent and lucid when you spoke to him. Wherever he went, he went alone for his own reasons. And he's not suicidal, Commander."

Neither looked inclined to believe her last statement. And she wasn't entirely certain herself.

"Let's go back in. I can't make Alyn more important than Governor Tanton," Kalison said. His eyes looked back towards the city. Fiona could see nothing moving in that direction.

"The Governor likes Alyn. She'd understand if we left," Talin offered. "I just don't know where we could go. Fly around the city and look for the aircar?"

"No. Let him go. He'll turn back up."

Fiona didn't understand Alyn Naevon. It wasn't wise to

annoy Talin and Commander Kalison. Wherever he went, she hoped it was important enough to compensate for annoying his few friends on Tempest.

Long shadows of the approaching night converged on the garden. Sunset. The service was about to begin. It was time to say goodbye to one friend. She would have time to worry about the other one later.

CHAPTER TWENTY-EIGHT

Alyn carefully settled the borrowed aircar down at the Port Tower. The night was coming fast, and dark clouds were sweeping toward the city again: Good and bad, good and bad. This was an active storm pattern. The settlement didn't need more rain and even a couple centimeters would cause overflows in most areas.

The rain would, however, dissuade the troublemakers from roaming the city. He only hoped the storm held off until after Ember Tanton's Memorial Service.

When he finally emerged from the aircar, Port Guards moved restlessly toward him, weapons in hand. These people came to Tempest only for duty, not love. Alyn showed his hands, wisely leaving the vidcam on the seat beside him. He didn't want them to mistake it for a weapon.

"Oh -- you." The woman in the lead signaled the other four to go back. "You're the Vidline reporter, Naevon."

The others muttered words of annoyance at the disturbance and gratitude that it wasn't trouble. Kalison obviously hadn't missed him yet since the woman didn't look ready to lock him up.

"Can I help you, sir?" the guard asked.

"Just came for a couple shots of the port," he answered. He drew his vidcam out, dusting the surface with a fond caress. "Sorry if I worried you."

"No problem. I heard you were in the hospital. You do look unsteady so don't wander too far. I don't want to go hunting you down."

"Thanks. Don't worry if it takes me awhile. I want to sit out there and watch the storm come in. You know, get the right shot."

"Yeah, right." She looked out at the storm and frowned. Apparently, she thought he was crazy for wanting to sit out in the weather.

If she knew the truth --

Alyn smiled and tried not to limp as he hurried away. He also tried not to look guilty for misusing their trust. He didn't look forward to facing Kalison later. Maybe the man would understand why *Alonso* needed to slip into the Maze for answers, but he didn't dare confess his identity before coming here. The Commander might want his hands on any De Velera right now and especially one who wasn't an artist. This *De Velera* had lied to his friends, making him suspect of any amount of evil. He didn't pretend this was a wise choice, but he wanted answers, and some Rats might yet talk to him. He had to find out about Sebastian.

All hell was going to break loose by the time he got back out ... if he walked out of the Maze again.

He had to enter the port tower lobby to get out into the grounds beyond. This was the easiest way for him to get to the Maze because the aircar would have drawn too much attention anywhere else. When he entered the nearly empty lobby of the Tower, Alyn still waited for someone to grab him. *Obnoxious reporter, lying Rat*: someone could come up with a reason to take him in by now.

The silvery walls didn't shine quite so brightly tonight, and it seemed the entire world was duller than when he had arrived. He remembered meeting Captain Bauer at that counter. Alyn hadn't thought he would consider the man a friend within a couple days.

Another guard stood at the service entrance to the Port grounds and frowned as he neared. Alyn gave a smile, although the bruise on the side of his face hurt.

"Just here for a couple shots of the port," Alyn offered. "The guard outside let me in."

The man keyed on his commlink. Kalison wasn't around. Could he bluff his way past someone else? Would they call Kalison, even though he was at Governor Tanton's? If they held him until Kalison came back, he would likely be off-world before he learned what happened to Sebastian and Caden Paris. There wasn't anyone else who could walk in there and have any chance of bringing back answers again.

"Naevon's here. Wants some shots of the port," the man growled. He held the earpiece up, shielding the conversation from Alyn's hearing. Didn't like reporters? "Yeah, out on the pad. All right."

The man's frown never wavered. Alyn couldn't guess the answer to his query.

"Twenty minutes, Naevon. We don't want you out there if we have an emergency landing come in. There's no one near right now."

"Thanks," he replied. His sincerity surprised the man. The guard even lost his sullen look for a moment as he palmed the door open and let Alyn through. Alyn walked away, the limp a little worse. A slow walk, until he was beyond the retaining wall, and out onto the well-worn concourse. It was a damn long trek from here to the nearest Maze fence line. With no other guards in immediate sight, he began a lopping run across the scared cement.

Under normal circumstances, the port would remain a hive of activity throughout the night, but Kalison had canceled the night shifts, keeping the Rats home after dark. Even during the day, the tension must be considerable. Citizens wouldn't do this work and probably didn't have the expertise to handle some of it. Kalison hadn't called in off-worlders to take over the work. Alyn suspected the man would let the port go to hell before he called in other workers to take Rat jobs.

Alyn paused to catch his breath midway across the long stretch of an empty pad. He looked back at the tower's brightly lit windows. Beyond the building, he could see the outline of the city, much of it still dark. Too much damage done, not enough time for repairs.

Then he started running again. He had to reach the nearest fence, find a passage, and get off the grounds before the guards started looking for him.

Or he could just take the shot of the Port Tower and walk back, innocent of everything except annoying Kalison, Bauer, and Fiona by disappearing.

How long would it take him to find out about Sebastian?

The residue of drugs and a surge of adrenaline got him to the fence but too many years had passed since he last came this way. Nervousness over the possibility of capture -- on either side of the fence -- didn't help. He forced calm and slid along the wire fence. He finally found the place he had used years ago, and carefully pulled aside a little piece of wire and pushed the rest aside. Once he was through, he pushed the wire back into place, indistinguishable from the rest of the line. Without knowing the trick, no amount of pushing would open the secret gate.

Beyond the opening stood a vast stretch of open ground, protecting the Port from its Rat neighbors. He left no distinguishing prints in the cover of hard gravel, but the rough, damp stones proved treacherous. Alyn covered the ground in an uneven jog, feeling the pains catching up with him. By the time he reached the first line of huts, he had only enough energy left to slip into the shadows and slide down to the ground.

Alyn sat there for a long time. He spotted Port Guards examining the pad where he had crossed. Annoyed already by the looks of them. They didn't go near the fence and soon went to look for him elsewhere.

When he finally stopped gasping and trembling, Alyn forced himself back to his feet. He couldn't turn back now without answers. Taking the vidcam farther wasn't wise, though. He didn't want the Rats thinking he came to spy. After leaving the equipment in the shadow of the hut, he started towards the inner Maze.

Alyn wanted to talk to one of his father's former councilors, but he didn't know if any were still around. He had seen some of their names on the lists of dead Rats when he'd studied on his way home and now wondered if the other deaths had gone unnoticed outside the Maze. Wiser, probably, to look for some of his old friends -- the ones who *hadn't* been involved in Maze politics and therefore unlikely to draw Miranda's attention. No use heading toward the bachelor's barracks, though: the unattached men and women moved too often. Alyn couldn't hope to find former companions where he had left them six years ago. He needed to locate the ones already married before his departure. They usually settled somewhere and stayed longer.

He shivered as a breeze blew through the alley. Though the night was already cold and muddy, at least it hadn't turned worse yet.

Despite tonight's somewhat good weather, few people walked through the Maze tonight. He kept his head bowed and none of the few people he passed looked closely. There was, in fact, a familiar feel to skulking around the Maze like this. He'd grown up a De Velera, and that meant he'd had enemies all his life. Ino Mythrin wouldn't likely be in this area, at least. He and his people ran the area of the Maze farthest from the port where his black market wasn't likely to draw port guards. Miranda hadn't moved against him. Even growing up, that part of the Maze might as well have been a different world. Though he could speak the slang of the south side, those who lived in this area tended to sound more like Citizens, for all the good it did them.

Alyn spent more than an hour wandering the alleys before he located someone he could trust. He saw Wakia entering her home with a small child in tow. She looked up with a start when Alyn crossed the alley at a near run and started to slam the door closed, then paused, surprised at the sight.

"Can I come in?" he asked, nervously glancing around.

"God, yes! Get in! You could get us both killed!"

"I know. I'm sorry," Alyn apologized. He darted through the doorway and caught his balance on the other side. The child looked up at him, mistrusting. "I just needed to find someone I could trust. I need answers. Is Syman home?"

"Go wake up your daddy," Wakia ordered. The child scurried away. Two others played at some card game at the table though they cast nervous glances at the unexpected visitor. It made Alyn very uneasy.

"What's going on?" Syman came from a back room and stopped in the hallway, staring. His dark hair lay disheveled across his shoulders, his green eyes wide with shock. "Damn, Alonso. What the hell are you doing here?"

"Trying to find out what happened to Sebastian," he replied. He leaned against the door and began shaking again. Alyn suddenly realized that Syman might tell him an answer he didn't want to hear. His head began to pound as he looked back at the worried man.

"Take your cards and your brothers into the back room," Syman ordered. The first sound of protest from the children won a darker look. "Now."

No one argued, though there were sullen looks at the man who invaded their home. They did not, however, look surprised or worried. That said something about the kind of life children had in the Maze these days. It hadn't been this bad before.

"Sit down before you fall down," Wakia ordered. She waved him toward the cluttered table and mismatched chairs. "Tea?"

"No, thank you," he replied. He felt like an intruder and knew they had little of anything to spare. He crossed to the table and sat with Syman. The dark-skinned man stared at him, curious and worried. "I only came to talk. I'm sorry if I put you in danger."

"Miranda always knew we were your friends and she watched us for a long time -- but she lost interest after the second kid," Syman answered. He finally gave a little shrug and dropped onto the worn plastic chair across from him. Wakia busied herself at the counter behind them. "You're here. I'm glad you thought you could trust us. There's damn little trust in the Maze these days. There's no telling who suddenly sides with Miranda and is willing to take down former companions for a smile of appreciation from her."

"That bad? Damn. What about Sebastian?"

Syman looked down at his hands. Rough and blistered, they belonged to a man who worked hard. Wakia and Syman both looked older. They'd aged far more than he had in the last six years.

And the silence spoke of everything Alyn feared. They didn't want to tell him about Sebastian.

"Miranda says he disappeared," Syman finally reported. There was a hint of anger in his voice, the quick words clipped and sharp. "And she is hinting that the disappearance has something to do with your arrival."

"Me? People know I'm back? What is she saying?"

"That he went to the city to see you," Wakia said. "And that you were afraid he would give you away."

"That damn little bitch! She sent him into the city. If I hadn't found him, by accident, he would never have reached the Maze again! But no one's seen him since, so I suppose it wasn't safe after all. He was going to Caden Paris. Any word on him?"

"We heard she wanted him removed. No one's seen him either."

"Why do you people follow her?" Alyn demanded. Then he stopped and spread his hands. "I'm sorry. I'm not here to judge. I left, and you stayed, and I know you just do what you must."

"She walked into the role, Alonso. I don't know why no one seriously challenged her," Syman explained with a shake of his head, clearly not understanding how it happened any better than Alyn did. "I never paid much attention to politics. By the time any of us had second thoughts, she had us in a war. What can we do now? If we back down, the Citizens will destroy us. Miranda is the only answer we have left."

"What about Caden?"

"People liked him. Miranda didn't. So where is he now?"

They sat in silence. Wakia placed a cup of tea before him despite his protest, and he sipped out of politeness. The bitter, hot liquid hurt the inside of his mouth. Everything hurt.

"What happened to my father's people?" he finally asked.

"A couple are dead, and the others are too scared to do

anything but back Miranda," Wakia replied. She settled in another chair. Her neat, short blond hair contrasted with Syman's perpetual disarray. Alyn -- *Alonso* remembered the many jokes made about the two in the old days. "If you want to talk to one, go see Bunlin. He still lives out by the Hostel. And I think Miranda is still a little afraid of him."

"Everyone respects him," Syman nodded. "And he is careful to remain on the right side of neutral in all this trouble. He's a wise old man. Some of us wish he'd offer to take over the government, but I guess he knows better than to pit himself against Miranda."

"Thank you," Alyn whispered. He suddenly realized the depth of what they gave him. They risked Miranda's wrath when he entered their home and what they told him now was treason against his sister.

He lifted the cup again. The bittersweet taste reminded him of days in the Maze, sipping tea -- and stronger drinks -- with friends. Talking about books, work, and the less life-threatening aspects of politics. He didn't understand how everything went so badly, so fast. There was danger in the days his father led the Maze: Alyn saw friends die. However, the friends didn't have to live in fear of their own people.

When he got ready to leave, Syman slipped outside and stood, casually by the door for a moment, before he signaled to Alyn.

He left quickly and didn't look back. The encounter with his friends left him feeling out of place, and he knew he no longer fit into their world. Alyn realized he didn't belong here any longer. He wasn't a Rat pretending to be something else. Alyn Naevon was a Vidline reporter, and Alonso De Velera was only a persona he called up for this unusual occasion. He had changed, and he didn't regret having done so. Walking here, fearing his sister and worried about his friends, he realized the choices he'd made had been wise. He never would have survived this long because he would have hesitated over taking their father's place and Miranda would have killed him before he could have gained power.

Alyn slowly worked his way toward the heart of the Maze. He passed down side alleys and through narrow crevices between buildings. At one point, he saw a clear view of the Hostel. Was she home tonight? Could he walk in and confront Miranda?

Probably. And die there too, if Syman's broad hints about what happened to Miranda's enemies were valid. Alyn didn't carry a weapon, not even a Rat knife. He slid along the buildings, grateful that no one was in sight.

Bunlin's well-kept cabin still appeared out of place among the dilapidated buildings around it. This area wasn't as neat as it had been when he left six years ago. No surprise. Somehow, he doubted that urban development was high on Miranda's list of necessities. The money for weapons and explosives must be difficult enough to find.

The man answered his door after two quick raps. Thinning white hair, lines around his eyes, across his forehead: Bunlin hadn't changed at all.

"Ah, made it at last, Alonso," he said. "Do come in."

"I tried to make certain no one saw me," Alyn whispered as he slid into the building.

"No matter," Bunlin calmly replied. He closed the door and took Alyn's arm, leading him to the sofa. Alyn felt as though he was the older, feeble one. Both sat, bathed in the glow from a blue cube placed on the low table before them. Pieces of the older man's life sat scattered around the room, less neat than Wakia and Syman's home. Beyond the shuttered window, he could hear the growing sound of the approaching storm. "You look much abused, Alonso. Or do you prefer Alyn?"

"Alonso, while I'm in the Maze," he confessed. "I never meant to forget or even stay away forever. However, chance brought me here in a way that made giving my true name . . . unwise."

"Well, of all three of Federico's children, you always showed the most wisdom," Bunlin told him with a bright grin. "You left."

That was vindication. Absolution. Alyn felt a little light-headed at the pronouncement.

"I came because I heard Sebastian is missing. I had nothing to do with it --"

"I don't listen to Miranda's propaganda. Those of us with any brains don't believe anything she says. Miranda takes too much for granted, especially when she thinks she's so wise no one would question her. I am sorry to say, though, that I have no idea where Sebastian is right now. Many of us fear the worse."

"He was in the city. Kalison and I got him back to the Maze because the city wasn't safe for him, even staying with me. I've made enemies among the Citizens," he said, touching the bandage on his forehead. "Sebastian said he was going to Caden for shelter."

"Ah. A brighter boy than we all thought," Bunlin replied. There was a whisper of a smile on his lips. "However, his timing was bad. You know Caden is missing too?"

"Yes." Frustration rose in him, and he caught his hands together and sat very still. "How the hell did Miranda ever get this much power? This *child* threw temper tantrums when she was sixteen! I remember fits if one of her friends got a new piece of clothing and she didn't. She was the one who only saw our father's work as a way for her to be important --"

"And there you have it, Alonso," Bunlin said and nodded. "It's an easy enough answer. She wanted all the fame for herself."

"I shouldn't have left," he admitted at last.

"You couldn't remain and play the part Sebastian has for the last few years, and I don't think you would have wanted the place she now has. Those were your only options. She was ready to take over when your father died, and you would have found yourself in a very precarious position. Or a grave," Bunlin replied. "Remember, it is not just Miranda you would face. She does have her followers and even that bastard Mythrin keeps out of her reach. You wisely left before you became another victim of the war. Ah, and I don't suppose you realize that your father covered for the loss of funds."

He felt himself go red at the reminder of how he left Tempest, and the creds stolen from the Rat emergency funds.

"I always intended to pay it back. Can I do it now? It's not like I'm poor anymore. This assignment pays very well."

"There's no need to become defensive, Alonso." The older man patted his arm, like a grandfather might give reassurance. "Few people knew what happened. Miranda never did."

"My father must have felt I betrayed him, leaving like I did."

"No." The one word won a look of disbelief before the man continued. "You are more like Federico than either of his other children. That's not to say there's anything wrong with Sebastian, mind you. The truth is your father told me he was glad you left when you did. Everything was coming apart, and Federico didn't like the changes any more than you did. He wanted out himself but knew he couldn't simply disappear."

"How the hell did Miranda get in charge?" he finally asked. He hoped this man would give him an answer he could understand. Alyn almost wished for the vidcam. Bunlin would show the Citizens there was still sanity among the Rats.

"The suddenness of your father's death shocked us all.

Rumor was that he wanted to step down, give the top spot over to Caden. Federico didn't have the heart for a real war, you know. His unfortunate death upset all the Maze and left us vulnerable to our own worst fears. Alyn, look at all this trouble as a Rat, and not just Miranda's brother. You'll see how few options we had."

Alyn nodded and felt relieved that Bunlin hadn't stated the observation a little differently. He didn't want someone else pointing out he wasn't Rat anymore.

"Miranda was *here* when your father died," Bunlin said softly. The older man leaned back, looking as worn and weary as Syman. "She holds a name some people willingly followed. Even today, many Rats still believe in her. They think the times need a strong, ruthless hand. They don't see that the troubles are a result of tactics used by the person they want to settle them. Those of us who actively don't like what's happened can't fight her, and we can't escape. Where would we go? To the Citizens?"

"You could go to Kalison," Alyn said. "He would stand by anyone looking to end the trouble."

"Commander Kalison arrived far too late to help most of us," Bunlin pointed out. "That isn't his fault. By the time some of us thought we could trust him, the situation was far beyond anything so simple. I could go to Kalison, as could a few others. It won't make any difference in the trouble on Tempest. Or we could possibly assassinate your sister and a few of her key people. However, the inevitable upheaval would leave us open to the wrath of the Citizens. Warring among ourselves is not the answer."

"What about Caden Paris? Is there any rumor about what happened to him?"

Bunlin bit his lip again, then ran fingers through his sparse white hair. More bad news.

"No one knows where he is. Rumor says Miranda killed him and his followers are hiding the fact in hopes of keeping her at bay a while longer. She'll go for them soon enough. She ordered Caden's death when she heard about his involvement with Ember Tanton."

"Who told her!" This news shocked him with the implications of a different conspiracy. "That's a tightly kept secret in the city."

"I don't know. Until now, I hadn't even thought it was true. This does substantiate the theory that Miranda has contacts outside the Maze. She's a surprisingly formidable woman, Alyn. And at least the Citizens fear her."

"Respect is better than fear," Alyn countered. "Some high-placed people respect Caden Paris."

"That's no help if he's dead," Bunlin replied softly. He leaned closer to Alyn, his pale eyes looking wild and lost. "Get out of the Maze, Alonso. Leave Tempest while you can -- before she kills you, too."

CHAPTER TWENTY-NINE

With his hands tied behind his back, Sebastian couldn't brush the hair from his face. In the darkness that distraction began to draw all his attention, helping him forget that he hurt nearly everywhere. Sebastian entertained himself by alternately considering how to deal with Miranda and in consideration of cutting off all his hair.

He tried not to wonder how long Miranda intended to keep him prisoner in the Hostel basement. Though few came down here, it still wouldn't be safe to leave him here indefinitely. And that, of course, worried him. He had never counted time in breaths and heartbeats before. They seemed too short, a fleeting way to measure any life.

His legs ached from standing so long. Shifting his weight or leaning against the cement wall didn't help. He didn't want to sit on the floor. He'd heard sounds around him in the damp, musty cellar of the Hostel, something alive tapping its way around the cellar. It tore papers for a while and later gnawed on harder material. Not a large creature, Sebastian convinced himself. Nevertheless, it was something he didn't want to encounter with his hands tied behind his back.

The sounds kept him awake for a long, long time. Then the animal grew quiet, and that lulled him to a restless, standing sleep.

Sebastian awoke when something brushed across his foot, then tugged at his pant leg. The gag in his mouth kept him from crying out. He kicked convulsively, upsetting his precarious balance. He tumbled, face-down, to the floor. At least it startled the creature away.

Well, what was one more bruise?

Maybe the fall knocked a little sense into him. Sebastian had realized he didn't want to stay here as Miranda's guest until she felt safe enough to kill him but hadn't really thought about doing anything about it. He harbored no illusions about his fate in her hands. She sent Niel to kill him once already.

The feeling in his arms hovered between agony and numbness. He tried to pull apart the ropes securing his wrists but quickly gave that up as futile since he couldn't feel if his labor made a difference. He did notice a patch of liquid warmth on his back -- blood from wrists rubbed raw by the tight restraint. If he became ambitious, he could probably kill himself that way. He wondered if the smell of blood would draw the creature back to him. There were such animals, even on Tempest, though they were rare in the inhabited areas.

He could hear the muffled sound of a storm blowing in, which meant the night had likely fallen again. Most of the rain on Tempest came after sunset this time of year when the atmosphere took a sudden drop in temperature and moisture suddenly -- and often violently -- condensed into storm clouds. The rest of the year they had morning storms which were usually not as violent.

Why he suddenly remembered that piece of trivia from school, Sebastian couldn't guess. Boredom, probably. Thinking about school wasn't unpleasant, though. He remembered how Alonso encouraged him to study Earth and to paint just because the colors fascinated him. His older brother was the first person to encourage Sebastian to be himself and not just another De Velera.

For all the good it did him.

That was unfair. For the last seven years, Sebastian had created art and loved his work. Sebastian doubted Miranda could say the same. Alonso might still understand better.

Light!

Brightness flooded the area. Still sprawled on his side, Sebastian tried to shield his eyes by burying his face against his arm. A new headache already threatened with a dull throb at the base of his neck. He couldn't escape the illumination and squinted across the room.

Miranda marched down the stairs and across to him. He didn't need to see her clearly to know she wasn't happy. Finely honed instincts tried to make him act subservient yet again, but that wouldn't do him any good. He might as well hold to a little dignity at the end.

"You little bastard!" Miranda bent and yanked the gag from his mouth, pulling out a few strands of hair as well. "Where the hell is he?"

"I really don't know what the hell you're talking about, Randa," he said. His voice was a dry whisper, uneven and harsh.

She stood again and kicked him. After what he already suffered through, it wasn't much of an attack.

"No one has found the body yet," Miranda finally spoke again. She leaned closer again. He could, unfortunately, see much better now and the fanatical hatred in her eyes made her seem inhuman. "Where's Caden Paris?"

"Niel killed him," Sebastian answered. No use antagonizing her by admitting he lied about the man's death. "What the hell do you have to be afraid of from a dead man?"

Her dark eyes narrowed: She suspected a lie, but that hardly mattered to him right now. When she stood again, he tensed, expecting a kick. Instead, she turned away as though she forgot he existed.

Sebastian didn't want to them to abandon him down here, alone in the dark. He fought very hard against the urge to ask her forgiveness because he knew those words wouldn't work this time. Miranda never really forgave. At best, she might find the scene momentarily diverting.

She walked away. Sebastian rolled to his back, and painfully lifted his head, trying to get a better view of the cavernous area, get his bearings again before the dark --

"Niel, grab him for me, will you? We're doing it tonight. This is as good a storm as any other. And if Caden Paris is still alive, we don't dare wait."

Maybe there was something worse than being alone in the dark. He didn't know what Miranda planned, but he didn't want to be a part of it.

Niel stalked across the room. Not a happy man, Niel Taress. He grabbed Sebastian under the arm and jerked him upward, taking considerable pleasure in the gasp of pain the movement won. Sebastian learned his shoulders weren't nearly as numb as the rest of his arms. Niel cursed when Sebastian couldn't his feet under him, and he dragged Sebastian to the far side of the room and up the stairs, gasping all the way.

The two paused at the top, listening for the sounds of anyone in the kitchen. Lauren stood there, guarding the way. She gave him a very bright smile. Sebastian considered yelling and decided there might be a better time. He could wait for somewhere that he might really hope for rescue.

When something tumbled noisily in the basement, all four jumped at the sound.

"You need to get that cleared out, you know," Sebastian offered. "There are rats in the basement."

Miranda and Niel scowled back at him. No sense of humor at all.

They dragged him through the kitchen and out the back door into the storm. He slipped on the rain-slick steps and pulled Niel down with him. The man pounded him several times in frustration.

"Just pick him up and carry him," Miranda ordered.

She and Lauren pulled aside an abandoned mattress, uncovering several new plastic crates. Neil shoved Sebastian down into the mud and retrieved three shoulder bags from inside the back door. Lauren helped pull out several large bundles from the boxes, slipping them into the packs her brother provided for them. They worked efficiently and obviously had practiced in the past.

Explosives.

"We don't have time to waste," Miranda warned. The excitement in her voice surprised Sebastian. "They could close the building in this rain and then what good would my work do? We need victims. Important victims."

She stopped and suddenly smiled very brightly. A flash of lightning made her look unreal, some phantasm in human shape. When she came close enough to lean down by him, Sebastian felt his heart start to pound with legitimate fear.

"We need victims," she repeated. "And I need a martyr. I let you live your own myth long enough, little brother. You became just what I wanted. What will the rest of the Rats think when the body of their perfect little artist turns up in the ruins of the Government Building, a victim of his own terrorism? It will start a considerable scandal and bring me even more followers."

He felt very cold and numb as everything began to make

sense.

"You want a martyr like our father was," Sebastian replied.

"*Exactly* like our father," she said and smiled.

CHAPTER THIRTY

By the time Commander Kalison reached the Port Tower, a vicious storm again assaulted the city. The already saturated ground couldn't hold any more of the precipitation and ponds of standing water quickly spread into dangerous, fast-moving streams. Though lowland flooding was endemic to this world, there hadn't been city flooding on this scale for half a century.

Kalison felt drenched and annoyed as he headed for his office and thought about all the work piling up at his other, temporary Government Building office as well. So much else to do -- he didn't need to waste time worrying about that damn reporter. He had ferried Bauer and Fiona to the Tempest Pride where the two would wait for Alyn. If the boy were wise, Naevon would go straight to the hotel and stay out of his sight for the next few days.

Kalison didn't need the report from his soldiers to know that Alyn Naevon was again in the Maze. There was nowhere else he could go that he couldn't have mentioned to them first. Neat trick, to head off across the Port grounds and disappear like that. What else did the Rats teach him when he interviewed Miranda?

Kalison's office felt oddly quiet after the intensity of the day. He looked out the window as lightning brightened the night. Thunder shook the building, and the wind blew hard enough to sound like some creature pounding to get inside. He wondered how the Maze fared in this storm. No one on the outside knew.

People moved quietly outside the office, expecting him to show anger over allowing Naevon through to the Port grounds. In the scheme of troubles, it was a little mistake. Besides, he trusted Naevon, even still.

Commander Kalison found it surprisingly hard to sit and wait for word on their wayward reporter -- as though Naevon was all the trouble he had to think about on Tempest! He had a night staff meeting in a few minutes to fill them in on the latest developments, and Kalison wished he had answers to give them. After the meeting, he could go home to his apartment for a few hours of sleep if he thought it worth the time. The weather overlays he looked at on his comp showed a line of clouds stretching several kilometers into the backcountry, and the night was young. More clouds would form before this storm died down. There was no use going home. Tomorrow's weather promised calm at last --

And that meant he would have trouble with the people instead. There was no way to win. Kalison pressed fingers against his temples and tried to demand calm of himself, at least, even if he got cooperation from no one else.

The comp screen began flashing a design of spiraling multicolor dots, intended to help ease stress and preserve the monitor. It always annoyed him. Kalison believed computers existed to do work, not sit and look pretty. He always intended to remove the program from the system, but never quite found the time to bother. He felt very tempted to gut the machine right now. Bare essentials --

He glanced through file listings and chose to do research instead of destruction. Maybe there was still something he hadn't quite grasped yet; some truth beyond the obvious ones that Rats and Citizens were pushing each other to mutual destruction.

Miranda De Velera: Kalison called up the file and noted that the picture was years out of date. It showed a sullen, glaring teen with long brown hair and no especially distinguishing features. He tried not to be critical just because he saw the De Velera name -- but she really hadn't looked like anything special. Kalison accessed the copy of Naevon's now infamous vid report, choosing a frame to cut into the older text file. They hardly looked like the same person, he realized. He laid the two pictures side-by-side and studied the differences for a moment. The younger version looked like a spoiled child. She could easily pass for a Citizen's daughter with that haughty, superior look.

The newer picture was of someone ... different. Not just older and certainly no wiser. However, there was a fire in the eyes that had looked dull in childhood. Kalison studied the woman, with her lips curled in a near smile as she pronounced judgment on Tempest. He completely trusted Alyn Naevon's judgment on Miranda De Velera. This woman was mad with power. Dangerously insane.

What the hell made Alyn go into the Maze, where this woman ruled? Sebastian De Velera? A boy he saved from the Citizens, only to see him fall prey to his own people? Despite everything, Kalison hadn't thought Alyn had become that personally involved in this story. Surely Naevon had experienced enough reporting to know he couldn't save everyone.

Kalison called Sebastian's picture up. This was a younger

version as well, but not nearly as changed. Whatever madness infected his sister, it had never touched the artist.

Strange family. Intrigued, Kalison looked over the file on their father, the infamous Federico De Velera. The man who appeared on his comp screen looked strangely familiar, though he had died before Kalison arrived on-world. The frame showed him with one arm draped across Sebastian's shoulder and his other arm over another boy. Curious, he clicked on the face of the second boy who stared at the ground, shy in the face of fame.

Alonso De Velera, son.

Damn. He never realized Federico had another son. No one mentioned him, and that probably meant the boy was dead. Had this one been another Sebastian or a Miranda? Did he die before his father, and perhaps in a way that finally pushed the man towards the acts of terrorism his daughter now fully embraced? Was that the secret Kalison sought? Even if true, this would be useless information of no immediate help, but Kalison wasn't like Jeffries. He wanted to understand the Rats, not fear and destroy them.

He typed in the name and called up a file he had never glanced at before. It came from the archive directory, which reinforced his belief that the boy had died --

Text sprang up, the picture a moment later.

Kalison stared at that screen and went completely away until his mind began repeating two words like a litany of madness all his own.

Alonso, Alyn, Alonso, Alyn.

"Damn!"

"Sir? Something wrong?" The man covering Shanley's desk for the night stepped to the doorway, looking worried.

"Nothing wrong," Kalison answered quickly. His fingers automatically blanked the screen as the man came into the room. Sgt. Janey was part of the night staff and not someone he worked with very often. Kalison wasn't certain why he protected Naevon just then. "I hit my knee on the desk. Do it all the time. How long until the meeting?"

"Another twenty minutes, sir. Still no sign of the reporter."

"He'll turn up." Sgt. Janey gave him a strange look. Everyone knew Kalison favored Alyn Naevon and the sudden unconcern did sound odd. "We all know he's in the Maze. He knows what he's doing, though I'm not certain Alyn realizes how much he's trying my patience."

Janey nodded and went back to his own desk.

Kalison watched the pretty designs for a couple minutes. They still didn't help. He finally keyed up the file again trying to convince himself he had made a mistake the first time.

No. *Alyn Naevon* still looked back at him. This was only a younger version of the reporter, with lighter hair and a nasty scar that ran from his left eye to chin. What in hell was going on? He scanned the text looking for answers to yet another problem. Alonso De Velera had disappeared six years earlier on the night of the first serious fighting between Rat and Citizens. The previous Port Commander believed Alonso somehow bought forged papers and slipped off-world during the panic. Kalison called up the manifest for the two ships that left that night -- and there was Alyn Naevon's name on one.

Did he work for Miranda, then? That didn't feel right. Federico still lived when his son left Tempest. Besides, that interview with ... with his sister had been too rife with antagonism. He had certainly done nothing to help her cause in the few days since his arrival.

A study of Naevon's current papers made it apparent that Vidline did employ Alyn Naevon and they had no idea of his real identity. They had sent all the proper files and codes when they assigned him to this world, and even Janith had double-checked to make sure of the authenticity. Work brought Alonso De Velera back to his homeworld. With a whisper of amusement, Kalison remembered how nervous the reporter had been that first night. Naevon had probably expected everyone to recognize him and to end up arrested or shot, depending on who spotted him first.

He almost chuckled, thinking about a De Velera at those conferences, in those offices of high Citizen officials. Then he felt a sudden chill. Damn! He had told Bramis to give the boy an interview, and even she liked him. However, that time alone with Governor Bramis Tanton could have done irreparable damage to this world --

Naevon didn't kill her. He didn't hurt anyone, in fact. Alyn made concise, even fair, reports on the trouble here. Some of the saner Citizen's had to look at those vids and see mistakes made by others.

He studied the older picture for a long time. He didn't have a newer one handy to add to the file. Smart boy: Naevon never appeared in his own reports. Some Citizen was bound to have an avid interest in the De Velera family and recognize him. There was, he knew, ID pictures on file with this Vidline credentials but no one outside his department was likely to look at those, and the Port Guards were from off-world and wouldn't recognize him.

Jeffries might have, though. That had been a real chance.

If he didn't work for Miranda, why the hell did he go back into the Maze tonight?

Sebastian De Velera is missing.

That last piece of the puzzle suddenly made Naevon's actions understandable.

"Sir?"

Kalison keyed off the file before he looked up. "Time for the meeting?" he asked.

"Yes sir," Janey nodded. He looked relieved to find the Commander calmer.

Kalison wandered down to the conference room and found that he felt slightly bemused and less upset. So far, Alyn Naevon had done nothing but help him. Nevertheless, it was time for a long talk.

Naevon finally showed up -- drenched, limping badly, and looking worried. Kalison looked up as Janey brought him to the door. Unfortunately, it was during the staff meeting, and there was no way he could take the reporter to task in front of everyone.

"Well?" Kalison demanded.

"Sorry. I thought I could learn something in the Maze," he said and sounded as worn as he looked. Amid all the other surprises, Kalison had forgotten that the reporter escaped from the hospital to go to Ember Tanton's Memorial. "At best, I talked to a couple people who admitted to views different from Miranda's."

"Did you learn anything about Sebastian?" Kalison asked.

Naevon looked back at him, eyes narrowing as he tried to cover personal emotions. Pain and worry passed there, evident to anyone who watched closely.

"Sebastian and Caden are definitely missing. Caden's followers are probably hiding the fact he's dead. The prevalent rumor is that Miranda ordered them both killed."

Some of the local people who worked in the Port and were in the room made impatient sounds, anxious to have this meeting done and go back to their own work. Fools. Even without knowing Naevon's secret, they should realize what a feat this boy had just accomplished. They only resented the time their Commander gave to the reporter talking about Rat things. It would be better to discuss the particulars of his trip in private. Obviously, Naevon had nothing pressing to tell

Kalison. He wouldn't keep any dangerous secrets.

"If you have any vid for me to see, leave it at my office on your way out."

"No vid. Didn't want them to think I was spying," Alyn said. "Just wanted some answers."

"I'll be in my office at the Government Building tomorrow morning, Naevon. I expect you to be there."

Naevon nodded agreement. Maybe there wasn't anything else for him to do, now. Kalison hoped he could convince the fool to leave world tomorrow. Chance alone had kept anyone else from learning Naevon's identity. What would happen if Jeffries took a sudden interest in the family? Only the man's single-minded incompetence kept him so focused on Miranda. How long could the Port Guard keep *Alonso De Velera* alive if he faced a determined Militia assassin?

Kalison watched Alyn limp away, his head bowed in weariness -- and loss? At least he finally understood why the reporter fought this war so hard.

CHAPTER THIRTY-ONE

Fiona leaned against the counter and stared at the people sleeping on the lobby floor again tonight. The groups huddled together, treasuring their few belongings. They reminded her too much of the refugees from her childhood. These people didn't understand what future they faced if they kept on this destructive path and Fiona no longer tried to tell them about the horrors they were creating. Inevitably, Citizens politely reminded Fiona this wasn't her own homeworld, as though that made all the difference in the way they acted.

Ember had understood. Ember had suggested they hold private meetings at the hotel with as diverse a group as they could manage and try to find some common ground on which they could work.

Fiona didn't want to see the madness of her homeworld take hold on Tempest. She had worked to prevent it, with other friends --

Most of them dead already.

"Let's go up to your room, Fiona," Bauer suggested. He laid a hand on her shoulder and gently massaged the tight muscles. "Your people will let us know if Alyn shows up tonight."

She hadn't told Bauer about the refugee camps of her youth: about fences, and inadequate housing, and fear of the people on the outside looking in with hatred.

Too much like the Maze. Except, for now, the Rats still worked in the city and earned a few credits of their own. They didn't survive solely on the charity of those who despised them and hold on to the faint hope that the Inner Worlds Council would give them a new world of their own.

That last hope would come later if nothing changed.

"Fiona? Come on. You're dead on your feet."

"Yeah. Sorry. I just wish Alyn would show up. He even has a message from Mars, from the IWC complex. It might be important."

She was only trying to make all this madness less monumental, and Bauer seemed to understand. Talin put his arm across her shoulders and pulled her into his comforting embrace. She laid her head on his shoulder and rested a moment. Too damn much emotional overload today. She didn't care what her staff thought, either.

"Pod coming in," Talin said with a frustrated sigh.

She automatically straightened her jacket as she turned around, as though she expected a new guest to register at the hotel. The pod slid to a slow stop, and the top popped open. Too many people stood in the way. Alyn was out of the vehicle and walking towards them before she saw who it was.

"About damn time," Bauer whispered. There was more than a hint of relief in the words.

The Captain caught Fiona's arm, escorting her out to meet her wayward guest. They negotiated the sprawled restless people far quicker than the reporter, who limped and walked with his head down as though he mistrusted his own feet.

"You are a fool, Naevon," Talin scolded as they neared. However, he took Alyn's cam case and slung it over his shoulder.

"I know. I know," the reporter answered. "I've already seen Kalison --"

"And lived through it?" Talin grinned. They maneuvered past two wrestling children, then around a group of adults who glared back at them.

"He was in a meeting. Said he would see me tomorrow. You want to have a go at me now? Or wait till after him?"

"I'll let the Commander take you apart first," Talin answered. He caught Alyn's arm when it looked as though he was going to sit down right there and led him the rest of the way to the counter. "You have a message from Mars, and it drove poor Fiona crazy all night."

"It has not!" she protested which won a grin from both men, lightening the somber mood. "You can take the chit and view it up in the room --"

"Let's just look at it here. I'm curious myself."

Fiona handed over the chit, still sealed in plastic straight from the computer. Naevon frowned as he pulled it open, then handed the chit back over to Fiona to drop in the comp on the counter. Apparently, the boy had no secrets.

"Hi Alyn," a pretty woman addressed him. A thin dark face filled the screen with bright gray eyes and a brighter smile. A familiar face, Fiona thought, though she didn't know anyone on Mars. "We just saw your first reports here at the IWC, and you have managed to stir up the competition yet again. Excellent work! The Tempest Ambassador is threatening to resign, by the way. And a subcommittee is in session and to consider sending in troops, although they weren't scheduled to meet for another two weeks. Thought you might like to know those little tidbits. Outside my usual realm of reporting, but I pick up a little information here and there."

Alyn made an amused sound. Fiona just watched the screen, still feeling as though she should know the woman.

"I noticed the fine vid work you are doing. The new camera suits you. I'm glad. Drop me a chit, if you get a chance. And let me know if there's any research you might need on this or any assignment. I like your style, Naevon. I hope to hear from you soon. You know where to find me. Bye!"

She blew him a kiss in parting. Fiona saw Alyn blush although he still looked amused.

"Who was that?" Fiona asked. "She seems familiar --"

"She's a well-known reporter," Alyn answered. "Her name is Marquesa."

"From Private Line!" Fiona exclaimed. "I watch her weekly reports whenever I can. She isn't normally on-screen though. If I closed my eyes, I probably would have recognized her voice."

"She gave me the new cam just before I came here," Alyn admitted. "My other cam is old, and she had a couple extras. Marquesa's really a very nice woman despite her reputation. I only had a chance to talk to her for a couple hours before I left Mars. I never expected to hear from her again."

"I'm impressed," Fiona admitted drawing the message chit back out. Alyn shrugged, but he put the chit in his pocket with a little smile.

"Let's go to your rooms, Fiona," Talin suggested. "We all need the rest. Alyn has a busy day tomorrow when he faces the Commander."

Fiona grinned as Talin carefully took Alyn's arm, as though he expected the reporter to slip away again. They almost reached the lifts without any trouble.

"Don't you dare walk away from me!" a strident voice called out.

Alyn and Fiona looked back, but Talin just scowled.

"Damn. I hoped we could make it before Janith spotted us," Talin admitted.

Alyn stopped and waited. Fiona felt more of an inclination to get into the lift and leave Janith ranting and raving, a bit of entertainment for the poor refugees. However, Alyn wasn't moving, and neither of the other two would leave him.

The woman marched through the ragged rows of people, oblivious to their stares. Janith tripped on one foot, snarled something at the woman, and kept going until she was within a few steps of the three.

"Janith, I'm damn tired of this harassment," Alyn told her. She stopped before him, shocked by the words. "I'm filing a complaint with Vidline about your unprofessional behavior. Take it up with them."

She looked at him with a stupid, empty expression as though it never occurred to her that anyone would attack back. A long moment passed before her mind kicked back in. Apparently, Janith wasn't used to anyone standing up to her. Fiona thought she would have enjoyed the show at any other time.

"I don't know what the hell your game is --"

"That's the trouble, Janith," Alyn replied. Fiona saw dangerous anger in his eyes that she'd never seen before. He took one step closer to Janith, meeting confrontation with confrontation. "This is just a *game* to you. You're not a reporter, you're a propagandist -- and a bad one, at that."

Fiona clamped her lips shut and cast a pleading look toward Talin. There were too many witnesses -- Citizen witnesses -- and she didn't want to see this turn into a riot. She was uncertain of Janith's popularity, but even a few irate people could turn this lobby into a new disaster.

Talin stared at Janith with a scowl akin to Alyn's angry glare. No help there.

"Janith, this isn't the time or place for this behavior," Fiona began.

"I don't have to listen to you. You're in enough trouble already. We know about you and your association with that Rat, Caden Paris. Did you know about their secret meetings, Captain Bauer?"

"Yes." He grinned at her glare. "And don't forget the association included Ember Tanton, Wintas, and Sonio."

"Who the hell told you, anyway?" Fiona demanded and startled the woman. Rage finally surged over her tired resignation and Fiona only barely worried about what the others in the lobby heard, which hardly mattered if Janith already knew. "Those meetings were not common knowledge!"

"We know more secrets than any of you imagine!" Janith gloated. "None of you are going to walk away from this one. I'll bring you down, Naevon. You aren't going to turn everyone against me!"

"You've managed that all on your own," Alyn replied. The fire in his dark eyes lessened as weariness came back. "Go away, Janith. I don't have to listen to you."

Janith made the mistake of grabbing at Alyn's arm. Naevon surprised her by easily evading her hand, and Talin pushed her backward a step. He was Alyn's guard, after all.

"Listen to me, Janith," Talin said. His voice was low, and he spoke slowly, which Fiona realized was his own show of rage. She had never seen that reaction before. "Unless you want me to run you in for disorderly conduct, you will back away right now. And I have the authority to lock you up, Vidline credentials or not!"

A quick succession of emotions passed over Janith's flushed face as she forgot her attack on Alyn. Captain Talin Bauer drew all her attention now. They were attracting the attention of some people who whispered and pointed, and

Fiona didn't want to be on show here and looked back at the lifts, wondering if she could draw the other three in that direction.

Fiona suddenly spotted a new reason to get Janith out of here. A man stood at the edge of the lifts, looking at her with wide-eyed worry of his own.

What the hell was Caden Paris doing here!

"Look, people," Fiona suddenly spoke. Her voice remained remarkably calm. She slid up beside Talin, effectively blocking Fiona's view of their more serious problem. "I want this arguing to stop now. If that's the only reason you came here, Janith, then I suggest you march right back out. Or go on to the bar. Tell you what. I'll even give you free drinks for the night. Just stop bothering me!"

Janith looked around at the three, her hazel eyes narrowing in a moment of uncertainty. Fiona pulled out her pocket comp and keyed the orders over to the bar, silently praying that the woman took the bait. *Quickly.* She could feel Caden standing at her back, a new apparition of disaster.

"Those are your choices, Janith," Talin told her. "Arrest for disorderly conduct or free drinks. Either way, you won't bother us again tonight. I'll admit, locking you up would brighten my night. So, give me *one more* excuse to call in a patrol to take you away."

She finally took the Captain seriously. With a little-concealed growl of anger, Janith spun and headed toward the bar. Fiona held her breath and didn't even dare glance at Caden. When Janith slipped through the doors and into the crowded restaurant area, Fiona sagged against Talin.

"What's wrong?" he demanded. His hands caught Fiona in a protective grasp.

"Sorry," she whispered. She gave her hand a little wave toward the lifts.

"Caden!" Alyn softly whispered. He looked around with a quick, nervous glance as they headed towards the lifts. "What the hell is he doing here? Everyone in the Maze thinks he's dead!"

"Is that where you went tonight?" Talin demanded.

"Yes. I needed answers," Alyn said, unconcerned with the Captain's response. "I thought I had them."

Caden waited, leaning against the wall with his head bowed. He looked as anonymous as he could manage in a nondescript raincoat, but if Alyn Naevon recognized the man, some Citizen very well could do the same. Although Caden Paris was a Rat outside Miranda's circle, he still was known.

Fiona realized he had entered the hotel through the service entrance like he would have during the meetings. With no one down at the room where they met, he must have come up here hoping to find her. Standing around in the empty lower halls would have drawn someone's attention. However, a little warning would have helped her nerves.

Fiona hit the key for a lift and then fretted at each second it took to arrive. Alyn moved closer to Caden, his hand touching the man's shoulder.

"What the hell is going on?" Alyn asked softly.

Caden looked up and gave the reporter a worried look. Too pale, his breathing shallow, his eyes glazed with pain. Fiona hit the key again wishing something would cooperate tonight. Too damn many shocks --

The doors slid open to an empty lift. Alyn took Caden's arm and steered him into the opening. Fiona and Bauer followed. Fiona keyed the door closed and locked the lift against stopping before her penthouse.

"Safe," she whispered. That was all the word she could manage.

"Did Sebastian reach you?" Alyn asked.

Strange question, Fiona thought, although Caden didn't look surprised. He nodded, still intent on Alyn and the reporter's question.

"Miranda came for me," Caden whispered. He leaned back against the wall, and the little movement was apparently painful. "She knew about my connection with Ember --"

"Janith knew about mine," Fiona offered. She carefully took Caden's arm. "Are you hurt?"

"Damn lucky to be alive." He pulled back the edge of the coat. The dark discoloration of a laser burn showed across his shirt and Fiona could see the outline of bandages beneath the cloth. "She came to kill me. Niel did the actual work, of course."

"And he didn't check to make certain he did it right?" Alyn asked.

"They had Sebastian to deal with," he replied. He bit his lip. "I was almost conscious when Sebastian told them that I was dead. I do remember something peculiar that Miranda said as they left. She said -- Sebastian was -- the most uncooperative martyr she ever knew."

"Martyr. Damn. Her actions begin to make sense," Alyn mumbled. "That's why she sent him into the city the other night. She wanted him to get killed."

"Planned it and wasn't counting on Citizen's to do the work, either. Niel tried to knife him, though he failed with that one too. I can't believe she hasn't found a better assassin."

"Sebastian didn't mention that when we found him," Alyn answered softly. "I wouldn't have sent him back into the Maze --"

"Sebastian decided his own actions," Caden answered. He reached out with a shaky hand and touched Alyn Naevon's arm. "She took him alive, and she hasn't killed him -- yet."

The lift slowed as they neared their destination. Alyn took Caden carefully in hand, though the reporter looked unsteady as well. Talin took Caden out of his hold as the lift opened. In a moment they were in the living room of Fiona's suite. Talin lowered Caden to the sofa and dropped the vidcam equipment out of the way. He looked stunned by this new wave of lunacy.

"Why did you come here?" Fiona asked. "It was damn dangerous, you know --"

"I know. I'm sorry Fiona. I had to see Al -- Alyn. I had news for him. My people watched Miranda after she took Sebastian. Tonight, she came out of the Hostel with Lauren and Niel Taress, and Sebastian. My people heard --"

He stopped, catching his breath and stilling his hands by catching them together in his lap. Something seriously wrong, Fiona suddenly realized. She saw Alyn lean closer, a hand dropped gently on the man's shoulder, like an old friend might, who knew that bad news was coming.

"She took explosives. Several bags full, from what my people guessed. And she took Sebastian because --"

"Martyr," Alyn whispered. He looked shaken by the information. "Where did they go, Caden?"

"We followed them into the city but didn't dare get too close. They went within a block of the Government Building before they disappeared. We never had a chance to take her without the risk of Miranda setting off the explosives and taking out everything within reach. I sent my two people back to the Maze to try and talk sense into some of the people there, and I came straight here, to the only people I can trust outside the Maze. We must stop her."

It looked as though he had spent the last of his energy on those words, but they gave Alyn new strength.

"Bauer, call Kalison. Tell him to quietly evacuate the building," Alyn ordered. Really ordered, and Talin only nodded agreement as he headed toward the comp. "Tell him to do it very carefully. If Miranda suspects anything is wrong, she'll trigger the explosion early. Make certain he understands how delicate this situation is."

"I will."

"Fiona, can you help Caden?" Alyn asked. His dark eyes darted to the man on the sofa. "Don't let him back out."

"I'm -- not going," Caden whispered.

"Good. We'll talk later."

The reporter darted toward the door. Talin was on the comp, clear across the room. Fiona tried to reach him, but the lift was still waiting, the doors open. He threw himself in, keying the door closed.

"Damn! Alyn Naevon!" she shouted uselessly.

Gone. Headed straight for trouble --

And his cam still sat by the sofa.

CHAPTER THIRTY-TWO

A lyn heard the echo of Fiona's angry yell as he rushed out of the penthouse. He was honestly sorry that he'd annoyed her again and by now, Captain Bauer probably intended to shoot him on sight.

He would have to leave Tempest soon. Miranda's actions and his reactions meant he couldn't hide his secrets much longer. When his friends learned ... well, he might not really need Miranda's help to turn them against him. He was doing a damn good job on his own.

The lift stopped at the lobby. Fiona could call down at any moment and have security detain him, but he trusted that Talin would consider the message to get the Government Building cleared more crucial, giving him a few more seconds. Alyn hurried across the lobby, trying not to attract more attention. When he had entered this building a few minutes ago, every step felt like an ache through his entire body. Now he darted through the crowd, a surge of panic impelling him to forget his former weakness.

Sebastian had still been alive when they left the Maze. That was probably a precaution Miranda had to take. If, for some reason, her plan to set the explosives tonight didn't work, having Sebastian already dead would be a waste. Alyn had one chance to rescue him.

Tonight's storm poured a new torrent of water into the streets and wide, muddy paths washed even through the heart of the City. As Alyn stepped out into the open air, he slowed to keep his footing. He could hear the rush of water filling drainpipes and overflowing into the walkways. He couldn't see well and rushing out into knee-deep currents wouldn't help him save his brother.

"You're either damn brave, or stupid, to come out here again."

Alyn spun, panicked by the voice to his right. He backed up two steps. It was stupid to come out without a weapon of any sort --

Then the light from the lobby window fell across the two men. Port Guards.

"There's trouble -- the Government Building," Alyn told them. "Come with me!"

They stared at Naevon. Alyn didn't dare waste the time trying to convince them of the danger. Then Bauer slid out of the building and caught Alyn by the arm.

"You take off like that one more time --" he growled, caught his breath, and continued, "-- you two come with us! We have real trouble! Damn -- no time to call in an aircar, and it could take longer to get a functioning pod this far! Naevon, you don't have to go --"

"I do," he answered. There was no time to explain, and this might not be the best situation for a confession.

Bauer didn't argue. They had no time. The difficulty of the water-washed terrain saved him from explanations about his actions as they had trouble keeping to their feet in the dark, narrow passages. He didn't slow for streams of water or Port Guard companions. Alyn took them along the paths that Rats knew best, the shortest way he knew to reach the Government Building. He stopped in the shadows across the street; a Rat move, afraid to be seen before that symbol of Citizen power. A couple clerks exited the front of the building, disappearing into the rainy night. He thought he heard curses. The pods were not working, and they probably didn't appreciate having to walk out in the weather on a night like this.

"How -- hell get in?" Bauer demanded. The Captain gasped for breath as he spoke. His companions just gasped. "They couldn't -- front door."

"Don't know! Damn!"

Alyn finally crossed the street, nearly going down twice in the rush of water. When he started around the side of the building the others followed as though he knew what he was doing. He'd never even been back here before and found the service entrance -- tightly sealed and no apparent way in -- and an aircar pad surrounded by a waist-high brick wall. In the dark, Alyn couldn't guess the size of the lot. Even the occasional flashes of lightning couldn't pierce the pouring rain and dark night.

Bauer and the guards stayed with Alyn as he inched his way forward. Alyn wished Kalison would show up. He looked up into the sky, but the dark clouds gave no sign of help. Time to slow down and think about this mess. How would Miranda enter a building where no Citizen could even walk in, unchallenged?

He spotted movement out on the nearly empty aircar pad. He caught the Captain by the arm and eased him down beside the protection of the wall. The other two mimicked the movement without orders.

"Two people," Alyn whispered leaning within centimeters

of the Captain so Bauer could hear. "That's probably Niel and Lauren."

"We can take them down," Bauer said. He pulled his laser and checked the setting.

"Too dangerous. Remember, Miranda has explosives in there. If they give any warning, she might blow everything to hell."

One of the two guards made a slight sound of worry, finally learning the nature of tonight's trouble. If it had been Alyn's choice, he would have sent the two away. He didn't want to sacrifice anyone to Miranda.

"If she set the explosives, she'd be caught there too. She'd kill herself?" Bauer asked.

"Hell, yes. She'd rather go up in glory -- and take as many others with her as possible -- rather than face a trial. Our best hope is to get close enough to grab those two, but they might have comm equipment linking them with Miranda."

"Rats with that kind of equipment?" a guard whispered.

"They have explosives. They have laser weapons. Smuggling in a commlink or two isn't beyond their capabilities," Alyn pointed out. All three men nodded, and Alyn finally began to feel as though they were grasping the entire situation.

"Crawl along the wall," Bauer ordered. "They can't see in the shadow. I hope the evacuation is going well and they don't notice that there's no one in the rooms this side of the building. Alyn --"

"I am going," he replied.

Bauer nodded.

The cement walkway felt rough beneath his hands. Alyn felt every bruise and battered bone as he crawled those few meters. He even felt the cold and the wet weighing him down until he thought of Sebastian. Perhaps she always planned to kill him, but Alyn still believed his return pushed Miranda to act now as payment to Sebastian for annoying her and pain for Alonso to show she ruled.

He crawled faster, nearly getting ahead of Bauer until the captain grabbed his arm and held him back. Alyn feared they would have to climb over the wall and risk detection, but Bauer must have known there was an opening. He led them straight to the far corner and then continued across the lot, still crawling and silent.

The last two aircars left behind were not close enough to give them any real cover. They had to depend on the darkness and the storm and the fact that the two didn't look for trouble.

Soon he could hear their voices over the pounding rain. Lauren and her brother were not particularly quiet. Too self-assured that they couldn't fail -- too much like Miranda.

"Damn," Niel growled. "I wish she would hurry! It's cold out here! I want back to the Hostel. That bastard brother of hers was heavier than he looks."

"I wish I could watch sweet Sebastian while she lays out the explosives all around him," Lauren said. Yes, far too much like Miranda.

Alyn's group edged a little closer, circling in from the left. He wanted to reach up and grab that bitch but restrained himself, knowing Sebastian depended on him. The boy was still alive if Lauren was right about what Miranda was doing. It sounded perverse enough.

Bauer caught his arm again, stilling his movement. He made a sign to his Port Guard companions. Those two drew their laser pistols with slow, quiet movements. When they were ready, both nodded. Bauer looked back at Alyn with a slight shake of his head; he didn't want Alyn to get killed in a battle. He was still taking his duty as protector too seriously.

Maybe that was wise, at this point. Alyn could let these three, with their weapons, handle Lauren and Niel. He still had

Sebastian to rescue. He felt strangely calm as he nodded to Bauer. Unnaturally so, though it did allow him to think more clearly. Alyn realized now that he couldn't just rush in after Miranda. The entire De Velera family would die in the explosion and probably take many more with them.

Bauer and his men stood and charged the last four meters toward the enemy. Alyn crawled closer, but the dark night obscured most of the action. Then he found one Guard down, a knife in his shoulder. The man softly cursed a whisper in the rain. He could hardly hear the muffled exclamations of anger and surprise. Alyn moved to help --

Lauren snaked her way out of Bauer's hold, spun, and ran. Bauer looked at Alyn, the man Kalison ordered him to guard.

"Get her!" Alyn ordered. "Don't let her get away! She might still warn Miranda!"

Bauer took off after Lauren. Alyn helped the other guard holding down Niel. Together, they got restraints around his wrists and ankles and a gag in his mouth. So, for a moment more he was safe from them giving away his secret.

He found no sign of Miranda or Sebastian, nor any indication of how they got inside the building. None of the permaglass windows opened on this side of the building. No other doors --

Alyn's foot slipped on the slick surface of the pad, and he sprawled. When his hands touched rough metal rather than concrete, he knew how Miranda had entered the building and why Lauren and Niel had been standing out here in the lot. She had gone in through the drainage system, and he'd found the cover to the circular entrance, where it had been pulled open. He found the opening with a heart-stopping fear as he nearly tumbled in. Alyn's hands quickly located the ladder leading downward. Water rushed over the edge cascading towards a larger current roaring below.

Alyn looked back at the two Port Guards. Bauer wasn't back yet, and the injured man couldn't climb down this ladder. The other needed to stay and guard Niel and help Bauer if he needed it.

They might try to stop him from going on alone. So Alyn silently slipped over the edge of the opening and down into the dark tunnel. No one called out in protest. Alyn escaped, unseen.

Bauer wasn't going to be happy. Again.

CHAPTER THIRTY-THREE

The ladder's thin metal steps proved slick and treacherous, and Alyn slid for a few steps before he caught himself again. Alyn knew he had to move slowly, holding tight with nearly numb fingers and fighting his own urge to hurry to danger and away from his friends who would try to stop him. He was more than a meter into the hole before he heard a startled cry from above. No one seemed to follow, though. It might take them awhile to locate where he'd gone.

His actions were probably foolish, thinking he could handle Miranda all by himself, but he owed Sebastian at least this much of a chance. Bringing others increased the probability of detection and of his sister reacting ... badly. He hoped Bauer would realize the problem and not try to follow.

When he reached the bottom of the ladder, Alyn found the rushing water was well over his knees, making it barely possible to move upstream against the current that flowed past the ladder and on to the lagoons and swamps far out of town. Small blue cubes embedded in the ceiling gave dim illumination along the wide tunnel that headed directly towards the Government

Building. Surely, it wasn't this easy to get into the most heavily guarded complex on Tempest! If there hadn't been the flood, this might be a dry, easy walk.

He struggled against the current and ignored his own pains and weakness, passing two smaller pipes that drained into this one. The current hardly eased but a few steps further he found another ladder leading upwards to the basement of the building. He grabbed at it and levered himself out of the stream, refusing to feel the cold or the fear.

Here he learned it wouldn't be easy to get into the building. Both motion and sound detectors lined the wall by the second ladder, but they were useless in this storm as the water rushed over their sensors. That explained why Miranda chose such a lousy night for her work. Usually, she wouldn't inconvenience herself.

There should have been one more obstacle, a palm-locked door at the top of the ladder. It had already succumbed to a blast that tore half the wall away and made the ladder feel loose as Alyn started to climb. He also found a security cam with some sort of box over the lens. The top was open to let the water run through and probably gave the impression of nothing wrong.

Alyn started to pull the box away and then stopped. It was probably a Rat reaction, but he didn't trust guards who might rush in looking for trouble. He wanted to get Sebastian clear, and he would leave the rest of the mess for the others. Miranda was still inside. He had time.

Alyn wondered who gave that vital secret of how to get in here to Miranda De Velera. They had to realize the consequences. What Citizen offered this treason and why? Or was it some outsider, the same person who sold explosives to the Rats because there was profit in a war, so long as they didn't have to live with it.

Alyn Naevon might want to learn those answers and report on them ... after Alonso De Velera saved his brother.

As Alyn started to pull himself into the basement, he heard the unmistakable sound of Miranda's shrill laughter. He scrambled upward and found himself in an area of stark gray walls lacking decoration, a vaulted ceiling evenly lit with blue cubes, and a maze of reinforced arches that obviously helped support the tall building above. There wasn't anything stored down here, and water ran in little rivulets across the floor and down the small openings, the area built for drainage from the outer edges of the large building, funneled in here and out of the way. This place was an excellent target for mayhem.

Unfortunately, the plethora of gray arches made it impossible to spot Miranda and Sebastian. Alyn darted to the nearest column and stopped with his back against a wall, his breath coming in short, nervous gasps. He'd never liked clandestine work. He hadn't ever intended to be a rebel like his father.

Miranda laughed again followed by a snarl of words he couldn't understand. The sounds bounced and echoed around the cavernous area, disrupting any sense of direction.

A trail of damp footsteps led away from a rivulet and off toward the right. Alyn carefully slipped off his shoes and headed in that direction. As he put a few archways between him and the opening, he began to hear a little clearer.

When Alyn spotted a flicker of movement at the next intersection, he quickly slid into the nearest crevice. There he found something troubling. Attached to this arch was a gray lump of putty, little larger than his hand. Stuck in the middle of the mass were a black radio needle, yellow wire, and an ominously blinking red diode.

Explosive. His hand reached out before he wisely hesitated. Anything might set the charge off or possibly alert Miranda in some other way. A glance to the right and left showed more of the gray lumps. He might have missed a few in his rush to get to Sebastian. Caden had mentioned several bags of explosives. With a little shiver, Alyn wondered how many of these traps were hidden around him. How many could he hope to defuse even if he thought the action safe?

He hoped Kalison got the building cleared.

Alyn stepped around the edge of the arch and started towards the moving shadows and whispery sounds.

He found Miranda first. She sat on the floor, carefully putting rods and wires in more lumps of gray clay. Beside her sat a hand-sized black device with a glowing blue screen and a couple buttons. The trigger, he suspected. Beside it was a silver laser pistol, the trigger glowing red and showing the weapon was primed and ready to fire.

She looked up and grinned. Alyn's heart pounded with fear until he realized she wasn't looking at him.

"I'll finish here in a couple minutes, Sebastian," she stated happily. "Well, at least neither of us have to play games anymore, right?"

"I don't have to play stupid, and you don't have to play sweet."

The bitterness in Sebastian's voice surprised Alyn. He didn't want to see a change in the one member of the family who never committed any crime.

"You really shouldn't provoke me, little brother," Miranda said, her hand caressing a lump of the gray clay.

"Oh, really?" Sebastian mocked. "Why the hell not? What have I got to lose?"

Alyn wished his brother calm, especially when Miranda scowled. With her attention focused on Sebastian, Alyn dared work his way to the next set of arches. From here he could finally see Sebastian. The youngest De Velera sat against a damp archway wall, his hands tied behind his back. The boy's light brown hair lay in wet snarled strands covering most of his face and Alyn couldn't see the expression, but Miranda didn't look pleased. She made a little sound of anger and laid her hand on the laser beside her.

Damn!

Then she grinned and drew her hand back.

"No, no. A laser wound would be too noticeable, wouldn't it? People must believe you died down here, setting these wonderful little bombs. Won't everyone, Rat and Citizen, be shocked to learn how you lied to them all these years?"

"Not everyone is that gullible, Miranda."

"No, not everyone. However, there will be enough of them to create the chaos I want."

"Alonso will never believe it."

"Do you think I give a damn what Alonso believes? And I'm going to make certain no one else cares what he says, either. After this explosion word is going to get out of who he really is. I doubt he'll make it out of the city alive."

Those words didn't surprise Alyn. He had wondered what was taking her so long to make the announcement. It would be wonderfully dramatic coming right after the bombing.

"And they can't find you tied like that, can they?" Miranda continued. "I do want the show to look good."

Miranda carefully laid aside the latest lump of explosive and pulled a small belt knife. She crawled forward, still smiling. The movement looked predatory and inhuman, even when Miranda rose back to her knees. She gently leaned Sebastian forward and quickly sliced through the ropes that bound him. Sebastian made a little sound of pain as his arms fell forward. Alyn could see blood on one wrist, and swollen fingers.

Alyn held his breath, mistrusting her and wondering if he could move fast enough to save his brother. Not yet, not yet.

Miranda had more of her explosives to plant.

"There, is that better?" she asked. Her fingers brushed at Sebastian's hair, and Sebastian pulled away with a curse, almost falling. "That's not very polite, you know. And that's always been your problem."

"Sorry I never bowed to you."

Alyn watched her face redden with anger. Then she blinked and smiled again and plunged the knife into Sebastian's right thigh and then the left ankle, cutting downward with two quick sweeps. Sebastian cried out, and Alyn moved -- and stopped again when Miranda slid back and grabbed her pistol.

"Can't have you running around while I do my work, can we?" she asked.

Sebastian made a soft sound, and his arms moved, but he hadn't the control yet to even reach his wounded legs. Instead, he fell to the side.

Miranda laughed and shoved the pistol into her belt and the knife into her pocket. She moved cautiously as she gathered up a few of her little bombs. That reaction told Alyn all he needed to know about the explosives and his chances of defusing them. She almost left what must be the trigger behind but grabbed it up at the last moment with another little laugh. That would have been far too easy.

Then she headed out of sight around the ubiquitous arches.

Alyn didn't waste time. He slid forward, as silent and quick as he could manage. Alyn didn't know how long it would take Miranda to place those six small lumps of destruction. He wasn't even sure if she was alone down here. Or one of his own companions could come in through the tunnel at any moment, creating more problems, though that might distract her. He could wish for that kind of help right now.

Alyn startled Sebastian who gave a single yelp and then looked at him with shock bordering between hope and dismay.

No time to be gentle. Alyn only noted that the cuts in Sebastian's legs seemed long but relatively shallow. Neither wound bled heavily. The trouble with his brother's arms proved more serious. Niel had carried him in, and that was the only way Alyn was going to get Sebastian back out.

He wished Miranda had left the laser or the remote. Preferably the laser because with one shot all this madness would finally be over. Alyn knew he could do it this time, too. He felt no sentiment towards the woman who wanted to destroy the world around her. He might not even feel any guilt.

Neither Miranda nor a weapon was in sight just now. Perhaps saving lives was a better choice. Alyn caught Sebastian under the arms and lifted him as he concentrated on saving them both.

It wasn't far back to the drainage tunnel, and Sebastian moved in quick limping steps with his arm over Alyn's shoulder. Unfortunately, they had no idea where Miranda might be working. Alyn didn't dare rush forward and chance stumbling across her. He moved as quickly as he could while taking cover from archway to archway --

He heard Miranda's shout of anger from behind them. She knew Sebastian was gone even if she couldn't guess how he escaped.

"Go," Sebastian whispered. "She doesn't have to know you are here."

"No."

Sebastian started to fight and changed his mind, helping as much as he could as Alyn dragged him toward the tunnel. The roar of the floodwaters and the occasional pounding of thunder made it impossible to hear more than a few feet away which meant he couldn't hear Miranda now. She must, Alyn knew, realize there was only one way out of this place. He had to get there before she reached them.

Miranda raced around an arch, running in rage and not considering what she would do if she caught up with Sebastian.

It was the best chance she could give them.

Alyn dropped Sebastian and swung. His blow caught her on the left cheek and staggered Miranda backward though she didn't go down. Her eyes went hard, and her hand went for that laser as Alyn threw himself at her, caught her arm, and forced it away from the weapon. She fought harder, her left hand getting free of his grasp and he couldn't catch it again.

He felt a sudden surge of fire in his side and remembered -- too late -- that other weapon she carried. *Knifed.* He didn't dare let the wound stop him, and he tried one daring move, letting go of her arms and reaching for the laser pistol --

But she moved quicker, slapping at his hand and sending the weapon clattering across the floor. Miranda brought the knife around and slashed down his arm. Frightened, she fought with the ferocity of something wild, finally driving him back a step. He looked for the weapons in one quick sweep --

Then back at Miranda. Her sudden smile was the most frightening sight he'd ever seen. Miranda pulled something from her pocket and held the device out of his reach, a small plastic square with a glowing blue screen. The trigger.

That, finally, held him.

"Well, this is even better, isn't it?" She gasped, her hand going to her bleeding cheek. He hardly remembered hitting her and regretted that he hadn't gone straight for her throat, instead. "You and Sebastian found in the ruins --"

"I have no intention of staying. And Sebastian is coming with me."

She frowned. Alyn took a step closer to the laser and kicked; it sailed out across the floor, and down the tunnel entrance, splashing as it hit the water.

"Now how are you going to keep us here?"

She snarled, and then her face cleared his own words came back to haunt him as she lifted the trigger again.

Hell yes, she'd rather go up in glory -- and take as many with her as possible -- rather than face a trial.

He leapt, and they collided. The force of his attack sent her flying backward against an arched wall and her head hit with a dull thump. Miranda's thin face went slack as she slid to the floor, unconscious.

He grabbed the remote out of her limp hand, but it was too late; numbers changed, time slipping away, second-by-second. Less than five minutes now. Maybe she only hit the button in reflex at the end, but it didn't matter. She won.

Alyn shoved the remote in his pocket. Maybe Kalison could still do something.

"We have to go," he told his brother.

"Triggered," Sebastian said and nodded. He tried to sit up and failed. "Damn, Alonso. I can't move --"

"You are going out with me," Alyn replied. "Why the hell do you even think I'm here?"

Sebastian looked at him with a touch of surprise and stopped arguing. Alyn caught his brother under the arms and dragged Sebastian to the edge of the tunnel leaving an ugly blood-red trail behind where their blood mingled. The water below looked higher, and the roar made it impossible to hear anything else. He quickly anchored his own legs on the ladder and then pulled Sebastian across his shoulders in a precarious balance. He had trouble holding on to the rungs with the added mass of legs, arms, and head, but Sebastian did his best to hold on.

Then, as he started down. Alyn looked back at Miranda, lying there, unconscious and helpless.

"Damn, damn, damn!" he mumbled, then shouted, "I can't carry you both! Miranda! Get up!"

She moved, making a slight sound of protest.

And time sped away, resting in his pocket. He felt Sebastian tremble again and grab feebly at his arm. Time to go.

Climbing down the rungs proved difficult with Sebastian's unwieldy weight pulling him off balance. Alyn did his best to ignore the fiery pain of the knife wound in his own side and hadn't even dared to look at it. There was damned little time left for anything but running.

When he reached the motion detectors and the cams, Alyn took his feet from the rungs and slid down into the water. That was far quicker than climbing down, and he knew the distance wasn't dangerous. The water rushed around him as Sebastian moved to try and get his footing, though Alyn held him up. At least he didn't have to fight the current this time, though his balance felt precarious. A dozen steps into the tunnel, and Alyn went down on his knees with a wrenching fall. He barely caught his brother before he slid off in the watery maelstrom. Sebastian lifted his head, which had momentarily slipped into the stream, and coughed as he grabbed his brother's arm.

"Thanks. I'm awake now," Sebastian mumbled in a halfhearted joke. "Let's go."

"Not far to go."

Time.

Alyn fought his way forward, wondering if he really hoped to hear Miranda coming down the ladder behind them. The thought of her at his back wasn't reassuring. It did get him to move more quickly though. His hand found the next ladder before he saw it and pushed Sebastian ahead of him, hoping his brother could pull himself out of the tunnel. Climbing upward proved far harder than sliding down the last one.

Time.

"Yes, sir! Someone is coming up!" a familiar voice said.

"Bauer!" he shouted. Tried to shout. The sound came out

in a hoarse croak. "Help me get him up."

He could see the dark opening above, and the movement of other people as hands reached to help. He took the next four rungs in swift succession as someone caught Sebastian, lifting him upward with a quickness that startled Alyn.

"She set -- set the timer. I have the remote," Alyn gasped. He came over the edge of the opening with Kalison's help. Good to see he had gotten here, though it might be too late to help. "Don't know if you can do anything. Need to get back in - -"

Kalison took the device from his hand, the dull glow from the LCD reflecting in his face. The Commander blinked once.

"Get the hell back!" he shouted.

Alyn looked at the opening, wondering how long that journey had taken for him and Sebastian. Wondering if he had time -- if Miranda was only a few steps behind them --

"Grab him!" Sebastian shouted. "Don't let him go back after her!"

"Naevon, you fool!" Bauer bellowed. He grabbed Alyn by the arm, energetically pulling him away from the opening though they both slid and stumbled on the rain-slick cement. "There's barely twenty seconds left!"

He didn't want Bauer caught here on his account. Someone else carried Sebastian, moving ahead of him. He kept his brother in sight and tried very hard to banish the face of his sister from his mind.

He had thought maybe Miranda had done something wrong, that it wasn't going to explode -- and then he heard a muffled roar, like an ancient, mythical dragon of Earth, awakening from a long sleep. The ground swayed, and he went down to his knees along with everyone else.

By the time he looked back over his shoulder, the lower floors of the building were already sliding into the ground, sending up a puff of gray dust, like a cloud touching the ground. Higher walls cracked, and windows shattered before they, too, began moving downward. The building moaned and growled in protest while the rest of the world stood silent witness to its unnatural destruction.

Another explosion shook the night. Alyn threw an arm over his face as several large pieces of debris landed around them. Something struck his left leg, numbing it from knee to ankle, and another hit the side of his head with a dull thump that made his ears ring. When he looked up again, flames rushed through the crumbling ruin, bright in the dark rainy night. Alarms rang all around them.

The ground trembled, and cracks appeared in the cement before the entire pad around the tunnel entrance collapsed, leaving a dark empty hole several meters across. They had barely made it out of range.

Miranda wasn't coming out.

"Damn, I'm sorry," he whispered. Kalison, who had crawled to his side, looked surprised. "I tried. I honestly tried. I found some explosives, but I didn't know what to do -- didn't dare touch them for fear of setting it all off --"

Kalison placed a hand on his shoulder, holding him steady. The man looked grim but not angry.

"You and Caden saved more than two hundred lives tonight, Naevon," Kalison offered softly. "The two of you did the best anyone could under these circumstances. Your idea to quietly evacuate the place was brilliant. All we lost tonight was an empty building and some equipment. We even had time to tap the comps and get most of the files out! If you and Caden hadn't thought so quickly, we would have lost far more than that empty shell. And by the way, Governor Bramis Tanton is very grateful. She was working late tonight."

Alyn looked back at the fire-wrecked ruin of the building,

remembering the office where she graced him with an interview. He felt suddenly ill.

"Naevon?" Bauer called to him.

He tried to answer, but he wasn't really there any longer.

CHAPTER THIRTY-FOUR

Detainment in the sterile, white room of the hospital was an entirely new experience for Alyn. He didn't complain for the first two days. Every time he awoke, he hurt too much to care where they held him. However, by the third day, the constant pains began easing to a dull, tolerable ache and his mind began to sort through the events of the last few days. He was lucky, all things considered, to have any medical aide considering how much he'd annoyed people. At least over the previous three days, no one had tried to kill him. He decided, still half in a haze of drugs and pain, that maybe he shouldn't fuss too much over his present quarters.

Besides, Sebastian often sat in the room with him. His younger brother's wounds proved less severe compared to the frequent misuse Alyn had suffered since his arrival on Tempest. The meds and their assistants showed mistrust, if not dislike, for Sebastian De Velera. Alyn, when he finally noticed, felt a surge of anger though he hadn't the strength to complain. However, it was Sebastian's continued patience that finally won most of them over. The others just stopped coming back to the room.

Sebastian remained, and Alyn gradually became aware that his presence was his brother's own choice. He wanted to complain again but learned from Sebastian that they were both safest here. This floor remained under heavy security for the safety of Sebastian, Caden, and Alyn Naevon.

Caden left the hospital on the morning of the third day. By that afternoon, Alyn began to feel extremely restless. They wouldn't let him watch the news, and he knew essential stories slipped by every hour he remained here. Alyn suspected Kalison's involvement in the injunction: probably punishment for having driven the man crazy during his few short days on the street. The meds claimed it was because he had suffered a blow to the head at the explosion and should only rest.

However, as the drugs wore off, Alyn became anxious to know what was going on. Even Sebastian obeyed the injunction and refrained from telling his brother anything important. He did assure Alyn that all was going very well. That only intrigued him more.

At sunset of the fifth day of confinement, when the guests arrived, Alyn knew something monumental must be happening out there. Commander Kalison entered the small room first. He carried a large box and looked very pleased. Alyn hadn't seen that look before. Captain Bauer, Fiona Salend, and Governor Tanton followed him through the door. Bramis still wore black, but there was a lighter movement to her step and the whisper of pleasure in her eyes. Fiona and Talin held hands and grinned in greeting.

"What's going on?" Alyn demanded. He anxiously propped the bed up into a sitting position, ignoring the protest in his back and leg.

"Yes, it's good to see you too, Naevon." Bauer grinned at his discomfort. "Why we've been fine, thank you."

He blushed. Bramis Tanton laughed aloud and patted his

arm. Then the woman crossed to the window and held out her hand to Sebastian. He looked at her, stunned by the gesture.

"I'm Governor Tanton," she introduced herself, as though Sebastian didn't recognize her. "You must be Sebastian De Velera."

"Yes. Yes, I am," Sebastian finally answered. He stood and took her hand and held it for a moment.

"I've heard nothing but good about you in the Maze. They are anxious to get you back. And Caden said to tell you that he would really like his wall finished. That's gorgeous work, though Earth isn't nearly as pretty as you picture her."

Sebastian grinned, then tilted his head as he released her hand.

"You've visited Earth?" he asked.

"Damn, Sebastian -- pay attention!" Alyn mused. "She just said she *visited the Maze*!"

Sebastian went wide-eyed, and the woman laughed.

"Yes, to both," she said. "I've visited Earth three times. And I went to the Maze this morning. Caden Paris invited Commander Kalison and me to tour the area. We looked for a spot to build the new school."

"New school?" Sebastian repeated.

"Bramis is putting up the money from her own funds," Kalison explained.

Sebastian looked at his brother as though he expected Alyn to explain this oddity to him. The Commander began pulling white plastic chairs closer to the bed. Alyn felt very self-conscious as the group settled around him. Governor Tanton smiled and patted Alyn on the arm as she came back to the bed, Sebastian beside her.

"By using my private funds, we don't have to go through the Council," Bramis explained. She and Sebastian sat side-by-side. Luckily, there were no other locals here because someone on one side or another would have had a fit. "Though, quite honestly, the Council and the citizens as a whole are far more cooperative right now than ever before."

"Caden also sent you these, Sebastian." Kalison handed the box across the bed, and Sebastian took it carefully into his hands. "He said you must be going crazy without them."

Sebastian opened the top and grinned with delight.

"Art supplies, obviously," Alyn said.

"Right," Sebastian agreed. His hand rifled through the contents. Then, with what looked like a force of willpower, he placed the box on the floor beside him.

"Now, are you people going to tell me what happened out there? I noticed the streets remained quiet the last two nights. And we're close enough to the ruins that I heard heavy equipment working at the site."

"You really are a good reporter," Fiona said.

"Just too damn bored," he answered with a shrug. The movement sent an ache through his neck, but he ignored the pain. The last thing he wanted was for the others to leave because they thought he wasn't up to the visit.

"The time went quicker for the rest of us," Kalison told him. "First, we finally found Miranda De Velera's body yesterday."

Sebastian bit his lip. Alyn touched his brother's arm, offering what little comfort he dared. Governor Tanton took Sebastian's hand in hers.

"It's all right, Sebastian," she offered. "Whatever else she became, she was your sister first."

"That was a long time ago. Miranda hated me and all I loved. She severed our family ties with the blood of others. I never followed her. I'm not mourning for Miranda's death. I'm only sorry it took so long to bring her down."

Bramis nodded and released his hand and looked at Alyn as

though she expected some reaction to the news from him. Alyn felt nothing more than a wave of relief knowing the trouble was over. He couldn't feel sorry since Miranda chose her path and the consequences. This death or a public, and probably bloody, trial was all she had left in the end. It was easier on all of them this way.

"She went back into the building, didn't she?" Alyn finally asked. Kalison nodded. "Then her death was her own choice. She knew the place was about to blow."

"You tried to go back in for her," Bauer reminded him.

"A moment of madness. I didn't want Miranda's blood on my hands if I could save her. However, even without knowing she purposely went back in, I had managed to reconcile myself with the death."

"The situation in the Maze is already better. Caden Paris is doing an admirable job of calming the people and helping them adjust to the news," Fiona offered. She grinned with a little self-conscious embarrassment. "We always knew he would do well if given a chance."

"A lot of people in the Maze thought so, too," Sebastian added. "We just couldn't get Miranda out without losing far too many of our own people. I offered Caden what little help I could, but Miranda never trusted me with anything significant. And she had that damn army of fanatics following her. I sometimes feared that if she died, one of them might take over. Most of them have even less sense than Miranda."

"We have many of her followers in our hands now," Kalison explained. He leaned back in his chair, straightening his tan uniform jacket. "We're not certain what we'll do with them yet. Caden said I should tell you that we have Lauren Taress as well."

Sebastian blushed and bowed his head in embarrassment.

"Someone close to you?" Bauer asked.

"No," he answered emphatically. "Lauren was the person Miranda sent to keep me busy and out of her hair. Lauren hated art, and I wasn't very fond of her. I did worry about going back home with her loose, though."

"All right, Alyn. Are you ready for the final rundown on this situation?" Kalison asked.

"Is my vidcam around?"

"I'll give all the facts to you, and a few more details, later in an official interview. Right now, I thought you might just want to hear the situation."

"Fine. I'm sure Janith has filed the report already, anyway. She's probably thrilled that I'm not there to usurp her work again."

"Janith isn't pleased at all right now," Bramis answered. She grinned, though there was an edge of anger in the look. "Kalison, would you like to tell him all the particulars?"

"The first key we found in this mess was Wintas," Kalison explained. "He didn't work for the Education Department, like the people in Fiona's group supposed. He had worked there for a short time, but Nedra dismissed him. Wintas went to work for Jeffries right afterward, and Jeffries managed to fix the comp records."

"Oh." Alyn nodded. Then he felt a sudden surge of surprise. "Then he was a spy."

"Yes. From what we've put together, Sonio saw him report to a member of the Militia. Sonio told Ember about what he saw, but both were uncertain if it was really a sign of trouble. After all, people talk to the Militia every day. They didn't want to risk trouble within the group at such a precarious time. That got them killed. Jeffries had a tap on Sonio's comp -- but we learned that later. First, we grabbed Wintas, and he admitted to working for Jeffries. We hadn't had time to act on it before the explosion, but afterward, we confiscated everything in his home and office. He kept extensive records. Jeffries was the one supplying arms and explosives to the Rats."

"What!" Sebastian exclaimed. "Why? He hates us!"

"Very much so."

"He never gave the Rats enough to win," Alyn answered. He understood the ploy. "Only enough to make trouble and draw the hatred of everyone else. Jeffries wanted the war. The man's only goal was to destroy the Rat community."

"That's the consequence he wanted, yes," Kalison said. "He also made a tidy profit on the deals. Many of the Citizens are doing considerable soul-searching tonight. Knowing that one of their own leaders tricked them into this war brought most to their senses. There's talk about starting changes they've needed for a long time."

"And besides, they see their world trembling on an abyss," Bramis added. "They don't want to go down for the sake of pride. We will have substantial new legislation before we forget these last few days."

"How did Jeffries sell us the weapons and explosives?" Sebastian asked. "No Rat trusted him, and I can't see how he could offer any of them weapons, especially to Miranda."

"He brought the supplies in with Militia invoices, most under his own signature," Kalison explained. "When we caught him, Jeffries decided to take everyone down with him. Maybe he thought we would go easier on him if there were other people to prosecute. He was wrong, of course. Jeffries organized a committee as a balance to Fiona's group. Niel Taress regularly attended, as did a few middle-management officials from several government departments. We suspect Niel was one of his main contacts for getting the weapons to the Rats."

"Miranda kept that quiet," Sebastian said. "Even she couldn't have painted Jeffries as on our side."

"We suspected as much," Bramis replied. "Ah, but the last irony of all of this insanity is yet to come."

Kalison grinned and nodded to Bramis to continue this time. Alyn suddenly felt as though he sat in the middle of a drama that was being carefully played out on a stage around him. He leaned back against the pillows and enjoyed the show.

"Jeffries didn't trust his own people," Bramis said. Alyn saw a hint of wicked amusement in her eyes. "So, he had his closest conspirator keep vid records of all their meetings in order to blackmail the others into continued cooperation."

"Vid records," Alyn repeated. It was so obvious and so wonderful that he began laughing. "Janith!"

"Right again." Kalison nodded no longer hiding his own grin. "Janith hasn't filed any reports since just after the explosion. She's sitting in the Port Tower holding cells with Jeffries and a few others. Jeffries supplied the weapons to the Rats and Janith fanned the flames of hatred against them. We're calling it a conspiracy with intent to incite riots. We'll add murder charges later after we've done some weapons checks. I've been looking for some laser rifles used in several assassinations. It won't be long before we have their weapons hordes in our hands."

"Janith spent all those nights in the Tempest Pride bar to watch what my group did," Fiona added with her own smirk. "Hell, we could have held the meetings in the lobby, and she would have been too drunk to notice! And now we know how she found out about my involvement with Ember."

"Jeffries got the word to Miranda about Caden, as well," Sebastian said. He still looked uneasy about speaking in this group.

"I guess Vidline will start looking for someone to take Janith's place," Alyn said and grinned. "Maybe I should apply for a permanent post here."

"Do you really think that's wise, Alyn?" Kalison asked. His eyes flashed with amusement. "Are you going to stick around until someone else happens to take a really close look at the files on the De Velera family?"

Bauer, Fiona, and Bramis looked at Kalison with curiosity. Alyn stared in shock. He felt uncommonly shaky, and Sebastian caught hold of his shoulder, as though they faced some dangerous creature.

"Are you all right, Alyn?" Bramis asked. She took his trembling hand in hers. "You look very pale. Should we call in a med?"

"No, no," he answered. He didn't want anyone else in here now. He looked back at Kalison and tried not to show his fear. "When did you figure it out?"

"That last night while you were in the Maze. I didn't know why Sebastian De Velera's disappearance bothered you so much."

Alyn nodded. Then he looked at the other three and shrugged. There was no use keeping the secret now since they would all leave and head straight for the nearest comp to look at the files. And, honestly, he had no reason to hide from these people.

"I'm afraid I kept one secret," he offered. Bramis still held his hand, looking concerned for his health. "I am a reporter for Vidline, but I only took that job a few years ago. A few years before that I had changed my name to Alyn Naevon. I was born Alonso De Velera."

The Governor's fingers went limp around his hand. Her eyes darted from Alyn to Sebastian, and back to the reporter again. Fiona and Bauer stared at him in disbelief.

"De Velera," Bauer repeated softly. "Related --"

"My older brother," Sebastian explained just as softly, his eyes watching the closed door as though he expected someone to rush in and attack. His own hand tightened on Alyn's shoulder. Sebastian didn't know he could trust these people.

"My God, boy," Bramis whispered. She finally released his hand, giving her own nervous look around the room. Alyn tried not to feel paranoid just because everyone else suddenly looked so worried. "You took a hell of a chance, didn't you? Why?"

"I thought I came to Tempest because Vidline offered me a chance at a freelance job. They don't give those chances twice," he replied. He didn't need to dwell on the fact that he'd botched his only opportunity to go full time with them. "I honestly intended to do a couple quick reports and leave as quickly as possible without risking my career. Only Janith was so damn incompetent, and there was so much I needed to tell. And -- I found I wanted to make a difference here. What good is fighting the war for everyone else if you can't help your own people?"

"We needed to get that business out of the way," Kalison explained. "The truth about your identity will come out in the trials, and I didn't want Bramis blind-sided. We have several of your sister's people coming up before the judges. They wouldn't keep a secret like that out of respect for you."

"True," Alyn said. He leaned back against the pillow, feeling very drained. "You can't imagine what a strain this secret has been."

"No, I can't," Bramis admitted. She still looked at him with surprise but not anger. "That was quite a game you played. And you did it damn well."

"Thank you."

"The meds are letting you out of the hospital in a few minutes, Alonso," Kalison told him. "I suggest you spend most of your time at Fiona's hotel until you get your next assignment -- unless you really do intend to stay."

"I'll apply for another job. I'm not suicidal."

They all laughed.

"Hell, I thought you were suicidal before I knew you were a De Velera!" Bauer replied. He looked back at Commander Kalison and shook his head with an exaggerated sigh. "I suppose you still want me to keep an eye on this fool for a while longer."

"Might be wise," Kalison agreed with a nod. "I'll come by the hotel tomorrow and give you an interview, telling you the details on all this."

"Vidline probably doesn't expect anything more from me, considering how long it's been since the last report."

"They're patiently waiting, Alyn," Governor Bramis offered. "Or should I call you Alonso?"

"Alyn," he replied. "Alonso makes me nervous. They're waiting? *Patient* is not a term ever used to describe Vidline."

"Alyn," Bramis said and nodded. She also looked less nervous with that name. "I sent a private message to your main office explaining that Janith is under arrest and you were hospitalized. I told them not to bother sending any other reporter because we wouldn't talk to them. This is your report, and you'll get to finish it properly."

He tried to imagine what must have happened when the Vidline Office received such a report for the Governor of Tempest and nearly started giggling. He'd suffered too many shocks lately and felt a precarious shift in his emotions. Well, this turn of events couldn't hurt his reputation.

"Sebastian, you can stay at the hotel with us," Fiona offered. "If you'd like to spend some more time with your brother."

"I would, thank you," he answered, bowing his head. "It will be nice, neither of us having to pretend about anything any longer."

"Then we better get out and let the meds finish their work

with him," Kalison said. He stood and glared down at Alyn, looking quite serious and fierce. "Bauer will wait here for you, Alyn. I suggest you stick with him this time. If I find you out on the streets, unguarded, I'll shoot you myself."

"I thought it would come to this." Alyn laughed and met the man's stare with a grin. That finally broke through the Commander's icy façade to win a smile in return. "Isn't shooting a Vidline reporter harassment of the press?"

"That's protection of our own sanity," Bramis corrected. She laughed as she stood. "And believe me, no court on this world would convict Kalison after they heard the facts. Better not tempt fate, boy. You seemed to have used up more than your allotment for a lifetime when you stepped foot on this world."

He nodded agreement while wondering how long it would be before he got used to the idea of being friends with the Governor of any world, let alone this one. He wondered if she was feeling the same way, knowing his true name now.

"Take care, Alyn," she said. "I'll see you later. I thought all of you might come out to the estate for breakfast tomorrow. I can give Alyn my report then, and we can discuss how to help this world."

He smiled agreement and watched the others leave, although his brother lingered at the door.

"Are you all right with this, Sebastian?" Alyn asked. He felt a little twinge of guilt and worry, seeing his brother pulled into political games that might not suit him. "You can go back to the Maze."

"No. I want to help put all of this right." He took another step and was half out the door before he stopped and stared at his brother. The brighter light from the hall made it hard for Alyn to see his brother's face and he wasn't certain what emotions passed there in the moment of silence. When he spoke again, Sebastian's voice was softer. "I wasn't strong enough to take power away from her. No one would have listened to me. No one outside the Maze ever offered to listen to Miranda, either. She could only destroy and create hatred. Miranda never had the power you do, Alonso. I guess you're Federico's heir after all."

Sebastian slipped out of the door, and it closed before Alyn could answer him.

The End

ABOUT THE AUTHOR:

Hello!

I am an eclectic and prolific author who has published in several genres, including Young Adult Mystery, Urban Fantasy, Epic Fantasy, Science Fiction and numerous works on writing. While I started on the outer edges of traditional publication with sales to small press and magazines publishers, I have since moved most of my work to the Indie world and I am madly in love with the new world of publishing and the direct contact with readers.

I live in Nebraska with my husband, my cats and a small but entirely useless dog.

I also own Forward Motion for Writers and the ezine, Vision: A Resource for Writers.

Connect with Zette:

Web Site: http://lazette.net

Twitter: http://twitter.com/lazetteg

Facebook: http://www.facebook.com/lazette.gifford

Joyously Prolific Blog: http://zette.blogspot.com/

MORE NOVELS BY LAZETTE GIFFORD
AVAILBLE IN PRINT AND EBOOK AT
LAZETTE.NET

An angry goddess, a vengeful ghost, a spell that threatens the world . . . and one stranger who might save them all.

In the future, after humanity has spread across the stars, the Norse Gods ask a former companion for help, but Loki isn't ready for another round of Ragnarok. Reluctantly drawn into the battle against the Chinese Pantheon, his connection to chaos might be all that saves the Norse Gods and humanity from destruction at the hands of an awakening elder god.

Half-fae, genderless and mistrusted by his fae relatives, Skye is unexpectedly drawn into a dangerous magical power-play.

Skye's human half-sister has disappeared, drawing Skye into contact with their bitter mother . . . and into a trap that reaches all the way to the fae world.

When humans found the abandoned -- and ancient -- space station, they moved in to study the place they called Xeno-Station, and then shortened to Xenation. Following them came three other races, all intent on learning secrets. Only now one of the humans has a dangerous link to the heart and controls of this alien place, and he's learning there are secrets and dangers no one imagined.

A talented writer with a gift for world building -- C.J. Cherryh

Lord Micalus Raventower is a genius at creating clockwork creatures and tinkering with steampunk engines, but that doesn't explain why Atiran assassins are suddenly intent on killing him. Trouble is brewing for the city of Kamere. Atrian warships stand off the coast, and Merriweather may have quite a job keeping him alive as well as hiding his more unusual secrets. She soon learns there may be very good reasons for the Atrians to want Lord Raventower dead.

Find works by Lazette Gifford

Smashwords

A Conspiracy of Authors

Barnes and Noble Nook

Amazon

Amazon Kindle

Lazette.net